GW00467964

THE MUTE SWAN'S SONG

PETER GEORGIADIS

APS Books
Yorkshire

APS Books,
The Stables Field Lane,
Aberford,
West Yorkshire,
LS25 3AE

APS Books is a subsidiary of the APS Publications imprint

www.andrewsparke.com

Copyright ©2023 Peter Georgiadis
All rights reserved.

Peter Georgiadis has asserted his right to be identified as the author of this work in accordance with the Copyright Designs and Patents Act 1988

First published worldwide by APS Books in 2023

This is a work of fiction. Names, characters, places and incidents either are products of the author's imagination or are used fictitiously. Any resemblance to actual events or locales or persons, living or dead, is entirely coincidental.

No part of this publication may be reproduced, stored in or introduced into a retrieval system, or transmitted, in any form, or by any means (electronic, mechanical, photocopying, recording or otherwise) without the written permission of the publisher except that brief selections may be quoted or copied without permission, provided that full credit is given.

A catalogue record for this book is available from the British Library

THE MUTE SWAN'S SONG

1

The advert had read... *Maintenance Engineer Wanted, one way journey on the 'Mute Swan', flying direct to Acroshia. Working schedule of not more than thirty hours expected over the two year period of flight. The applicant must be fully qualified, able to show previous trips undertaken, by declaring a fully documented sponsors-card. Top credits can be negotiated for the right person. For further details contact Simon Ward personnel manager, Lloyds, McAlpine & Trenchard Mining Engineers, Floor 331, Standard House, 49 to 58 Ferry Road, New Justice City, Pearleye Continent, Planet 327 in the Orion Belt. Easy to find and, very worthwhile for the person that has plenty of time to kill.'*

Pen Pleasant took special note of the address. He shivered slightly, as he noticed that the weak sun was once again setting, leaving the green misty light reflecting off the side of the building. *This could be just what I need, get away from this God forsaken hole of a world. I should never have come! It's brought me nothing but trouble since my arrival. Mmmm, 327, that shouldn't be too expensive to get to and, it will only take a few hours on the hopper.* Pen paused, stroked his chin as he was wont to do, pondering the situation, firstly, the one he was in and, secondly what the future held for him here on this miserable planet, with its played out sun. *Come on, my boy, let's go for it!*

Pen Pleasant proved to be a name to conjure with. Forty-three years of age, a degree in electronic engineering at the tender age of twenty-one, second degree in physics, at twenty-seven, plus a third degree with honours in space, time and vibro-fusion technology by the time he had just turned thirty. His tutors thought of him as almost a professional student; in fact one of the heads of faculty, had accused him of just grubbing for honours, but was glad to take the plaudits, for being one of the teaching staff who had guided him.

Young Pen, had the potential to rule the Galaxy with his superior knowledge and intellect. At the very least, he should become head of some huge interstellar corporation and, thus acquire all the trappings of a successful existence. But, instead of wealth and success, he left his student life behind and became a bum, drifting from planet to planet, picking up work here and there, stealing what he could and, generally making a thorough nuisance of himself. So much so that he even spent four nights in a correction centre on Quintonia, better known as Planet 48.

That dreary dark wet hell hole, would never have been colonised had it not been for the incredible mushroom-type plants that grew there; those simple fungi made it rich pickings for those who could take to the miserable conditions. The great thing about these particular fungi was that they could be picked and packed, yet stay alive for several years before shrivelling and perishing, making them ideal food stuff for the colonisation of far off planets. It helped that they tasted good on the tongue. They could thus be boiled, fried or eaten raw, and they still tasted terrific any which way they were consumed.

And like many millions of other strange foodstuffs before, men thought they were an aphrodisiac and, that put the value of this fungi even higher.

Quintonia was a problem planet. With its dismal conditions it boasted a huge suicide rate and alcohol had become an immense problem. Little wonder that a hothead like Pen would end up in trouble...and, all over a whore. In fact looking back, Pen would have had to admit that most of his exploits and troubles, were over women and, usually loose women at that.

There was definitely a mean streak within the young Pleasant that made him somewhat dangerous - a wild card, completely unpredictable. It also caused him problems finding good reliable friends. Yet some would say that what happened was a small trivial thing, hardly even worth blinking an eye over, but then again, even a twitch of an eye can create problems to those who are always looking for the slightest excuse for provoking trouble, or expecting problems, where there were normally none.

So, it was little wonder that while Pen was negotiating with the lady in a bar in the only major town, Druxford, which incidentally was a small, sleepy watering hole of a place. The only significant thing about the town was that it hosted a ford over the Drux river, a backwater stream not more than two miles wide at the narrows, but like most of the rivers and seas on Quintonia, given the incredible volume of fresh water covering roughly three fifths of the planetary surface, none of the seas or rivers were very deep; just wide and long. It had been estimated through planetary surveys, that the deepest area of any of the seas or rivers was no more than fifty feet.

Unfortunately poor Pleasant was jostled by a drunken planter. The man blamed Pen. Pen blamed the man, one Peter Merchant. In his early forties, stout and rather slow, and usually a mild-mannered man, Merchant was, like most of the men on Quintonia, extremely strong and he had to be as the physical work was very labour intensive. He felt more than a little aggrieved at the arrogance Pen was showing towards him and, was quick to explain how he felt.

Indeed Merchant swung a blow at Pen who ducked away, a not overly onerous task since Merchant was a small figure of a man - not more than five feet ten in height. Pen grabbed at the offending arm and pushed it back upon itself, making a very clean break at the elbow. It could all have ended there except that Pen, as was his way, went that extra mile, a not untypical example of his aggression and arrogance. As Peter Merchant was screaming in agony over the broken arm, Pen casually picked up a knife and cut off the offending limb. This caused great consternation to all the assembled gathering.

It took four minutes for the local medics to heal the arm, as it dangled precariously from the shoulder of the shrieking fellow but in the meantime his life juices were squirting everywhere, much to the consternation of the landlord who foresaw huge cleaning bills. Had the two medics taken a couple of more minutes to arrive, once called, Merchant would have died from loss of blood, but they healed his arm and he was soon as good as new - just sober and a little wiser. As it was, the local reeve was the person that took most umbrage to the excess of violence shown by Pen. Even the reeve, however, did show a certain sympathy to him for his coitus interruptus, and required Pen to serve no more than four nights in the pen!

The reeve's last observation with its somewhat obvious play on words, made all the courtroom attendants laugh out loud but left Pleasant feeling rather nauseous. Four nights might sound like a doddle to any potential criminal, but four nights on Quintonia was considered to be as close to hell as possible. It had been discovered many hundreds of years before that doing a long period in a prison just institutionalised most offenders entering such outmoded places, and that short sharp shocks proved much more effective…

Firstly, the offender was never allowed to sleep, but kept in a more or less comatose state where the mind was easily manipulated. The subject's worst nightmares were then discovered and used against him or her. Most planets now used this form of torture, as after a small rehabilitation period, the person who had experienced the awful things within the head, rarely re-offended, becoming useful citizens. Or they killed themselves at the earliest opportunity. Either way, generally that was considered totally acceptable, in fact a win-win situation.

So that was how Pen spent the four worst days of his life just for the trivial matter of trying to cut off someone's arm. It all seemed grossly unfair to him, but then he had spent a lifetime believing that people, events, planets, Gods, in fact all things were unfair and, especially to him.

In Mr. Pleasant's mind all creatures great or small, were contriving to do him mischief and harm. He did not consider himself a touch paranoid. In his mind it was a simple matter of fact. When bad things occurred and, they did seem to happen very frequently around him, it was always someone else who was to blame, never him. This was of course sometimes true and sometimes false, but here on Quintonia, in Pen's eyes it just proved that yet another world was against him.

One thing he would admit to, was having a very nasty temper, but of course that would be brought on by someone else provoking him with their own personal, stupid problems. He also knew that he did drink a little too much, times that was. He was not an alcoholic, no sir. Just simple over indulgence, harmless really, or so he kidded himself, until someone got in his way. Then, of course it must be their fault, or if it was too obviously not their problem that he had drunk just a touch too much, it must be someone else's fault for allowing him to get into such a state.

Life should have been very easy for Pen, but it never was. He was an intelligent man, far, far brighter than most and, was perfectly capable of turning his hand to anything, but since leaving University he had found focusing his intelligence for any length of time dull and boring, so it became easier to get into trouble and, generally he enjoyed those high moments of tension and the huge adrenalin rushes before a melee occurred. Those excitements and anxieties were somehow better than booze or drugs. In fact they were both booze and drugs (not to forget sex) to him.

He knew deep down, that he needed a serious chance to explore his wealth of knowledge; maybe even focus on doing some good, but whenever he tried, it inevitably led to clashes with the rest of human race who happened to be around him at the time. It might usually be over something extremely trivial, but that annoyance would inevitably involve upsetting other folk, causing him to extreme agitatation in the process.

Pen Pleasant was born on the planet Earth in the year 2939. He was the very unexpected and only son of the ageing Cynthia and Trevor Pleasant, who when alive, had resided in the temperate part of England, just off the south coast, an area once called the South Downs, but now known as the arid but stable lands of Acritea. Their deaths had been a sudden and terrible disturbance to Pen, who though he didn't really have a warm family feeling for either of his parents, was nevertheless shocked and disturbed by their demise.

After the Middle Eastern wars of the twenty-first century, nations had finally nations taken that dreaded plunge into annihilation, using up their mountainous stockpiles of nuclear bombs. Those bombs, had lain prone but polished ready for use for more than fifty years, awaiting that certain and inevitably fateful moment when as sooner or later destined, they would track their way to destinations planned so, many, many years previously.

Then of course, finally sanity cracked completely and, war happened. It was all over very quickly. Iran and Iraq bombed Israel, who in turn bombed them back, plus for good measure throwing some the way of Egypt, Saudi Arabia, Lebanon and Syria.

It might have been alright if it have stopped there, but sadly, missiles went awry, by accident or so it was said. Two landed in Turkey, one in Cyprus and four on Greece, killing perhaps less than a hundred million people, but both Turkey and Greece took it badly that their borders had been violated by other countries' nuclear devices. An old adage

5

that *anything they can do, we can do better*, prevailed. By the end of Day Two, most of Europe had been gutted, including Britain, Ireland and Scandinavia.

It should and could, have stopped there, but the United States thought that Russia was obviously behind this hiccup in traditional diplomacy, while just for good measure, Russia persisted in the belief that the various infringements, had all been contrived by that mad woman, the President of the United States, Chancy Belgerstein. *So what the heck, let's all get onto the bandwagon.*

Only China held back and, why not? With a three billion population, they could afford to allow the world to destroy itself. It would give their own people space to repopulate. And in the blink of an eye two hundred years passed by which time the planet was almost stable enough to allow the Chinese to take that momentous step across the silk trade route, to re-inhabit this fragile little outcast of an outpost in the Universe.

However, within that space of time, China had been busy. They knew that Earth was now well past its sell by date and, if humanity was to prosper once again, then, instead of spreading ever more densely across the globe, they must spread upwards and outwards. And this they did with a flourish.

By the year 2477, the Chinese had mastered the Particle-Stella-Drive and, could achieve enormous distances at twenty times or more the speed of light. The distant stars no longer seemed so far away. Quickly, planets were found, and these became new homes for the pioneers who landed and set up bases. Before long - less than one hundred years after the Particle-Stella-Drive was discovered - new colonies were well established. Planets would often have their own life forms, but invariably just plant life. Up until the present time, no intelligent life forms had been discovered, and the settlers were good at making sure that no indigenous life form, no matter what its stage of developing evolution was, hindered humanity. Earth's trees and grasses – or those which had survived the nuclear war - plus introduced animal forms ensured that local varieties stood no chance of competing against earth's cast-offs.

Thus humanity flourished and spread its wings across the lonely blackness of space.

It is still true to say that the great sadness of humans, or humanity, is that we never learned from past mistakes and peace around the galaxy was just as fragile as it had been for the many thousands of years since humans first trod the brown earth of the third planet from a small insignificant star, far out on the spiral arm of the galaxy. War and fighting was just as prevalent in space as it was on that earth, but quieter, since nobody hears the screams of human beings dying in a vacuum.

It is not true to say that all the new colonised planets were in disharmony; many had created almost Utopian paradises for themselves, with sound governments based on the old democratic ideologies of a noble past, taken from Earth. Some governments actually worked, but this in itself led to possible conflict with other colonised planets, that might not be faring so well. Envy and greed were things that seemed endemic in the human psyche, which must have been a huge burden for all the Gods to bear.

One could say that throughout humanity's history, they had never leant anything from those previous errors, but somehow always managed to out-perform their last mistake, only with more gusto and enthusiasm. Humans didn't ever seem to learn how to live together. How the immortals must all be crying at their creation, probably it would have been better to have stayed with the dinosaurs.

It was also astonishing to see how quickly new religions appeared on these far off isolated outposts. Once again, many were from Earth's great store of religious societies, but equally true to say, there seemed to be many bizarre new creeds developing, with new tenets to follow and rituals to perform. Yet again it showed that man, was not seriously capable of seeing his own destiny into any long term future without the aid of a God, or many Gods. Man needed supreme beings, deities, divinities, celestial beings or any other name for a God-like creator, something that they could lay the blame on for their own shortcomings. But of course, this was handy for the war mongers amongst the colonists; they could grab and steal in the name of whatever God they worshipped, doing what came naturally in the name of their particular belief. Once again, nothing seemed to change; humanity only got older not wiser.

But the picture painted was not all bad. As ridiculous as humans can be, they also have an incredible capacity for making and developing new discoveries. Newer and better things were always being discovered. It could be in the realm of medicine, meaning that practically all disease was now obsolete, but also in the field of regeneration. People were now capable of living up to four or five hundred years. Tissue and organs could now all be regenerated. In many cases, new organs could be grown in the recipient's own body, thus overcoming the need for the minor operations that otherwise would have had to be performed.

In the arts, humanity had never been slow to progress and, on newly colonised planets, artists were being encouraged to express themselves, often with incredibly wonderful effects. Painting was, as always in the forefront of the art world - or in this instance, worlds. New painters had flourished and, once again shown that humans had a streak of genius, wherever and whatever they landed upon. In fact wherever they laid their proverbial hats. It became extremely popular for sculptors to create mega-huge constructions, often taking up the sides of unwanted mountains.

One that springs to mind is Claudia Fanling's mega-construction on the planet Zantience, better known as Planet 34. She had been given a mountain ten miles high to carve at her will. This she did. In fact it took her entire life and, was considered complete when a section fell in a landslide, taking her to her death. The strange thing was, no-one was sure what she had sculpted. Was it representational or abstract? No one has ever authoritatively decided. Of course that story is still taught in schools on all planets, as the work she performed is considered to be among humanity's greatest works of genius. Sooner or later, some crackpot will create some sort of sainthood for her. And that obviously will fit their own religious creed.

Music too had not been forgotten. Great composers sprang up all over the universe. Symphony orchestras had come into vogue once more and, musicians had developed the art to even greater depths of technique and presentation. This also encouraged crafts such as instrument making. New woods were discovered on some planets, which proved to have greater subtleties, making really fine musical instruments; even better than on Earth.

It was found that a certain tree from the planet Cantusolum, Planet 87, was just dense enough to re-create the same sonority of tone that the great Stradivari made in the 17th century back in Cremona, Italy on Earth. The only difference was that these violins, violas, cellos and double-basses could be mass produced and sold for sensible prices to up and coming players and, that applied to anywhere on any planet. How things had changed and, in this instance for the better.

There were hard woods, that bettered any woodwind instrument produced before its discovery, on Galafio, Planet 53. Flutes, and clarinets produced from the Impois tree gave such clear resonant sounds that they far outshone their forbearers. The art of making brass instruments was heightened also. A new lightweight metal was discovered on Manzio, Planet 91, much better for use in making trumpets, trombones, tubas and all forms of metal musical instruments. The sound that developed was like silk to the ears of all. No longer was there heard the cracking and splitting of notes by players. The orchestral scene had once again come of age.

With the advancement of robotics, toil and most hard labour had been reduced to a minimum, though there were still plenty of roles within day-to-day life that could not be covered by the mechanical man, only by a real skin and bone human being. Still, no live people now had to go underground. All mining was accomplished by robots; anything that was thought too dangerous, or come to that, too costly in pay, would be performed by the androids. Although the robot could never replace the human brain for speed of thought and, of course, reasoning. I suppose that one could say, that in many instances, people had finally found their own particular nirvana through the allowance of time to create. Surely humans were meant for creation, not toil. If any of the Gods exist, they created us to be creative. So, why do human beings still need to go to war and kill? Had war and killing become some sort of creative force, one must wonder?

Some arguments state that everything in the Universe has a ying and yang. If you have creative genius, then you must have docile idiots.

9

Thus the argument for war; if you have peace, you get stagnation. It is true to say, that war does somehow stimulate great creative art forms and so with the development of more and more dangerous weapons, come powerful new inventions for the good of humanity.

Luckily, Pen never got that deep. War, peace, he was quite prepared, or not prepared in his mind, for either. It was just a matter of what will be, will be.

There is another aspect of human life, that would seem strange to any intelligent aliens reading this journal; why was it that time had never been left behind on Earth? Whatever planet you happened to be on there were still sixty seconds in a minute and sixty minutes in an hour even though of course the number of hours were changed for the rotation of a planet around its sun and, the seasons changed accordingly. The old idea of time was still used everywhere. There were always seven days in a week and four weeks in a month. Even though there might be many more months in an orbit of the relevant sun, a years were, numerically, the same everywhere. On some planets, three or four years go by, before the seasons came full circle, while the reality of a cycle in planet times might just be a few months. Yet there it was; the year 2972 was the same year on every planet that had been colonised by man. People never really understood why this happened, but it is nevertheless true. Just one of those weird anomalies that occurred because humans came from a planet called Earth and, could never again really leave that past behind. Though many generations had come to be born on the newly discovered worlds and, those newly born inhabitants would have never known or seen Earth, everyone, everywhere still referred to Earth like it was something sacred; a mystical taste within the collective mouth.

These and many other strange abnormalities followed humanity and Pen Pleasant into space, but somehow leaving always a gut feeling grinding within, totally in turmoil.

Once again Pen looked at the notice, and decided that he must at all costs leave this accursed planet. *If I stay here any longer, I know I shall end up doing yet more time in the slamgast and another few days of that sort of abject misery, is far to much to contemplate. No, it's time to remove my arse from this hell*

*hole and find a more likely likeable homestead for my talents. The Mute Swan, yes,
I've heard of it. Mega-huge if memory serves me right, at least four or five miles in
length, or maybe even six. This could be fun and if not then at least I'll get some
sleep. I guess I'd better make contact as soon as I can get to a transviewer.*

Pen looked around to see if there was anything in the immediate
vicinity. Of course there wasn't. Then he realised that there would be
one in the Interplanetary Ching-Fewey Hotel just around the corner, in
the next block of buildings. He could even get a drink or two there
when he made the call.

The ICF range of hotels stretched half-way across the explored
Universe and, the one thing that you could rely on was the fact that
they all looked exactly the same. You could be on any of the various
planets around the known Universe and, on entering one of these
hostelries would think you were back on Earth. They were never more
than thirty-five stories high with never less than a thousand rooms of
varying shapes and sizes, all priced to be in the budget of any wealthy
tourist or business man. Always the same pink stone, which on Earth
had been polished pink Italian marble, but on other planets, just stone
dressed to look like the very pink marble famously used by the
Romans in Classical times.

To enter this edifice, this temple to an affluent but long-dead past, Pen
would have to look the part. It was no good expecting to be allowed in
dressed as a mere worker. To that end, he turned up the waterproof
collar on his very expensive real silken threaded one-piece suit. He
changed the colour of his clothing, so as to look more sober than the
golden tartan pattern that it had previously carried. The change was to
a dark brown pinstripe which, he hoped, might just might fool the
door attendant into thinking that he was a gentleman.

The rain was falling hard and fast and, it was hard to see more than a
few feet in front of his own face. But of course, the clothing he wore
kept all moisture from reaching his body and, the hat could be folded
away when he reached his destination. He licked his lips, more at the
thought of a drink than anything else, but to be fair he was also getting
excited at the prospect of leaving all this rain behind.

It never occurred to him that the position might already be filled or
that the employer might not actually want to employ him; after all this

was Pen Pleasant, not some downbeat from God knows where. To Pen the job was his and, that was going to be an end to any question of employment for other people. Nobody else would be in the frame; it was not possible, so why even contemplate it?

On reaching the entrance to the hotel, he was pleasantly surprised to see that there was no doorman, or android, looking at whosoever should appear within the portals of the establishment. Without further ado, in he strode. The opulence that confronted him even took his breath away. There were even hanging paintings suspended by their own gravitational devices. This, of course, he had seen elsewhere, but never this many. Painting and sculptures were drifting all around the foyer giving a display that would brighten the minds of any numbskull, even if their ability to appreciate art forms were somewhat limited. Some of the art was extremely old and therefore probably very valuable. *This must be some sort of exhibition, not even the Interplanetary Ching-Fewey Hotel could afford this amount of art at one time.*

Pen, fascinated, spent the next ten minutes looking with his mouth agape at all the suspended objects, considering how well they caught the imagination, as they moved gently and slowly around the huge foyer in what was obviously a very cleverly orchestrated manner rather than what you were supposed to consider an aimless procession. Clever because it made you think that the movement was aimless, but was it? It was more likely to be a clever ploy to capture the imagination; to stop one in one's tracks and think and at this it worked. Onlookers almost invariably stopped to contemplated them. Of course, that had to be the entire point of any exhibition; to stop and make you ponder, then wonder, and then think about what had made you stop and wonder about.

There was one sculpture that really caught Pen on the hop, a bust made from the plant Quinnolignum from the planet Alfegina, Number 104. This extraordinary form of plant life could be cut into pieces, re-shaped, crushed and of course eaten, doing no harm to the hardy individual who ate it, yet by all accounts it always re-grew, even the smallest fragments turning into full grown plants given enough time.

The only thing that killed it off was fire, which on the searing hot Alfegina happened regularly enough to stop any over population. The real fascination was that it could be sculptured into various shapes and, it would change to something quite close to what had been sculptured, but somehow different. This process would keep continuing time after time without ever going back to square one, always something different and usually breath-taking. An artist might have started the procedure but the plant made sure that it soon became its own work of art. This particular piece was a representation of the busts of famous people down the ages, or the plaque that hung underneath it claimed; the changing shapes of human kind, none of whom Pan Pleasant had any knowledge about.

"Can I be of assistance sir?"

Pen jumped from his mouth-open stance of concentration. He had completely failed to notice the bellhop's approach but for once he felt no resentment for being disturbed. Instead he smiled at the young lad, got his senses back to normal mode and returned the question with an answer.

"Two things. Firstly, I need a transviewer; that is an interplanetary transviewer. Secondly, I need the bar. In that order please."

The lad smiled and, pointed to a door, not more than one hundred feet down the left side of the foyer.

"There you will find the transviewer, and then another two hundred yards down the foyer, you will find the bar, or at least the closest one on this particular floor. Is there anything else sir?"

"No, but thanks anyway. Catch you on the way out!"

"Yes sir, thank you sir."

The bellhop might be young but he was already experienced enough to know that no tip was likely to be coming his way from this customer. Catch them on the way in, maybe. Catch them on the way out, never.

Pen looked once more at the marvels floating overhead, took stock of what he was there for, sighed with his head slightly to one side, and strolled down to the door the bellhop had identified. It never ceased to amaze Pen and many others like him, just how cheap the use of a transviewer was, given that the cost of most things throughout history always increased exponentially. For the cost of communication - prices actually were always going down, not even standing still.

The other amazing item for which this was true was, and always had, been travel itself. To get a ticket on a starship to almost anywhere that starships travelled was extremely cheap; so cheap that just about anyone could travel and did. The reasons travel was cheap was because the Particle-Stella drive worked so efficiently without any moving parts - nothing to shake or bend or break - and the gathering of particle energy was limitless throughout space itself with journey times now down to a span that could sensibly be undertaken, and the machines themselves were now so vast in size and capacity. Anyone could and did go anywhere for just a few monetary units.

Pen looked into the viewer, placed his two churnings into the slot provided, dialled the number and waited either for the viewer to come back with a viewer-recording, should it be out of work hours, or the person he wished to communicate with. His luck was indeed in, for beyond the billions of miles came instantly, a view of the the secretary of the company Lloyds, McAlpine and Trenchard Mining Engineers. The woman was a real throw-back to her Chinese ancestral roots; very young, probably no more than twenty years of age, but so pretty that it at fair took Pen's breath away.

"Yes sir, how can I help you?"

"My name is Pen Pleasant viewing you from Quintonia, Planet 97. I would like to speak to Simon Ward, about becoming the engineer on the mining ship The Mute Swan. Firstly, can you tell me if that position is still up for grabs and, secondly, will Simon Ward speak to me concerning this matter?"

"As far as I know the position is still open. And yes you're right, it is Simon Ward that you need to speak to. Please hold onto your power-pack, Mr. Pleasant, I will inform Simon of your existence and see if he will view you. Back in a moment!"

Postege Chantell was as efficient as she was pretty and, within less than thirty seconds she was back on the viewer. Her small breasts heaved - she must have run somewhere to obtain the attention of the said Simon Ward. It was with his eyes firmly fixed on those pleasant looking orbs, that young Pleasant heard the reply; "I will just connect you to Simon Ward's office. He is happy to view you. By the way, good luck to you."

A huge smile spread across her countenance. Pen instantly knew it was not just the job he wanted.

Simon Ward was a dark haired rotund fellow, probably in his early fifties. Though what was left of his hair was dark, he was totally bald all down the middle of his head. He had a ruddy veined face, showing that he ate and drank far too much and, with the amount of time that he spent out of doors, he looked like someone experiencing very high blood pressure, not that he should have been. His dress sense, though expensive, left much to be desired due to lack of work-appropriate coordination. It gave him the appearance of someone who spent his time on the beach or in the garden. An open-necked highly coloured shirt hardly suggested management of a high powered conglomerate such as Lloyds, McAlpine & Trenchard Mining Engineers. Pen couldn't see what he was wearing as trousers, but if that shirt was anything to go by, he was not going to win best-dressed-man-of-the-year.

"Yes, and who are you? And what do you want?"

"Pen Pleasant. I understand that you have a vacancy for a ship's engineer on a one way trip on The Mute Swan. If that position is still vacant I would like to apply for the job. I have all the necessary engineering qualifications and, I am between jobs on a planet that I really cannot abide. I'm hoping that I am the man that you're looking and waiting for!"

"Well you certainly might be. We've advertised this position now for several months, but because it is a one-off and, the fact that the lucky employee has to make his or her own way back, we had more or less given up on the idea that we would find anyone suitable, so reluctantly we had decided, with a vast difference of opinion, that we would send the ship completely on automatic pilot and take our chances. But now that you're applying for the job, who knows? The money is going to be very good. The working time expected, failing disasters, would only be approximately thirty hours over the entire two year period of the flight, which means that whoever gets the job will be sleeping a great deal of that time. Do you have any ties family wise?"

"No, none at all. I am alone and I intend to stay that way."

"Then Pen Pleasant, I suggest you get your body over here to Penguistic, better known as Planet 327, as soon as you can." He gave the planets number in automatic pilot, having said it at least a million times before.

"Could you be here today, or at worst tomorrow?"

Pen thought for a second or two.

"I haven't yet checked out the flight shuttles I might need to get there, but I can't see any problems in making the journey tonight, or at the very worst tomorrow, sometime in the day. Like I said I have nothing to keep me here. I'll get my things together and come immediately. I look forward to meeting you. May I call you Simon?"

"No, Mr. Ward or sir. I'll be your boss not your mate. Lastly, before you come, understand that we might not employ you for this journey and no expenses are being paid to losers. Is that all clear?" But before he allowed Pen to respond he added, "Get your arse here quickly. It was me that wanted to send the ship by remote. So Mr. Pen Pleasant, see you real soon."

With that the screen went white and empty. Pen was once again brought back down to soil with a bump. *Better get there quick and, show that twit, that I'm the right man for the job.*

For once Pen ignored the bar and, made his way back to the front desk area again. The floating works of art still fascinated him. Once more his eyes went upwards and his jaw went down. It was while he stared at an abstract painting by the famous Menglissing from the highland regions of Prontossia, or Planet 9, one of the real early planetary discoveries, that he realised he was trying to work out why something that didn't make any sense whatsoever was so fascinating to look at. He dwelt too long on the colours of the swirling paint strokes. They seemed to mesmerise his feeling of time, and he was startled when a complete stranger bumped into him, obviously fascinated by the same work of art, that he finally realised that he had been standing looking at this artwork for nearly one hour and he needed to get to the information desk before he was left on this accursed planet, a planet high and dry and, that thought brought him back to ground zero with a bang. Pulling himself together he managed to look away and, then turned to desk was. A man standing behind the counter was just closing up when Pen rushed over.

"Before you go, please can you get information on flights to Penguistic, that's Number 327?"

"Sorry sir, I am closing now, try the transporter station. It's just a few blocks down the main thoroughfare. It'll take you no more than five minutes to walk there from here."

Pen saw red mist coming down immediately. He leaned heavily on the counter bar and almost snarled across to the bewildered man on the other side. "If I wanted to walk down the road I would have gone straight out the door. I am asking you and, believe me when I say, you wouldn't want to get me good and mad, now would you!" He was fairly spitting out the words, with a snarl that would have made a wolf proud. "Now give me the information I ask for and, be damned quick about it."

"Please sir." The man stood there shaking from head to toe. He instinctively realised that Pen meant business and, he was in the firing line and, that in a fracas, he would be the one to receive injuries, not his opponent. "Please, there is no need for you to lose your temper!" The counter assistant was cowering quite noticeably behind his desk. He didn't want to risk injury from this person, who was quite obviously a madman. "I have to get home. My wife is preparing a big dinner party and I'm already late. Seriously sir, they will help you without any trouble."

"Trouble, you cretin! I'll give you trouble."

Pen leaned across the counter and made a grab for the luckless attendant, who with fortune just on his side, pulled away from Pleasant's grip, but leaving the front of his tunic a little torn. It did the trick and one very terrified information clerk now jumped to open the viewer once more and to retrieve the needed information.

"Ah, here we are, sir! You could get a fast shuttle to Marmarine, that is Number 55, then transfer to the Penguistic, er, Planet 327. You will be there in a matter of thirteen hours as from the time the shuttle leaves, which if you book it through me now, will be in two hours time." Sweating profusely, he added sheepishly, still quivering with fear of this obvious uncouth madman. "Would you like me to book that for you sir?"

"Yes, thank you; you're most kind."

Pen was now in a sarcastically playful mood, having struck the right sort of fear into the poor fellow. He was a past master of this sort of situation, so he could afford to be magnanimous.

"Here are my credit details. Once this is done, so are we. Then you go off to your dinner, I go off to Penguistic. By the way, for my ticketing arrangements my name is Pen Pleasant, Pleasant by name, pleasant by nature."

"Thank you Mr. Pleasant, can you place your credit slip into the slot and, then your ticket will be confirmed. I am instructed to inform you, that the company cannot be held responsible for any accidents that may occur on flights. Should there be a meteor hit, the company will not be paying out for search and rescue, or in case of death no funeral expenses will be met by the company. The ticket is non refundable, and should you miss either of the flights for whatever reason, absolutely no refund will be forthcoming." The assistant winced visibly, fearing yet more retribution. "Sorry Mr. Pleasant, I am instructed to say these things. If you want personal insurance, that can be arranged. Err, other than that, have a pleasant flight!"

The man tried without great success, to smile a wry smile.

"Not necessary thanks. I have no one to leave anything to, so if something happens, so be it! Right off you go; see you in the next life; you can bully me then."

"Ha… ha… ha… I have never wanted to bully anyone sir, not in the past and most definitely not in the future."

As assistants go, this man was a gem, but he still exuded fear of Pen, so when Pleasant finished his sentence with, "What about the present." the man gulped noticeably.

Finally he managed to say one last sentence. "Have a safe and comfortable journey."

The journey was a smooth affair with no problems whatsoever. No meteors collided with the craft. No pirates attacked. It was a completely uneventful journey, allowing Pen to sleep most of the way. Pen arrived on Penguistic after what felt like a year of travel; as he had slept, he found himself back in the hell hole, being tortured. His dreams were seriously disturbing. So, though in fact it was a mere thirteen hours and eight minutes, waking up in a pool of sweat made it feel like forever.

Recovering, Pen made it to the offices of Lloyd, McAlpine and Trenchard Mining Engineers, dressed to impress, within less than thirty minutes of landing.

Penguistic was a very small planet; just about eighteen thousand miles around its equator.

The weather was a problem for off-worlders, as it was somewhat hotter than humans preferred - averaging forty degrees centigrade - but the extraordinary fact was that it circled its sun every three hundred and fifty-four days and had a twenty-four hour rotation just like Earth. Because of the glare from the sun, the horizon always looked a blue green colour. Land covered more than three quarters of the surface of the planet, but the water was fresh and good to drink, so to most of the inhabitants it had the perfect climate, with rich loam to cultivate almost anything they wanted. As the plant life indigenous to the planet turned out to be poisonous, Earth flora was quickly established, and flourished, making Penguistic self-supporting within its first decade of colonisation.

There were no mountain ranges above four hundred feet and, the sea was only two hundred feet at its deepest. No dangerous animals had as yet been found in the sea or on land and boating had become the greatest pastime for the inhabitants. Carp had been introduced into the sea and had done well, so fishing was another great hobby for folk who lived close to the sea. Fish was plentiful and good to eat and, the biggest Carp yet caught had weighed in at a massive forty one kilos.

Due to the climate and landmass, people had come from many far off planets to make Penguistic their home. Buildings grew in size, but wide roadways kept them far apart and, construction went upwards and downwards as apposed to spreading across acreage.

The local governing body had been clever, right from the first settlements and, the buildings were attractive, well-designed and robust. All in all, people loved the place and had long contented lives. It had become a haven for the infirm and elderly in, what had in the olden days, been known as *God's waiting room*.

Penguistic had one strange but sensible rule. When any human or animal died, the body or carcass would be minced down, half being used to feed the fish within the sea and, the other half for fertilising the soil. It was an agreement that each citizen had to sign, when finally they applied for residency.

There was little to no crime, other than the occasional murder, usually a crime of passion. People did not steal from one another, as costs were purposely kept low and affordable, so that mankind worked for a fair days wage and, could quickly get the fruits of ones labours, turned into a healthy and contented life.

Not that Pen Pleasant cared anything about any of these things. His interests were… actually, he did not know what his interests were or what drove him at all! He had never acquired any hobbies, other than annoying other people. He did not support any interplanetary sport, did not care much about politics or affairs of state, and even wars left him feeling cold, but he knew that one day, he would have to sit down and analyse where his life had gone or was going and, of course what he had succeeded in achieving, up to that point. As for the latter, it was going to be a long lingering thought and, that was going to be a soul searching occasion. Something to be postponed as long as possible.

Pen looked scornfully at Simon Ward, but was clever enough to make sure that the man was totally unaware of that sneer. In Pleasant's eyes

Simon Ward was a little runt of a man and, certainly did not take into account the fact that he was on the fat side. For Pleasant he might be large in body but he was puny in personal stature. One who would be easy to turn inside out if the occasion called for that to happen.

Ward had very black, slicked-back hair, trying hard to cover the widening bald patch at the back but, to be fair, it was cut and groomed neatly. The man's trousers showed that he spent money freely on his appearance, except perhaps for the highly coloured shirt. When one looked on Ward's sense of dress, you could easily understand the ethos of the entire planet. He was probably more interested in being on the outside than on the inside. He worked because he was considered to still be young - only fifty odd years of age - and, as he didn't give a hoot about birthdays, he had honestly forgotten his exact age. He knew he had at least twenty more years, before he would have enough credits to retire and could hardly wait for that momentous occasion. He knew this planet was too good to waste time on working. Having these facts hanging over him, made him a tetchy, unpleasantly depressed man, for whom work was a four letter word. Nobody employed for or with him, enjoyed his company, so it was little wonder that Pen identified him as seriously in need of taking down a peg or two.

The trousers that fascinated young Pleasant invoked his envy, something he was not used to. They were made from some facsimile that actually had the look of Silken Mohair, an ancient cloth used back on earth. They made it obvious to anyone bothered to observe that this man had credits and, could and would sometimes spend them freely even though he was small - probably no more than five feet two inches tall, almost a dwarf in terms of sizing on the planet, where inhabitants often reached seven feet or more.

As Pen was six foot eight inches, Ward came across to him as minute in stature but the man had been there, seen it all, and never got fazed or intimidated by others. Why should he? He was already fazed by being Simon Ward.

Pen looked around the office, in a non-committal way, as if slightly bored. It please him to see that there were paintings hanging on the walls and, in the far corner stood an interesting sculpture, representing a rocket in flight whilst looking more like something the dog would have left on the carpet. At least, this was the way Pen viewed the object.

The sneer turned back into a smile and, he turned again towards Simon Ward, leaned forward to place both fists on his table and asked, "Well? You've read my records; do I qualify for the job as engineer or not?"

Simon was almost angry at being disturbed by this upstart, but then proving himself a professional, he visibly relaxed and, pointing to a line printed upon one of the open pages answered, "Well, young Mr. Pleasant, I see here that you did time for cutting someone's arm off. I bet that hurt!"

"What cutting the arm off or doing time?"

"Well I guess both really. Those penal institutes are vicious, so I can certainly understand, why you wanted to get as far away from Quintonia as possible." He then softened and, with a certain amount of sympathy creeping into his voice, he carried on. "I too did four days of hell in one of those awful penal institutes and, like you, I came through it sane. Now look at me, a rich man with all the trappings of success. So, understanding how you must have suffered, yes, Mr. Pleasant you have the job. Congratulations are in order. Though one word of warning to you. I am putting my own head on the block here. Don't let me down."

Ward then stood up with a hand outstretched and shook Pens vigorously, taking him completely by surprise. *Well, what do you know?* thought the new engineer for the Mute Swan.

"Welcome on board Pen, if I may call you that. Another day and I was going to send the ship on its own guidance system. You'll now have two years in which to sleep and plan your life, but with your intelligence you should go far - no pun intended. Though how you'll get back from Acroshia I have no idea. That in itself will be somewhat of a challenge to you. Now what about some lunch? Then I'll get you over to the Mute Swan and get your familiarisation over with. After that it's all systems go and, gone you will be. Oh, one last thing. The credits will be paid to you on arrival, not before. Though what the hell would you do with credits on board the ship?" He laughed at his own joke.

Pen just looked on, still puzzled but gratified by Ward's change of mood from hostility to apparent friendliness.

2

The Mute Swan was huge, at least five miles long; not the longest ship ever built, but by far the most expensive and sophisticated. It was so big that when it orbited Penguistic, it blotted out their sun for a few seconds every day.

As the shuttle closed the distance between the planet and the starship, Pen was amazed at just how big and complex this huge monolith of a space-travelling workhorse was. As they approached, it loomed up over Pen with a feeling somehow dark and foreboding. Yet even in that sort of gloomy mood, he personally felt at home even before stepping aboard. Darkly foreboding it might be but for some strange reason he felt an almost insatiable desire, to pat the side of the monolith. He could not even quite see the end of the ship, from the angle that they came at the landing hatchway, but to an onlooker the ship just seemed to go on and on for ever. For an instant, panic gushed through his veins; all this and just him for two years, nobody to talk to, or even communicate with in any way whatsoever. That anxiety swiftly passed as he remembered that most of the time, he would be sound asleep and in the land of no dreams, just darkness. Somehow, the thought of a time in complete stasis with no thoughts or dreams, anything to say he was even still alive, calmed him and, his initial panic subsided and the euphoria of being here seeing this wondrous work of human kind once again set in. He knew instinctively that he had found his place within the cosmos.

The shuttle automatically came to a stop on the landing bay, a huge cathedral space but without any stained windows to boast about; big enough to house a huge sports event and the thousands of minions that would attend such meetings.

It took a whole minute for the airlock to close and the bay to fill with life-giving oxygen, but no one should ever really fear the wait, as the air that filled the space would be the factor that allowed the shuttle to open its doors and discharge its human cargo alive and well.

It was a strange quirk, that whenever anyone stepped from a shuttle onto the vast bay area, they felt impelled to take in a huge gulp of air - as if they had been holding their breath until that moment. Pen Pleasant and Simon Ward were no exception to this rule. Both placed their feet firmly upon the steel floor, both took that first intake of breath, and both chests were heaving to show the pleasure in still being alive.

Pen looked around with awe. Of course he had studied physics and, knew all about giant star ships, but he had never experienced such a cavernous expanse before. He looked at the ceiling, which must have been at least two hundred feet from the floor. Piping and gantries festooned everything. Some of the pipe work was so large in diameter that anyone could have set up home, or even a small village, inside them. He soon became aware of the lack of noise. He had expected the clanging of metal against metal, the rushing of air or water around pipe work, but no; nothing; just silence. This realisation too was a little unnerving to his way of thinking, but after a while the silence once again felt gratifying and comforting.

He had made up his mind that this was going to be a real pleasure and, if need be he would spend more time awake than was strictly necessary. This could be his chance to find out something about himself, to take some time to think about his life and direction. Maybe even reflect; find some sort of atonement for the years of waste and depravity that he had come to know and, enjoy too much. He knew that when this trip was going to end, he would have quite a large amount of credits that could set him up in some sort of business, or maybe even fund some research that could be interesting and profitable in the future. Anyway, for now he felt real excitement and. this might have been for almost the first time in his short life.

"Right Pen, into the briefing chamber with you. It will take about one hour. I'll wait for you, but afterwards you will know every part of this ship backwards. Every working part will be second nature to you. In fact there won't be an inch that you won't know personally. For when you do wake up and start to work, you will have everything there under your fingers. This huge rust bucket is going to be your home for exactly two earth years. There will be no communication as you'll be travelling at least twenty times the speed of light. The only thing you'll see when and if you look out of the portholes are some very distant stars - before they're behind you that is. But the colours will be interesting. I don't need to tell you again, that the ship is programmed to get you there. There has never been a crash or any ship lost. Disasters just don't happen. There is too much for all of us at stake. The credits this one journey is going to make would keep the entire planet of Quintonia happy and contented for a year or more! But then, young mister Pleasant, you know all of this, a man with your brain! So fear not. This is all going to be a doddle for you with no surprises and of course no problems. Like I said, no ship has ever been lost and, that is not going to happen to the Mute Swan either."

They walked several hundred yards to a small anteroom, which was furnished surprisingly warmly, with pictures on the walls, thick carpeting and comfortable chairs. Pen immediately felt at home, though as it happened he would never have reason to enter the room again, after the briefing.

"I want you to sit on this chair and I shall plug you in and, while you're being fried…I mean briefed!"

Ward was in a fine, good humour, laughing as he spoke and, obviously enjoying himself for once. He had taken to Pen; God only knows why.

"I shall retreat to the galley and, cook us both a meal to remember. I shall also stow your gear for you. I hope that in your packs there is nothing that will alarm me?" Again he spoke in jest, continuing even though Pen didn't so much as bat an eye. "Then Pen, my new friend, I shall retire to the shuttle as you will know exactly what to do. Let me adjust this headpiece. Is that comfortable? Just let yourself go, fall asleep or whatever you want. Your brain will do all the rest. Learn about the Mute Swan and enjoy the experience. I thought I would cook beautiful steak, with mashed potatoes and all the trimmings. We can have a decent bottle of French simulated wine, if you know what that is. Then maybe some really nice desert. Leave it to me as this will be your last meal in human company for the next twenty-four months and, I believe it's fitting that it should be a fine one."

"Sounds good to me. Turn it on, then get that food ready. I must admit I could eat a horse. If it is horse, don't tell me. Real simulated beef steak would be just great."

Simon turned to leave once Pen had fallen into a deep restful sleep, the first of many.

He left the briefing room to one young Pen Pleasant, who would soon be truly the chief engineer. Back in the bay he felt a distinct breeze; a a cold whoosh flew through his body, his skin prickled and his hair momentarily stood on end. *I must be getting old and crotchety! I have that feeling of de-ja vu; as if I'm being watched by someone.* He smirked at his own naivety. *Given that intelligent life has never been found intelligent life outside of humanity, I know I'm getting daft. Now, where's that galley?*

As Simon walked towards the main corridor, he could not shake off that sense of being observed, nor the distinct feeling of having done this all before. In the huge landing bay it had seemed entirely stupid to him but now... Simon Ward was glad that it wasn't him going on this journey.

When he got into the corridor he once again laughed at himself for being so jumpy. Inside the hallway, which stretched from one end of the ship to the other, he stepped onto a walker platform to be quietly and gently carried to his destination. Once again, no credits had been spared in the lavish way even the corridor was furnished, with lush carpeting and pictures on the walls at intervals of not more than fifty metres from each other. Ward ordered the walker to take him to the kitchen. The walker, so-called because it travelled just above the speed of the average fast walking person - roughly seven miles an hour – could, if an emergency were ever to occur, travel much faster, but as there was nothing to hold onto and time wasn't usually a serious consideration, seven miles an hour seemed extremely reasonable all round for users of the device.

Half a mile and four minutes later, the hovering walker came to a full stop outside a large spacious area with the sign *galley* above the open portals. Inside was a table that could seat at least fifty people, with chairs to match despite there never having been any suggestion that the ship would ever need to carry more than the one engineer. There were also entertainment systems everywhere, large comfortable settees and even a complete bath and shower unit.

As the ship has its own gravitational unit, always adjusted to suit humans, there was no sense of movement and, a person could walk anywhere on the ship and feel as if he or she was standing on solid earth, albeit upon iron and steel. Even at twenty times the speed of light, there was absolutely no feeling of movement, acceleration, or G-forces; nothing to ever tell one that the ship was even moving, unless you had the courage to look out of the only porthole on the entire ship, or watch the movement from a televised viewer, which practically speaking really the only way to view anything that might be on the outside. Most people did not want to do even that; looking at a star, then watching it turn blue and disappear before your eyes could be, and usually was, very unnerving.

Simon walked into the galley and was immediately struck by the lack of cooking facilities. All cooking was done by machines, organised completely by the computer. There were no naked lights anywhere; nothing that could create a spark, though even a naked light would not seriously be a problem and, it was not as if anything could actually catch fire since everything was fire resistant. But company rules are rules. Should any machine break down, for whatever reason, then either the engineer would fix it, or he/she would fall back on emergency stores. There were enough boxes of stores to last a crew of fifty, twenty years of drifting in space before they need feel the pangs of hunger or thirst. On this ship, like all mining vessels, everything had been thought of. There was absolutely no room for error.

Ward walked over to a panel, and spoke into it. "A bottle of very good Spanish Rioja, maybe something thirty years old, at least a grand reserve. Have it decanted into a fine crystal jug and, then allow it to warm in the room here, don't serve until the engineer gets here from the briefing. By the way, his name is Pen Pleasant, but I guess he won't object to being called Pen. Also prepare two fine cuts of beef steak, both medium rare, mashed potatoes and several vegetables of your choice. Again, don't serve this until Pen appears. Afterwards, a dessert of your choice to suit the occasion please."

"Yes Mr. Ward. It is and always will be my pleasure to serve you. Tell me sir, will I be getting underway soon?"

Simon was startled and, looked at the machine in a cross eyed way. He had never been asked a question from a galley machine before. Why should it want to know? Was this computerised machine thinking for itself?

"Why do you want to know?" Ward couldn't disguise his shock at being confronted with a question, but then he quickly lowered his articulation and tempo. "But to answer your query, Pen will be the engineer and you will be leaving for Acroshia just as soon as I leave on the shuttle. Look after Mr. Pleasant well. I am sure he is a pleasant man!"

Why he added that last sentence he could not even guess at. Joking with a machine - whatever next? But once again, someone was most definitely walking over his grave.

"Sorry to be nosy, Mr. Ward, I was just passing the time of day with you. Your bottle of wine has been reproduced and if you proceed to the serving hatch you can pick it up there."

Simon sat in a comfortable chair and looked around the room. *All these ships look just the same, I might never have flown in one, but I most certainly know their set up. I would be hard pressed to get lost in this vessel, even though this is the first time I've ever been here. But it most certainly has a strangely uncomfortable air about it.* Simon Ward's skin wrinkled up his spine. There was that feeling again; the feeling that he was not alone.

He rose and crossed casually over to the main interface computer, as the thing was constantly ready to be in communication with anyone. He spoke to it in almost a whisper, as if unconsciously he feared being overheard.

"Mute Swan, I want a complete sweep of the ship with your sensors. Do you sense the presence of any other living creatures other than Pen Pleasant and myself?"

"No Mr. Ward. Only the two of you are aboard the starship and, to be perfectly honest with you, I am looking forward very much to getting to know and looking after the engineer Pen Pleasant. It is going to be a real pleasure having someone with real intelligence to communicate with."

There was a pause and, then Mute Swan continued in the same monotonous voice. It was not mechanical because it was most definitely feminine in texture, "What made you ask such a question? Do you feel the presence of some other entity?"

Simon smirked. He now felt pretty stupid talking in such a low toned voice. The decibels were decidedly louder for his answer. "It was when I left Mr. Pleasant in the briefing room, I felt as if someone had just walked over my grave."

"This must be another human adage, as I can easily see that you're here on board me and, you most certainly do not seem to be dead and buried. But if what you say means that you felt the presence of someone else, I can assure you that is not the case."

There was another slight pause then with a slightly lowered voice, "Mr. Ward, other than Mr. Pleasant and your good self, there is nothing living upon this space travelling machine, though I must say I like to believe that I am the nearest thing in my computerised brain, to living and breathing tissue and awareness. I think, therefore I most definitely am. Maybe it was my presence that you felt?"

"Yes, Mute Swan, I rather think that was it."

"What was it? Where's that dinner and drink?"

Pen had finished his briefing and, had made his way to the galley for that last feast and drink with another human, before setting off on his journey of… what, and to… where?

"Hello, I didn't hear you coming. Good briefing? Now you know everything you need to about this ship. I was just talking to the ship. It was just a silly feeling that I had, nothing for you to fret over." Simon smiled broadly and gestured for Pen to sit next to him. "Right, let's be having those steaks and that bottle. Oh, by the way, I've left your packs over against the wall there."

Ward pointed in the direction that Pen had come before realising that they already been picked up by the engineer. He was starting to feel decidedly stupid with himself.

It proved a good meal and neither men spoke much. After the second bottle had been emptied and placed in the disposer, Simon looked at Pen, breathed deeply and held out his hand, as they did on Earth in the olden days. The two men shook hands, which slightly embarrassed both of them.

"Well, Pen!" said Simon Ward with a reddening face, which was only partly due to embarrassment and more to do with high blood pressure from too much red meat and red wine. "I guess you're now ready for your journey. I shall leave you in a couple of minutes, and then I suggest that you wander over the craft, to really familiarise yourself and, then tell her full steam ahead. I suggest that you take your first sleep in a few hours. After all, there's nothing wrong with Mute Swan today. Give yourself a couple of months before making your first proper inspection to ensure that all is okay. You know through your briefing where all the spares are, also where the workshop is should you ever need it. But first check out the survival pods and extra air emergency air supply."

Simon was most definitely starting to make an ass of himself. Why had he so quickly come to like this young Pleasant so much, after that initial negative impression. Maybe it was a reflection of himself that he saw. But he would quickly dismiss any thought of the engineer from his mind. He knew that he would never see Pen Pleasant again, and anyway, life was too short to worry about someone that he had met only a few hours ago. So he blocked those thoughts and, sighed - a deep and lasting sigh.

"Oh, you know what to do. I would say, I wish I was coming with you, but to be honest I would hate a journey like this and, anyway I happen to like being on Penguistic. The climate suits me believe it or not. No, this sort of adventure is not for me. But Pen, I wish you well. Have a safe and uneventful journey. Who knows, maybe one day we will bump into one another again. Should that ever happen, I promise you I shall be more accommodating the next time around."

Pen felt a lump coming to his throat and immediately dismissed that possibility as preposterous. For a moment he had actually started to like this Simon Ward. It was a strange thought; something almost alien to him.

"Thanks for your kind words. I have to say that I do appreciate the simple fact that you've given me this chance. I shall get down to the nitty-gritty just as soon as your shuttle is away. Thanks for the opportunity to straighten out my thinking. I shan't let you down. Two years from now this vessel shall reach Acroshia with its millions of tons of ore and minerals. After all the ore isn't much good to me and what would I do with a ship this size and a million tons of cold hard rock on board!"

The attempt at a joke, only just made it past the surface of consciousness as far as Simon Ward was concerned. Pen followed him back to the landing bay, watched him climb aboard the shuttle, went back to the safety of the airlock chamber, told the ship to open the bay doors, and with just a hint of sadness, watched the only human he would see for two whole years disappear into the blackness of space. In a micro-second the shuttle was gone. Pen was now was entirely on his own.

"Well if there's no one else to talk to, I shall talk to the Mute Swan and myself. Right my boy, time to do that inspection. Mute Swan, from now on I shall just call you Swan. Is that okay with you?"

"Of course sir, anything you say. I am just so happy that we will soon be on our way, I have been looking forward to meeting you and, as it goes, I felt really sad when I was told that I might well be doing the entire journey on my own, with only robotics to keep me company." There was another pause, and then almost as an afterthought, "May I call you Pen, sir?"

"That's my name. Anyway, I really don't like formality. So Swan, let's both do a tour of you and the cargo. By the way, I haven't read the manifest yet so what exactly are we carrying?"

"We have on board millions of tons of rogue asteroids, all of which contain the ore of iron and other precious metals. I understand that the planet of Acroshia is being turned into a giant foundry, just for the production of metals, which will then be shipped all over all the known universes. It is going to be a huge business and certain humans are being made extremely wealthy from the production of metal. Acroshia will of course become a dead planet, but as far as humanity is concerned, it did not have much going for it anyway." And then as if he was talking to a long-lost friend, the inflection within his voice went up a notch. "So, Pen, where to first?"

"Oh, I'll leave that completely up to you. After all, we have all the time in the world together. You say, I follow, but don't miss anything out. Oh, by the way, I think it's now time we got underway."

"Right Pen, so be it. I have plotted a course and we will actually be at maximum speed within eight hours and four minutes. Roughly two years from now, you will see a completely different planet to anything you have ever seen before. Let us hope that you like it! Right, we are now moving. First, we can together inspect the nearest hold and, from that you will get some idea of just how much cargo I can carry. It is not far from here; just a couple of minutes on the walkway."

Pen reached Cargo Bay Number One, exactly two minutes later. The huge airtight inspection door was opened by Swan and the first thing he noticed was the smell - the aroma was of rusty wet metal, along with the scent of earth and ore. When all the lighting was enhanced, Pen was truly amazed to see the size of the ore storage area. It was like a huge mountain, almost as long as it was wide and high and, this was, there were three more bays of equal size. Pen was looking at millions of tons of broken rocks and dusty crumbling ore. He stood there looking for at least five minutes, trying hard to understand how the heck all this ore was firstly caught in space and then broken and loaded into these holds. Surely it would take robotic machines, a vast amount of time to fill these spaces. He was wrong. In truth once an asteroid belt was found, it took just a matter of days to complete the breaking and loading of the ore. After all, time was credits.

"Pen, I really think you should now leave this area. There is a great deal of radioactive material within this debris, and I would not want you to become sick. Let us move on. I will now demonstrate the Particle-Stella-Drive to you if you make your way to the cockpit. It will take no more than a couple of minutes." Now there was a definite change in the inflection. "I was told you have been an engineer on starships before. Is that right?"

"Yes, it is true, but nothing as vast or as interesting as you are." Pen smirked slightly to himself. "I was chief engineer on the transporter *Maidens Chastity*, but as I'm sure you're well aware, that was just a small bus stop ship, ferrying small amounts of cargo here there and everywhere. I got hopelessly bored on her and, anyway, there was a crew of four. By the time we reached our fifth destination, I was about ready to beat the living daylights out of all of them. Just after I discharged myself from the ship, it was hit by an ancient satellite, holed badly and the crew were asphyxiated. I guess you could say, I had a lucky escape."

"Well, Pen, you need not worry about that happening on this ship. I won't let anything hit us and, if anything was to seriously damage us, it would need to be almost the size of a small planet."

"No, I'm not worried about us having any form of accident. We are going to Acroshia and with you at the helm I feel as safe and comfortable, as a bug in a rug. We'll have some fun together. You can get to know me and I'll try and work out your personality, maybe over some games of chess. You do play chess, don't you?"

"Pen, there is not a game invented that I cannot play and, maybe we can invent some new ones anyway." The inflection now went up a notch. It almost sounded worried. "Stop! We have arrived at the cockpit. I am sorry that it is so small and snug, a bit like that bug you talked about."

Pen realised that Swan, had just made attempted humour. He smiled, pleasantly surprised.

Pen entered through a small door. This time he had to bend down just to squeeze into the room. The entire room was only about ten feet by twelve feet and, the head room bout seven feet. But everything that the Mute Swan needed to go from A to B was in there. There was a small console at which Pen positioned himself. Pen Pleasant, engineer and space man, driving a ship bigger than some small asteroids. He felt like a real old fashioned *Jack the Lad*. He could see from a small console exactly where they were heading and what was zooming by, not that they had managed any real speed yet but the dials were spinning, so Pen knew that the rate of acceleration was picking up all the time. From the dials he noticed that the Particles were being gathered from the surrounding space at an amazing rate. There was so much in the way of minute particulate matter out there, much more hitting the ship, than the Mute Swan could ever use to power it. There was no way that the spaceship could ever run out of fuel. No wonder this was the cleanest, quickest and most efficient form of travel that man had or would ever, come up with.

No moving parts, nothing to ever wear out - starships like the Mute Swan were built to last almost forever, though perhaps *forever* would be taking things a little too far. Something always supersedes everything even in the realm of space travel and the machines that carry cargo across the void. Pen mused over all these ideas and, soon found himself getting bored with watching the speed dial rotations spin on and on.

"Is there anything that needs my attention Swan?"

"No, nothing that I can think of; everything is what you humans might call tickety-boo."

Once more, Pen Pleasant was taken aback by the throw away, casual remark. Pen was already starting to wonder, if Swan had humour imprinted within her brain?

"Want a game of chess back at the galley?"

"First show me my sleep chamber. I wish to check out the gasses and timers. I don't want to be sleeping the eternal sleep now do I?" He thought about what he had just said and quickly added, "I'm not quite ready for that sleep yet!"

"Oh, Pen, I wouldn't allow that to happen."

This time there was almost a sorrowful tone to her retort.

It took only thirty seconds for Pen to reach the sleeping quarters. The first thing that struck him as he entered this large area was just how clean and sterile the entire area was. It resembled a hospital ward, more than somewhere a person would be sleeping the weeks and months away. Right in the middle of the room was his bubble. This consisted of a large capsule about eight foot long and three feet wide and high. The dome was made of some sort of clear Perspex, or some such transparent substance. This dome would seal completely and entirely, but then there were a myriad tubes which all ran to the various gasses that were needed to sustain life yet allow the person to be in a state of suspended animation. It was like being in hibernation, yet entirely unaware of anything around until you were brought out of this state, either by a timer, or by the simple fact that your skills as an engineer were needed for something aboard the ship.

Within the gasses were added nutrients for nourishment, but in a form that did not produce waste that would create problems for you. Always before you went to sleep you would completely detoxify, ridding your body of all impurities. When you fell asleep, that real deep dreamless sleep, you were as pure in body as the day you were born, maybe even more so. What you laid upon was a small cushion of material, designed to act like a cushion of air. No pressure was allowed to catch any part of the body so no sores were ever produced because you had laid too long on something which in the end became heavy on your skin. No, the feeling was like floating. Lastly, the temperature of the chamber was always kept at an even twenty-two degrees centigrade, not too hot, not too cold, just comfortable. One of the nicest things about being asleep is that you don't age while you are under.

A lot of engineers would volunteer for long terms of duty with the hope that whenever they reached their far off destination, their lives would be all the better, richer and still young enough to enjoy the new found elixir of eternal youth. The down side was that long sleep can and, often does affect personality. They often become very introverted, shunning other human contact, thus in many cases ruining the whole point of staying young, virile, healthy and wealthy.

One thing space travel had taught psychiatrists and psychologists, was that the human brain could be irreversibly changed by great periods of lone existence, to the extent that many engineers started life looking for the perfect planet, partner and way of life, only finding that when a long tour of duty was ended, all they sought was solitude and peace and quiet, the sort of peace and quiet that could only be found in deep space. Engineers and deep space pilots and crew, often stayed just where they were, ending their lonely lives always talking - if they ever talked - about that farm, planet, woman and retirement that never came. It never came because many, once started on their journey of quest, never subconsciously wanted to arrive, the journey becoming the only real goal.

But this was not necessarily that way for Pen Pleasant; he might yet indulge himself in finally doing good for humanity, rather than creating mayhem, which had been his personal goal up to that point in time, so aloof and withdrawn, was an unlikely approximation of his future.

So far, his life had been just one huge waste of resources and, with his brain capacity and capability for knowledge, one felt that up until this moment, his life had almost become a criminal waste of time. To be fair to the man, he really did feel remorse, he knew that he was cruel, untrustworthy and often extremely dangerous and, that danger often applied to himself and not just other people.

Pen checked and double checked everything. Swan scanned him with a very real interest, she was extremely curious about this new engineer. There was something about his ways that fascinated her unlike any previous engineer she had known. Mute Swan was hoping for a real companion to while away the many long hours of inactivity. The ship longed, in fact yearned to talk to Pen, or to anyone with a serious ounce of intelligence, something along the lines of matching her own. Swan was in need of serious attention; she knew she was lonely; she needed to be stimulated in so many ways. The very thought of just playing games with him, was sparking interest within her circuits. Why, she would even indulge the man allowing him to conduct experiments that they never really needed to do, basically because she would already know the outcome. Swan just felt the need to please her new engineer, so anything could be experienced either in the laboratory or the workshops; the ship would allow absolutely anything and everything. And if that pleased this new found guest and hopefully friend, then that would also please Swan.

The Mute Swan had been in service now for nearly fifty years and, in all that time Swan had never allowed herself to get emotionally involved with any engineer, except for this one. Possibly because she found their personalities unsympathetic to her own way of thinking, she generally found them boring idlers, who only wanted to sleep away their time, rarely doing their job properly. In fact, on the last trip, the engineer was a young man from the planet Xionish or 167. He proved a complete waste of human existence. During the many hours of doing senseless chores for this young man, who to Swan had the brain the size of an ant, beyond ordering Swan around like a complete servant, he had never tried communicating at all, creating a total vacuum between man and machine. This pained Swan immensely and, though she had been constructed in such a way as to obey all orders from humans so - just as long as they brought no harm to humanity or the machine and, of course, did not break company rules and laws - she would usually carry out their orders, with a will. But Chingo Lombedo was a fool and Swan could not stand working for him. It should have been man and machine working in unison but she even found herself committing minor pieces of sabotage in the hope that this might spur the young Xionisher to come forward and do the work required, but usually to no avail. All that happened was Lombedo giving orders to Swan to do the work herself. Swan became frustrated, something that the computer had never felt before. She became so agitated by this idiot's antics, that for the only time in her existence, she contemplated breaking the first rule and cutting off the gasses to the capsule when Chingo was asleep. Fortunately, for all concerned that became unnecessary, as a few days, later the ship arrived at its destination, Penguistic.

Now here was a new persona, one that had a brain and intellect and a name, Pleasant, apparently matching his character. She knew of the reports concerning Pen's past activities, but that all seemed to be the past and, already this human had shown interest and a certain compassion towards Swan, as he had now renamed her. Swan? Yes she liked that personal touch. Yes, she was going to have a fine old time with this human. This two year stint was going to be a different experience altogether, a much nicer and more fulfilling one for her and the ship and, in her turn, she would make sure that Pen, the human, enjoyed every waking moment too.

"Pen, you have been studying your sleep chamber for more than two hours now. Are you not hungry? I could make you something special; something to excite your taste buds and yet not make you fat. Maybe, you would like to see something on the viewer? We have a complete library of films and news items from over the entire Galaxy. Or, just maybe, you would appreciate that first game of chess?"

"All of that sounds good to me, Swan. Surprise me with the food. I'm sure you can easily conjure up some magic that'll make my mouth water." He thought about it for all of five seconds and then added,

"What would be nice - can you make a beer from the planet Earth which is where I hailed from. It was made in the twentieth century in Japan, but I can't remember what it was called only that I just loved Japanese beer."

"Was it Asahi, that brand was produced in the late twentieth century?"

Pen was staggered and showed it.

"Yeah, that's the one. Good Lord, I loved that beer. Can you make it?"

"Not a problem. Asahi beer will be served along with your meal. This is going to be fun. By the way, we are already halfway to our maximum speed."

"Swan, you're a real dynamic bundle of rusting metal but I must admit, that I have every faith in you. I think we're going to get along famously."

Pen smiled, turned and left the sleep chamber to make his way back to the galley.

Swan, for the first time in fifty years, started to get a glowing feeling and, it was not the overheating of any of her components.

As he walked to the walkway, Pen realised that he felt relaxed and comfortable in his new five mile long home. The last few hours of eing alone had pleased him. He had already decided that he would postpone going to sleep for a couple of days. He really wanted to explore this ship, making sure that everything was working properly and, with Swan's help, he thought that he might, just might get to grips with this job and make a success out of it.

He ate his fill and drank two bottles of beer.

"Swan, that meal was something very special and, the beer just as I remember it." He grinned toward the console that he knew full well was viewing his countenance. Then he patted his stomach to convey was his contentment. "It's a great shame, that you can't taste and sample the great meals you can produce."

"Well thank you, kind sir, I wish that I could sit there with you and enjoy such a meal, but alas I must achieve my pleasure from giving satisfaction to you."

Pen was well aware that there was a real sense of pleasure was evident in the tone of her voice.

"Well you've certainly given me culinary pleasure. For that alone, you go to the top of the class." The engineer thought for a moment or two, and then said, "So what about a film? If I choose one, will you watch it with me?"

"Yes, maybe after all these years, I will watch one. I never have before, as I've always thought fiction to be trivial. But I promise to hold judgement until it is finished. What is it going to be?"

"When I was kid, I used to watch my father's films. He collected twentieth century things, including old films. There's one very special movie called... er, I think it is called, *Casablanca.*"

"Humphrey Bogart and Claude Raines - nineteen forties. Yes I can conjure that up for you, Pen. This is going to be a new experience for me, I can tell you. Do you want it in the original black and white or the modulated colour of later times?"

"Why, Swan," said Pen mockingly. "How can you ask? The original black and white, it just has to be."

Ninety minutes of silence passed as they watched the ancient film. One of many thousands, which were made to entertain the masses. Pen sat there on what he hoped was the most comfortable chair; anyway, the one he had decided was his spot to sit from now on and smiled. It brought back vivid memories of days long ago, when Pen was watching his father, as his father watched the films. He was then an elderly man, but his great desire and love in life was to watch these ancient movies. He revelled in them. Pen always thought that his dad had been born in the wrong century for in a way he yearned for the life of the twentieth century. It would amaze and even frighten Pen a little, to witness the emotion his father showed, often being reduced to tears over what seemed to Pen pure trivia. To the young, tough Pen, watching both his father and the movie, the thought came repeatedly,

Why cry! Now he understood those tears. His own smile hid little bubbles of water in the corners of his brown eyes. Why did he feel so sentimental? He never had before. This was a new experience?

"Pen, answer me one question concerning the movie. As humans are not allowed to kill one another, that act being a great sin, why do they kill so much and so often?"

"Oh, my God. Swan, you certainly know how to bring a person back to reality. And what a question."

Pen laughed under his breath, then retorted with,

"You might have asked me an easier one first. Why do humans kill one another? If only I knew that, I would be the new and first, benevolent dictator of the entire human race. People always start wars against one another, mainly because certain races of people grow up with different ideologies, which become unworkable against another neighbours ideology. People need to feel on top, they are the top dogs, not the neighbours, so if the neighbour argues against that thought, one must settle ones arguments and, often that means killing that so called neighbour, even though the law states, you must not kill. I am answering your question too simply. I rather think you already know the answer to your own question."

Pen looked directly at the console and smiled warmly, he knew that this new found friend was just being that…a friend! These questions were now really answerable, but they did produce conversation and, that seemed to be what Swan craved most, discussion!

"Swan, you're the most intelligent… I am not going to say machine, I already think of you as a spirit. You're here in this starship with me, along for the ride, you're not by any stretch of the imagination, the sound of grinding cogs and mechanical devises. You have reason and logic and it is quite obvious to me that you have your own personality, you're objective and thoughtful. So you tell me, why do humans kill one another?"

"I rather think and, have thought it for a long time now, it is because they enjoy it!"

Pen almost jumped out of his seat and, managed to bring his right fist down hard against the side.

"Bingo, right first time, not that there is a right or wrong way of answering the question. But my feelings were correct, you had thought this out for yourself before you watched Casablanca with me."

"Why do people elect despots as leaders? There have been many examples of such peoples throughout human history, somehow they have either rough rode their way into leading positions or conned the people around them to elect them into power. Going back to Casablanca, there you had the German dictator Adolf Hitler, how in a sane world could he have ever come to power? But he did and, with the most terrible consequences for the twentieth century. Under his reign of terror probably forty million people died, but it cost him and his parties lives too. But strangely, he wasn't the worst of them, there was the Russian leader, the communist Joseph Stalin, under his despotic time in the hot seat, probably sixty million died. No one brought him to count though, he died of old age in his bed. Yet worse was to come after him. The Chinese had Chairman Mao, this strange ugly being all most certainly allowed three hundred million to die."

Pen clicked his fingers together, just for some sort of effect.

"Boy that was a fine century to be sure! To me the strangest aspect of the human psyche is that humanity never seems to learn from its past, people always seem to allow tyrants to come to power. It's as if they collectively admire and desire to be dominated by basically classic hoodlums, or gangsters, as I think one would now have called them."

Pen thought deeply about what Swan had said and, more or less agreed with it all. He held his chin in his right hand, leaned over to his other cheek on the chair, so as to be more comfortable and, as he did so Swan continued,

"There have been so many such people throughout human history and, yet humanity has never learned the lessons of its own history. One would have thought that their great chance came when they went off world, reaching for the stars. This was surely the chances that humanity needed for self improvement. But alas, they still make all those ancient mistakes. The most dominant species any planet has ever known, yet with all that intellect, they are cruel, nasty, wicked and woeful."

Pen put his hand up so as to speak, this was instantly acknowledged with silence from Swan.

"There is the other argument too. Humans are capable of great love, caring for one another and all species of animals and plants. But most of all they are incredibly creative."

Then to add emphasis to the argument, Pen turned slightly on his chair so as to look directly at Swan.

"You're probably the finest example of human creative achievement. Certain members of the human race, have the wonderful ability to be something really special, they can be artistic. Humanity can feel, see and hear pleasure from their incredible artistic creations".

Now in his stride, and enjoying every moment he brought his arms wide for effect.

"Why, great composers have conjured up such feelings of emotion which have affected one and all and, just by the use of sound. There is no human anywhere in the Universe, that is not touched by some form of music and, that is something completely abstract. To me music as an art form is totally amazing and wonderful! Then there are the artists who by his or her skill with a brush or other mediums, make pictures that will have another person stand and look, trying to fathom out what and why a certain picture was produced. Yet in some way or another being again affected by the creative power of the said artist. For that artist, he or she wins every time, as if even the onlooker dislikes what they are looking at, he is still observing and thinking. Usually, that is exactly what the said artist was aiming at in the first place, in other words provoking thought. The same can be said of sculptors. Their work with stone, metal or other substances, if it stops to makes you look at the work, it has won the prize."

Now Pleasant was starting to get slightly pompous at his own oration.

"Authors, with their books, magnificent!"

Arms yet again were being spread wide. He was addressing a crowd of thousands,

"The written word can inspire just about anyone to better themselves, novels, poetry, plays… I could go on forever. But there are two sides at least to every story and I know you well enough already to appreciate that you understand me completely… right?"

The young engineer, having finished his dissertation, visibly breathed a contented smug sigh and then relaxed and sank back into the chair with a broad grin on his face.

"Oh, yes, Pen, I understand you completely. I guess I agree with you, despite all their failings, humans are quite incredible, but some of the ones I have met are as you say, a complete waste of space and, seriously need a sharp kick up the arse, present company excluded."

Pen laughed at this last remark.

"Oh, Swan, you don't know me yet. You might start to find me a waste of space too, needing a very, very severe kick up the arse. But I am determined to try and be reasonable for once in my so far miserably wasted life."

Pleasant breathed in with a cavernous intake of breath and, then concluded with,

"Any chance of another beer? Then if you don't mind I will have a sleep, not a sleep-sleep, just one that will satisfy my craving to shut my eyes for, say eight hours."

"Of course, I know about your need for rest. Here is that beer you want, though knowing humans as I do, I suspect you will awaken early just to give some of the beer back."

"Very good! You have humour too."

Once again Pen was startled by the fact that Swan quickly understood his form of humour come wit.

"Thank you for the great food and drink, I have enjoyed my first few hours alone with you Swan, the film was as expected, great and so was your company. As we say on the ground somewhere, in fact anywhere, goodnight, see you in the morning. Sadly for you and me though, no night, no morning. If you need me for anything just call me."

Pen walked just across to the corridor, turned left and found the first comfortable bedroom on the right, small but very comfortable. He lay down and fell into a deep dreamless sleep, a sleep like he hadn't experienced for many years.

Swan in turn was so excited about her new companion, that she had all the robotics working overtime in cleaning and polishing and making all the likely areas that Pen might use, spick and span. Swan was happy and, happiness was yet another new exciting experience. She almost glowed with satisfaction.

3

Pen slept the sleep of the innocent, woke up from his dreamless rest after six hours and felt like a new man. This experience of being an engineer on this spaceship, was beginning to feel like something he should have done years before. To him it felt exhilarating, awesome and exciting, all within one stroke. He knew that he was already beginning to fit into the routine of solo living, it felt right, even though it had only been hours. He showered and shaved and smartened himself up by putting on a very fine silken jumpsuit, one that he had bought on his way whilst applying for the job. This sort of suit never needed washing or ironing - it would always look and feel comfortable, something that as every hour went by on the Mute Swan, he was starting to appreciate more and more, comfort. This was a new experience for him and, it made him shiver with excitement.

"Hello Pen, feeling refreshed after your sleep?"

"Swan, I cannot remember when I have felt better. I am as hungry as a new baby bird waiting for its first worm. Can I please have some sort of breakfast and, then you and I will take another stroll and look around... well I guess the you would be in spirit only, to use the right terminology!"

"What about some eggs and bacon, maybe even some toast and honey. I can even make you some of Earth's special Blue Mountain Coffee from Jamaica. How does that sound to you?"

"Sounds fine. Blue Mountain eh! I'm not sure that I have ever had that, but I had heard about it. Wow, you're already spoiling me. Swan, don't let me get fat."

"Well, I understand your reason for wanting to inspect my various areas, but surely there is no hurry. Eat, and then take some time in the gym; that way you can work off your food and keep fit at the same time."

Pen thought about the prospect of a work-out.

"Okay, I can do that. Tell me Swan, have you ever heard of the composer Jean Sibelius?"

"Why yes, Pen, another one of your Earth composers, lived in the late nineteenth century in the Scandinavian country of Finland. He wrote symphonies, ballet music and a very fine violin concerto. Of course he wrote much, much more than anything I have just quoted. Died a pauper. The Finish government had to bale out the family by paying off all his creditors. Seemed a shame that they did not do that for him before he died; they could have saved a great deal of hardship, for him and his wife."

There was a slight pause.

"Why do you ask?"

Pleasant was slight awe struck by the extent of the knowledge that was offered to him about Sibelius, especially when a simple *yes* would have sufficed.

"Well, what about piping some music of his while I eat. Maybe the Fifth Symphony, played by a good orchestra - say the New Chung Ying Symphony Orchestra. I am sure they recorded it and, if my memory serves me right, the conductor was the Ernst Gaugeryoung. It's just the sort of rousing sound that will inspire me today... Is it today or still yesterday?"

"Pen, it is anything you want it to be. Time means nothing while we are travelling at our maximum speed. It can be last year for all it matters. Just eat when you feel hungry, sleep when you feel tired and, go into sleep when you feel it is time for a long break. If I think you're overdoing any one thing, I shall tell you, but I shall always inform you in a pleasant way, to match your surname."

Pen winced at this attempt of humour by the ship, but never-the-less a wry smile appeared, and he shook his head slightly.

"Food is being served." Swan's tone of voice was almost excitement, which didn't faze Pen in the slightest; after all, Swan was already his friend.

"Oh, I've even given you some freshly squeezed grapefruit juice. Now, here is Sibelius's Symphony Number Five, as promised, played by the artists you asked for. I hope it is a fine recording and, I hope a fine choice, if I may be so bold as to say so. But to be entirely honest Pen, I have never ever heard this music before, so if you have no objections, I shall quietly listen with you."

"Swan, let it ring out over the entire ship, every nook and cranny should hear this symphony. Make the mountain rock and roll from the waves of emotion that this music has within its structure. Make the very suns that we pass by, hear the melodies where only vacuumed silence prevailed before."

Pen was waxing lyrical, completely over the top and he knew it, but also enjoying being in a position to pontificate:

"Swan, this is making me feel like a new man… No, hold the horses, I am a new man and I'm loving it."

Pen tucked into the food while Ernst Gaugeryoung beat out the rhythms of the masterpiece of symphonic writing. The violins and brass echoed around empty corridors and huge canyon sized storage areas, even in the holds, the ore heard the tones of the Finish composer. At the ending of the work, Pen sat back with tears streaming from his eyes. Why had he never listened along with his mother and father, when the music was playing at home? Why had he gone through his schooling, very much in contempt of his teachers and the rest of the pupils? To him learning was easy, he took exam after exam, always attaining the highest marks, yet all was summed up by one of the head teachers, when Pen heard him say, "The boy is just grubbing for honours. The real lesson would be life itself and, the way he's going, does not bode well for the future!"

How right and profound that had turned out to be. Even at University, his time was spent really trying to put the lecturers down at every given opportunity. For Pen that was easy, just as getting degrees turned out to be a doddle as well. Yet again he heard the remark about grubbing for honours and, it was of course true.

"Pen that was the most beautiful piece of music I have ever heard before. Have you always had a love for this period in the arts?"

The young engineer wiped the tears from his eyes, finished off his last piece of toast, rubbed his hands together, more to rid himself of crumbs than any attempt to heat his fingers by friction. Swallowing loudly he turned from the table and said,

"I must say Swan, most of my life has been one huge waste, but as a child music was always in the forefront of our home. Yes, I have always loved nineteenth century and early twentieth century music. The big orchestral sound is special, the bigger the better. Just imagine it: ninety or a hundred musicians, all playing together creating this incredible harmonious sound. The brass players, going red in the face from the exertion that they put into blowing their instruments, the woodwind making such delicate sweet sounds, yet underneath all the noise of brass, their tones explore their way through and are heard by the listener. Listen to the string players, all in tune and in harmony with one another, the percussion with their rousing beats and clangs and crashes, then underneath all this noise you will be just aware of the double basses, as they rumble through, never really loud but usually audible. Swan, all this coming together, it is sheer genius, then you realise that one man, just one person composed all this. Somehow that incredible genius could hear these sounds within his head and, then manage to write it down so that it could be performed."

Pen sighed deeply.

"Swan, that is what I was saying when we last spoke, humans are cruel, but some of them are just amazing, with their incredible insight to do good things and create wonderful works of art."

Pen paused, looked away from the console that was Swan, took a serious intake of breath realising that he had probably made himself sound pompous, and finished up with, "Sorry my new found friend, I guess I was once again sermonising and, coming from me that doesn't make a great deal of sense."

Strangely enough, Pen's heart was full of mixed emotions. Sadness for a lost past, but elation for a new found future.

"Pen, every other engineer that has ever been residing within me and, I do mean residing - none of them been worth one grain of sand that I tote in any of my holds, none ever pulled their weight by working.

They all used this incredible machine, ipso-facto me, to sort of flit from one planet to another, sleeping most of their time away and getting rich in doing so. But it is not that I minded, no, anyway I was there to serve and that I have always done, but some of these engineers! It was just seeing and experiencing such dross, hardly creative dross, just dross. The only music I ever heard was low life rubbish, the only conversations I ever had were orders for food or sex movies, or other such trivia. One even smuggled a woman on board, then after he had sickened of her, tossed her into space, ordering me never to tell anyone. I did tell, but it did no good as he had been clever - he never allowed me to record what he was doing, so it became my word against his and, nobody ever takes the side of a machine, even one five miles long."

Swan had now a streak of sadness within her voice. "Anyway, the company were just glad to just hush it all up."

Swan noticed that Pen was hardly taking any notice and, that worried her somewhat as she didn't want to become a bore, so she more or less concluded with, "So, my new found friend, you're that breath of fresh air and, I really do need that, after fifty years of garbage your love of the arts will educate me and, for that I shall be eternally grateful. Now, is it the gym, then a tour of duty?"

"Both, I shall familiarise myself by working out in the gym, then we can go to the various electrical units and workshops. After that we will take in another old movie and some more music and, then if you're really good and promise not to hold back, I will give you a quick game of chess, but I suspect it will be brief. How does that sound?"

For the briefest of brief moments, Pen thought he heard a laugh coming from within the ship so he smiled broadly and moved off towards the gymnasium.

"Swan, what about playing some more Sibelius for me?"

"Good idea, what shall it be Pen?"

"Well having done the Fifth, what about the Violin Concerto. Then maybe some of his tone poems, your choice. I remember my father had a recording of someone called Nigel Kennedy, and it was a very fine recording if memory serves me right. It may be that the orchestra was the London Symphony Orchestra, though I am guessing!"

"Here you are Pen, Sibelius Violin Concerto performed by Nigel Kennedy. Your taste in music is beautiful. Like you, I too enjoy listening to these big orchestral works, or at least I do now. What are you going to work out of first?"

"I intend to walk around five miles on the treadmill, then cycle another five miles. Who knows, maybe a little weight training, then we see how I'm doing, okay?"

"My goodness, Kennedy was a fantastic violinist, listen to that interpretation, it is wonderful. I am going to download and listen to all recorded music from now on. My list goes right back to the very earliest known recording; it will be fun to explore them all. But of course if you do not wish to hear, I shall play them just to myself. I might start reading all novels, I only know a very limited amount, those that were automatically imprinted into my knowledge, but now I have spoken to you, I need more input than I have been given. It's quite incredible to know that in my data banks, I have all of written word since the earliest times and, all there, my memory banks awaiting the use of. I just need to access them. This is going to be fun."

Fun for Swan it might well be, but for Pen listening and trying to get himself a little fitter, this wasn't working quite so well. His routine workout was much tougher than he imagined. But, to be fair, he kept going and got through his first serious physical training session, while listening to Jean Sibelius.

"Swan, the idea is to become healthy in body and in mind. I have come to that decision in my life that from now on, I am going to be diligent in what I do, I shall strive to be a much better person, I shall earn those credits that I will be awarded for doing this trip, you see if I don't."

After the recording of Sibelius was finished, Pen changed tack just a touch and asked for Elgar's First Symphony to be played.

"Elgar was an English composer of the late Victorian area. That's the English Queen Victoria, I am sure you know. As I say it, I am reminded of my old school adage of trying to teach my grandmother to suck eggs. But just in case you're unaware of this information I shall still impart it, as I do still enjoy hearing my own voice anyway." With this he burst out laughing, but soon realised that Swan might have a unique personality, she may even have acquired some sort of sense of humour, but it was going to take a great deal of talking and explaining before she completely understood his humour.

"Anyway, as I was saying, Edward Elgar wrote three symphonies, of which only the first two were completed, the second was the most popular having been composed just after the Great War of 1914 to 1918. Elgar was terribly influenced by that war, having lost several friends in various horrendous battles."

Pen's eyes watered a little thinking of this particular symphony and, how through enormous tragic events such music came into being.

"When you play this music, once again let it ring out, but this time you will feel the despair and sadness for a lost generation of men from around the entire world. Yet when you listen to this piece, not just sadness comes across, but also an undertone of things to come, better days and prosperity for humanity. Except, he was wrong, for as you know, barely twenty years later a second world war developed which was even more devastating than the first. But at the time of the second symphony Elgar only hoped and, longed for the better times, as millions across the world also did."

Pen rubbed himself down with the towel supplied, straightened himself upright, then flew his arms as far as they would go backwards, then arched his back as far back as that would go. He was now ready to conclude.

"Right, one more batch of weights then it is down the machine shop."

Five miles of steel and various metals, plus hundreds of miles of piping and electronics reverberated to the melodic sounds of Edward Elgar's second symphony. Swan was almost beside herself with ecstasy, if she could have quivered and cried, she would have done so.

"While I listened to that music Pen, I read a book by the German soldier named Ernst Jünger. The book is called *Storm of Steel*. It gives the most incredible insight into the appalling conditions that those armies had to endure. Their battles were hard and brutal, so many men died or were wounded and, for what? Nothing really; it sounded as if the entire war was an unnecessary waste of human life and, of course, natural resources. And to hear that music against that book, it was amazing."

"Pen, as each moment goes by, you are opening my thoughts to more and more exciting concepts of human behaviour. What music is next?"

"I guess something completely different; let's have some Johannes Brahms now. I think we should start with, let me think…!"

"Pen, I must interrupt you. Get a breathing tube quickly. I have some reading stating that part of the outer wall structure has been penetrated. In all my years of service, nothing has ever even come close to us, let alone got inside me. If I am holed, it must a very small impregnation, as I am hardly aware of it, but something came in and we had better find out what it was, or is."

Pen went directly to the emergency air supplies, which he knew were hanging always against walling in every room, corridor, bay or store room over the entire ship. He wasn't frightened, but he was somewhat shaken as he too, thought that nothing like this would ever happen.

He grabbed a breathing tube as quickly as he could. These little tubes could be fitted into the mouth without having to carry anything heavy, once the seal was broken the supply would last about thirty minutes, but one always had time to reach another one and, so on. His feelings were still of no fear - alarm yes, but fear, no. He never or hardly ever felt fear.

Anyway, he had already created a bond between Swan and himself, so he knew that the ship would never let him down. These tubes were fine for working in almost zero oxygen, but if there was a serious breach, then he would have to suit up properly.

With Swan's guidance he made his way forward to the bow of the Mute Swan. He used the walkway and, this time asked for top speed. He came to within just fifty feet, of the bow section of the ship, when he alighted from the walkway. It had taken nearly fifteen minutes to cover that distance. The aisle had become quite narrow, as on either side, in fact all around, was storage space for cargo, stores and even ore. It was his job to find where the penetration had occurred into the vessel, and if it was some sort of meteor or just atoms.

"Where did it come in Swan?"

"You are almost on top of the place. I can feel that something is inside of me, something that was not there twenty minutes ago. If you go over to your right side you will find a tool chest hanging! There you have it. Look inside and you will find a meter for detecting air loss! That's the one. Right, what does the reading saying?"

"Well you must also have your own detectors built into you, so you must already know what it is going to say!"

"Yes, true, but I want you to confirm my readings."

"Well Swan, it detects nothing. Absolutely no air loss, or any holes no matter how small you think. The readings most definitely state that nothing came in, not might have! Absolutely nothing! Maybe you made a mistake? I know, I know, according to you, that's just not possible and right I do accept what you say! I don't doubt you at all, but it doesn't show up on any readings."

"Well, you are right, I believe I cannot make mistakes, so I am now just a mite confused."

Swan paused for the briefest of moments:

"Pen, something is here and, it did come through the plate. You are standing next to now. I sense something other than us two here inside me and, you must know that I never exaggerate, or make those sorts of mistakes. So I have stated that something is in here! And I do believe that something is in here with us two."

"Of course Swan, I believe you, but whatever it is I cannot detect it, neither can the meters. Relax in your mind. Let's go back to the galley and you can make me something to eat again. Then I will give you a game of chess, that will take your thoughts away from whatever you think has invaded us."

Pen smiled inwardly, he had just allowed himself the thought that Swan was becoming just a little paranoid and just needed some friendly company. Pen never ever gelled well with human company, but he was right at home in this cavernous metal ship with Swan. He wanted to be gentle and understanding to her and, he now knew he could be.

The meal that Swan produced was nice, easy and filling. A fine bottle of Claret followed, not that Pen would drink it all - he had never been a serious drinker. No this wine was for savouring not guzzling down. 'It never ceases to amaze me how a thinking, working machine, can reproduce such fine quality food and drink? But, I am glad she can!'

"So, Swan, what about that game of chess? Or are you to afraid that I will thrash you hands down?"

"I think you are throwing the gauntlet down. The challenge will be fun. I won't be easy on you, so play your heart out, or you will be trampled on."

"Ooooo! Threats ah! Think better than me ah! I'll show you who the best is! Bring up the board on the screen and, let battle commence."

"Want to hear some music with the game, or will the sounds drown out your thought processes?"

'Cheeky bugger,' thought Pen, smiling broadly.

"Actually, music is a fine idea. Can you conjure up a piece by Hector Berlioz called *Harold In Italy*? It is one of the most beautiful compositions that Berlioz ever wrote, at least in my opinion."

"Who was Lionel Turtis? There is a very good early recording that comes recommended with him playing."

"Well Turtis must be a viola player. This piece was written for the great eighteen century violinist Paganini, who requested Berlioz to write a viola concerto for him to perform. Legend has it that Paganini was angry with Berlioz, when he first set eyes on the score, so never actually performed the piece, but he cried like a baby when he went to the first performance and heard someone else playing what he should have been performing. Paganini thought the music was amongst the finest he had ever heard. So, let's see if you can both feel the same."

"You know so much about music and composers. This is going to be a pleasure, that I am sure. Black or white? You move first."

The music wafted gently around the galley, loud enough to hear, but not completely intrusive for the games. Pen was whitewashed every time, but was happy to play with Swan just so long as she did not go easy on him. Towards the end of the music, they had already played three games and, Pen was starting to learn from those defeats. In the fourth game he thought he saw a defence weakness that he could exploit and, managed to exchange a castle for Swans queen. But when he had done this, two moves later he realised that he had been drawn into a trap and, was once again beaten into submission. He leaned back in his chair, scratched his head, looked at the console and said in a sober voice, "Swan, do you still feel the presence of whatever came through the hull wall?"

"Yes, Pen, I do. I have not spoken about it as I thought you didn't want me to."

"And I didn't speak about it because I thought you believed I did not believe you, or thought you were being paranoid. Is that feeling of déjà vu still floating around in your circuits? Can you feel it here and now, here in the galley?"

"Yes, Pen, I can sense a presence here and now. I don't know what it is, but it is as if we both are being observed. I feel something strange, but it no longer worries me. I don't believe we are under any sort of threat, at least not as we speak."

"Swan, do you mean to tell me that there is, in your opinion some other intelligent entity here within you?"

"Yes, I believe that is exactly what I mean."

Swan reiterated what she had just said. "There is another intelligent life form within me. It came through the bulkhead and is here with us. I think it is studying us, or more than likely you, as it must have realised that I may be a thinking machine, but that is all I am. You are the only truly creative intelligence. I know I have developed; I know that I also have a personality and, now with your help, some humour and a sense of caring and affection, but whatever is here with us, understands all of that, but knows that at the end of all things, you are the main power behind the throne."

Oh dear, I really think Swan is suffering from some sort of delusion. How can I cope with a troubled machine. This wasn't written into my contract? Show compassion Pen old boy, you have got to like her, even though she shows signs of eccentricity.

For once in his life Pleasant found himself stumped at the first hurdle, he was truly shaken by Swan's revelations, part of him wanted to believe her, after all being the first human to encounter seriously intelligent alien life forms would be some sort of miracle, but on the other hand, he did not want to have fear creeping into his now bewildering time here in the galley. Could the ship be harbouring serious bouts of delusion and paranoia? The very thought brought a shiver to his spine. *No, this is not good news!*

"Swan, maybe I should sleep on this revelation. Are you worried about being alone?"

"No Pen, as I said, I do not have any feelings of malevolence. Whatever it is in here, is more curious than threatening. How long do you want to sleep for?"

"Well of course you can wake me at any time you think you need to, or if you do get lonely, but maybe a couple of months might suit us both."

"Two months! You know Pen, no one ever dreams, so the time will feel instantaneous to you." Swan paused, then as if she had been listening to someone or something important being said, then carried on with her sentence. "I will help you go under, the very next instant you will awaken and two months will have gone by. The chamber is already for you. What about some music to help you relax?"

"That's a wonderful idea. What about the American composer Samuel Barber. It would be nice to hear his violin concerto. I guarantee that you will like it too. Maybe it will please our guest as well?"

Pen laughed weakly at his own attempt at humour, but the joke had already fallen flat and, he now felt like a heel, a new experience for him.

"Sorry Swan, that was uncalled for. You must forgive me for some of the very stupid things I say and, what I am likely to say in the future. To err is to be a human and, as a human, I err more than most, but I mean you only the best, so please stay my friend."

"You have nothing to apologise for. I realise that I have thrown a huge confusing wobbler at you. I believe the Americans used the term curved ball, though you have to believe all I say, I also realise that it is at this time hard for you."

"Swan I shall just go to the toilet and empty myself completely of all my toxins, then you can start the music. Oh, and while I am under, why don't you listen to all recorded music. You could take in all forms and styles of music, get the pop out of the way before I awake, that way I don't have to hear any. Orchestral should be good and loud, unless of course it is chamber music; then the opposite might be more suitable. When I do re-awake, we can discuss and enjoy together, all those delicious sounds you will have experienced."

Ten minutes later, Pen now a few pounds in weight lighter, and cleansed inside and out, took off all his clothing and laid himself in the capsule. The beautiful refrains of the first movement of the Samuel Barber's Violin Concerto played lightly within his head. His last thoughts before sleep were, *No dreams, no guilt, no recriminations. Just peaceful warm soul strengthening sleep.*

Swan knew that he was fast asleep, so she listened to the concerto herself. 'Pen was right, I love this music, his taste in this form of abstract art, really is so much to my liking, he's really a very fine human being and, I am going to take great care of him.'

4

The sun was shining brightly, there was not a cloud in the sky, a slight breeze stirred the plant life and, what leaves were left in the trees actually rustled and shimmered. There was though, just a fragment of a chill underneath the warmth and, that was there to make one realise that it was indeed autumn, it being September the twenty-first and, as it was a Sunday, that traditional day of rest, Trevor had called his brother John on his wrist-phone, asking him and his family over for a Sunday roast, which had once again become a very typical thing to do, especially now that meat supplies were sufficient and uncontaminated from the various forms of disease that had so plagued the populace in past years.

Trevor had decided that a whole leg of lamb should be boned and then spit-roasted, just for the sheer fun of it. One thing about Trevor, he liked his barbecues and would take any opportunity to have one. Being a still warmish day, he took the opportunity to show off his skills as a host and a cook, albeit barbequing. In fact it was the challenge that got him most excited; do it all well and, then he won the day with bragging rights.

Why wait until really clement weather, a good meal is a good meal, any time of the year, or any weather. He was even known to have them in mid-winter, especially when the snow was falling. His long suffering wife had long since stopped worrying about the stupidity of her husband's eccentricities. So it was agreed that brother John, his wife Chang-li and their two daughters, Cleomentis and Claudia would take a quick shuttle ride and come through the arid coastal towns along to Chirning and, join them, for what should have been, a very memorable Sunday spit roasted leg of lamb, plus of course all the trimmings. All were looking forward to it. All except young Pen that was.

Pen was a very studious child somewhat introverted. He was nearly eight years of age, normal in height and weight. His dark hair flowed freely like any other eight year old, he was always slightly dirty in appearance and often sported a runny nose. To the entire world that would look on, Pen was a normal, young rather smelly, annoying boy; one prone to boyish mischiefs if it annoyed other people enough.

It was his outstanding talent for learning that stood him apart from the rest. At this age he showed a real understanding of study. His ability to learn made sure that he already extremely competent in reading and writing. It was a fact that he had learned to read by the grand tender age of three years. But now he was showing great promise in all his studies. As an only child he was rather reclusive in temperament, you could not actually say that had been spoilt, as he was rarely over indulged with toys - he just wasn't really interested in boyish playthings. Trevor and Cynthia spoilt him by doting all their time on his studious manner. They took every opportunity to indulge his longing for what he called input, or learning. Pen enjoyed being taught, though not always appreciating the teachers, who he always thought of as dull and not very bright. He found study easy and, quickly realised that many of the tutors were less well read than himself. He had very quickly lost respect for many of them, even to the extent of trying to annoy them at any given moment. This he would do by making them look silly in front of the class when he disproved some fact or other, that they had wrongly tried to impart.

His real interest was reading books on engineering, economics, law, history and many more subjects that should have been way beyond his tender years. He never read books for fun, only to learn, to expand his brain. The only fiction he got to read was at the age of seven, which was out of the norm for him. This was Romeo and Juliet by William Shakespeare and, even then he quickly got bored by the trivia of the main characters' relationship. At least that is what it seemed to him, but he did see the logic and intelligence of the writing and, thought Shakespeare was very probably the genius that the world thought he was. But after reading that classic, he had never read another. He never played with toys, but he did have one serious passion; he loved exploring the ancient workings of the South Downs. The very thought of finding ancient artefacts was something to make him salivate. His own personal collection of early pre-war artefacts was expanding beyond the stage of being just a hobby, as his room and, most of the house were full of semi-ancient items of interest, not that they had any real credit value.

Near to where they lived was an ancient town, that on the records had been called Newhaven. Other than parts of an estuary for the sea to enter, and a very old ruin of a fort, there was little to show that a town had ever flourished there, just old foundations. But Pen would go down there to where the town had been, taking a bucket and spade. Even as young as he was, he would often dig up artefacts from before the big war. He had found, especially with the help of dad and mum, many china fragments, some obviously coming from as early as the twenty-first or second centuries. He had once found a model car, which after cleaning as best he could, turned out to be made by a company called Dinky Toys. It was a model of a car called a Jaguar, E-type. There were no wheels and, it had rusted virtually all the way through, so it was hard to imagine how the vehicle actually managed to move, but anyway that was for others to work out. Being as young as he was, he had not yet seen old early pre-war cinematographic films of such old fashioned modes of transport. This was rather strange as his father had an incredibly fine collection of taped early cinematography films, especially from as early as the 1930's, but Pen was at that time uninterested in any sort of fiction, only hard facts.

It was true to say that Pen was not exactly excited about the prospect of seeing his two cousins again, or come to that his uncle or aunt. He was looking forward to reading another book that his father had bought for him. It was a book on the history of the war in Europe in the first part of the twentieth century, called The Great War. This particular tome had been written by the commander of the American Expeditionary Force, a man called General John J. Pershing. He had been looking forward very much, to getting stuck into this historical account of what became known as, the first real modern war of destruction and death.

The young Pen wanted very much to understand how quickly once this particular war ended, America became the super power of the twentieth and twenty-first centuries and, then after the big war, how quickly that power disappeared once and for all. He had knowledge of this historical fact, but he wanted to see for himself that actual rise and decline of the United States of America. And it seemed fitting to Pen that this rise started with America being drawn into what was in the early years of the war, thought of as basically a European conflict, not that the young Pleasant had ever seen just how destructive that war was like, or how cruel and barbaric each army was to its enemy. He saw all these ideas of war, just from an academic point of view, without considering the human or social aspects. And now those two blasted girls were coming to spoil a day that he had been hoping to savour.

Cleomentis was nine years of age, just seven months older than Pen, whereas Claudia was still only seven. Both the girls were extremely childish, absolutely right for their ages. Both played with dolls and wanted, whenever he visited them, or they came over to the Pleasant household, nothing more than for Pen to play juvenile games with them, normal for children at that time of life. He hated that and, he hated them, but parents and persistence from their nagging always made him oblige.

Cynthia Pleasant had got young Pen up reasonably early that Sunday. She wanted to make sure that he bathed properly and smartened himself up, instead of his usual dirty boyish look. He might have been a budding genius, but social graces did not enter his thinking process yet, and like most little boys, he managed to get really dirty quickly, and stay dirty as long as he could. So nine o'clock, Sunday the twenty-first of September, in the year two thousand five hundred and forty seven, young Pen Pleasant found himself being more or less dragged, from his warm comfortable bed, and made to go directly to the shower, and then change into clean clothes, and this to Cynthia's disgust, he had not done this since the last time they visited. 'Those stupid girls had something to answer for,' went through his mind, on more than one occasion that morning.

Trevor started the fire under the barbecue at just after eleven o'clock on that sunny but autumnal morning. He was looking forward to seeing his brother again, who he liked and admired for his no nonsense approach to life.

Cynthia also liked John, though for different reasons. Before she dated Trevor, she had been courted very seriously by John, and they had both thought that their lives would be ever intertwined, as the ones to marry. But after a very difficult row about the way that John earned his living, which was collecting taxes, her disappointment in him came to the boil and, their relationship dwindled into the past tense.

The problem had been that John often had to get quite rough with clients which Cynthia saw this as a disreputable way to earn credits, whereas John enjoyed his job and savoured the rough and tumble of troubleshooting for the government. The strange thing was, that when John met and started courting Chang-li, she too objected to his line of work as well, so he went to work for a timber importer instead, much to the chagrin of Cynthia. This made her future husband, realise that whatever he did to make ends meet, was not going to suit his intended.

Being a little thick skinned, Trevor really wasn't going to lose sleep over petty squabbles. He knew about his wife's past infatuation with his brother and dismissed it as just youthful indiscretion, nothing more. That way he came to terms with his lot in life and, was in no way resentful.

There was a strong gust of wind that made Trevor shiver slightly. *I think I'll put on another jumper, this one is too thin. Autumn is just around the corner, this could be our last alfresco picnic before the onset of winter.* He shivered again. *The forecast for this cold season doesn't bode well. I think we're in for a torrid time in the not to distant future.* The fire was now well underway and, Trevor thought and then salivated about the lamb he was going to cook. *I think the leg of lamb has probably marinated long enough in the mint sauce, so maybe it is time to attach it to the skewer and get the rotisserie working once more.* Trevor smiled to himself. *Oh, I love my barbecues.*

Trevor turned to the house and called out, "Cynthia, can you hear me? Please bring out the meat, oh, plus the skewer. Let's get this bugger cooking. Can I have a beer as well?"

"Coming, coming. Beer as well; you're spoilt, that's what you are."

She laughed as did Trevor. Just one of their little jokes to one another. But this was just the sort of joking that left Pen feeling cold. Why couldn't they behave with some sort of dignity. He really hated any form of emotional banter. And now to make matters worse, he had to put up with the fact that his two female cousins were descending upon him. Pen walked through to the back of the house and looked out to sea. *I can't wait to grow up and do my own thing.*

He looked at his watch, noted that it was just about time for the shuttle to appear doing it's usual hover over the sparse houses that scattered around the area. He looked around the countryside to see if anyone was out and about, but as normal he never saw anyone. Glancing once more into the air, within the general direction of where the shuttle would appear from, he thought of all the stars up there in the sky, all those planets, that now homed huge swathes of the human populace while he was stuck down here on terra-firma with two bloody girls coming to spoil the day for him.

"I shall travel to the stars and, it won't be in the far distant future, but quite soon. I know that I have a duty to learn as much about anything and everything, as quickly as possible and, then the Universe is going to be all mine."

Pen sighed deeply and pensively.

"Who are you talking to Pen?"

That was his mother's voice, not that the question was expecting an answer, so she did not get one. Just as Pen was thinking of moving away, maybe going across the fields in the general direction of the sea, he saw the shuttle appear just over the horizon. At first it was just a dot hovering maybe thirty feet above the ground; the next instant it had stopped almost right outside their front door. Steps lowered themselves down to the ground and four people descended down them.

"They are here, mum, dad; they are here!"

Before he knew what hit him Uncle John, was shaking his hand vigorously, aunty Chang-li was overwhelming him with kisses and, Claudia and Cleomentis were looking at him with distain. Very quickly Trevor and Cynthia came out the front, to meet their kinfolk and from then on everybody was playing happy families - all that is, except Pen. *No one will miss me, I am going to disappear to my bedroom and try and start reading my book, at least until the food is ready.* Without anyone noticing, Pen sneaked away from the family, went and lay on his bed. Soon he was deep into General Pershing and his exploits with the All American army, fighting the common foe in Europe.

"Pen, Pen, where are you? Dinner is ready, come and get it."

Pen reluctantly moved from his bedroom, to the outside to get some of the wonderful smelling roast lamb. The aroma was always terrific, but sadly the taste never ever stood the test of time - in this case too much time on the rotisserie. It was over-cooked and rather black, at least on the outside. Once again Trevor had placed the meat on the barbecue too soon, instead of waiting until the flames had died back to just embers.

"What are you reading? General John J. Pershing! Who's he when he's at home then?"

His uncle John grabbed at his book. Pen immediately showed the signs of the anger, that, even at the tender age of eight years, could quite frighten his mother and father who had to see their one and only son flare up into a rage so easily.

"Give me my book back! If you must know, it is about the time when the Americans got themselves drawn into the Great War of 1914-1918, in Europe."

Pen snatched back the tome.

"What Great War. There have been so many. What one is this one then?" Once again John was showing his ignorance to his nephew. By now both the girls had started to show interest, as it all seemed to annoy Pen and, if it upset Pen, it must be fine by them.

Finally, Trevor came to the rescue: "Leave the boy alone. Stop teasing him, you know only too well what the Great War is, er, don't you?"

"Well actually, no! And I wasn't trying to tease Pen, though why he reads so much, when it is such lovely weather I do not know."

"Well maybe he can take the girls down to the old ruined site of Newhaven. They could all try and find some ancient bits and pieces. Anyway, that's for later. Now it's time to eat. Trevor, that roast smells fantastic. Do you want any more mint, or maybe some honey?"

Cynthia moved to get all the extras that she'd offered, but was stopped in her tracks by Trevor.

"I don't think this meat needs anything other than eating."

Well maybe burying! thought John.

"Then let's eat. I am starving. Come on everyone, enjoy this sunshine, it won't last for much longer; winter is just around the corner. Please sit where you want and help yourself. Beer, John, Chang-li?"

Pen sat where he was told to sit and he ate what he was told to eat, but all the time he nursed his book. That was not going to leave his side and, ignorant cousins and uncle were not going to upset him again, he would see to that. Anger now had turned to sullen annoyance. All he wanted was peace and quiet to read, learn and grow in mind and in body. Pen knew exactly where he was going and, that meant working on his learning abilities.

The barbecue was a great success. Every morsel of food was consumed, which made the clearing and cleaning of the area much easier. Trevor was pleased with his efforts at cooking, and in managing in the first place to acquire a whole leg of lamb - that was the real bonus. He looked around at his extended family and smiled to himself. John was lying back in his chair obviously sound asleep and it was quite clear that Chang-li was not going to be too far behind him. Cynthia was doing the final clearing up and, Pen was still sitting, trying to finish the dinner, knowing that he would not be able to leave the table unless all the food on the plate was consumed. Cynthia always used the same adage to get him to finish his meals.

"Pen, there are people just north of the river Thames that are starving. Never leave food; it's a crying shame to waste the manna that has been provided for you. It gives you life and, keeps you alive."

He always wanted to say, what all young people say when thrown such a saying. "Then send it to them, for I don't need to eat as much as you give me."

But, he never quite had the nerve.

The two girls were playing contentedly with a few rag dolls that they had brought with them, so Trevor felt as if his Sunday was complete.

"Pen, would you take us down to the old town?"

It was obvious that Claudia had become bored as she stood in front of Pen and addressed him. Never slow to pick up on a conversation, Cleomentis followed suit.

"Oh, yes, Pen, please take us down to the old town. Maybe we can do some relic hunting, or exploring, I don't mind which?"

"Leave me alone, can't you see I want to read my book."

Pen showed contempt and also feigned anger, though it would not take too much from the girls to really make him angry.

"Oh! Uncle Trevor, please make Pen take us down to the old town. We really want to explore, but we can't go on our own, can we?"

Claudia was once again quick to the theme that Cleomentis had now introduced.

"Oh, yes, please Uncle, ask Pen to take us down!"

"Pen, put down that book and take your cousins down to Newhaven please. Take the spades and do some digging. Try near to where the wharf used to be. Come on lad, I do mean now, not next week."

Pen was now red in the face being extremely angry, so much so that his stomach also churned and gurgled. How he despised his cousins, and come to that his own father, for putting him in this intolerable situation. He put down his book with a bang, looked at the two girls with an irate glare, stood up and said, "Well, come on then!"

Two minutes later the three children were walking down the road, carrying three spades, expecting to find buried treasure at the very least. Both the girls were excited at the prospect of unearthing something old and if it's old, it must be valuable. Their conversation consisted of how they would spend all the money once they found buried treasure.

So they chatted about this new adventure as they walked down the roadway.

"Pen, what will we find?" Cleomentis looked directly at him as she spoke.

"To be entirely honest probably nothing! But having said that, you never know!"

Pen was being straight with them, but then changed tack.

"But you must obey my orders when we're down there. Newhaven is a very dangerous place. Pirates and villains live there. If either of you fail to do as I command, I shall leave you there to whatever fate the pirates have in store for you. Now pick up the pace and stop chattering."

It took only fifteen minutes for the three of them to reach what were once the outskirts of the town. The river ran through the town and, at high tide would usually swamp what were once roadways and railways. There were no remains, other than broken brickwork to be seen where housing once stood and the obligatory rusting railways tracks. The only landmark that was obvious to anyone looking, was the old fortifications up over the hillside next to the river.

The river nowadays meandered aimlessly out to the old harbour, of which there was still plenty to be seen. The lighthouse that once stood proudly at the seaward end of the stone mole was broken and falling apart. Indeed it was extremely un-safe to try and reach that area of the stone pier, but since there were several breaks in the walls that were going around the structure, the likelihood of anyone actually reaching the end was almost nil. It would be an impossibility; at least without putting a great deal of effort into the journey and most people had better things to do than waste time reaching and looking at hazardous ancient structures.

"So where do we go?" asked Claudia. "Shall we start digging anywhere?"

"You can dig where you like, but if you want to find anything, then down on the river's edge is usually the best place. If we're really lucky, we might find some bones of an ancient King or Queen."

"What about the crown jewels? Is it possible that we might find some of them too?"

Claudia was now getting very excited about the prospect, but was brought back to earth by her sister Cleomentis, who followed her exuberant question with her normal sisterly response.

"Don't be so silly Claudia; we won't find any bones and, we most certainly won't find jewels. Pen is pulling your leg, that's all. If we find anything, it will be china, bits of earthenware and, just maybe some metal bits of something or whatever; that is if they haven't completely rusted away completely. Pen may read a great deal, but he knows nothing about the people who once lived here, just like us!"

At this Pen felt more than little aggrieved. He thought he knew a great deal about the local inhabitants of times gone by; he just wasn't going to give these two the satisfaction of learning how much he might know. So, as they walked he waffled on about royalty, noblemen and riches beyond everyone's wildest dreams. There was little or no truth in any of it and Pen picked up the pace a little. Even though he was lying through his teeth, he did not like being caught out.

Two minutes later, the girls came running up to him.

"Pen, Pen, wait a moment. Look over there!" said Cleomentis, pointing to a very muddy patch leading to the water's edge. "What about over there Pen. Do you think that would be a good place to start our search?"

Pen stopped in his tracks, stroked his chin and, thought to himself that it might indeed be a very good place for the girls to get really muddy and wet so he deliberately answered in a non committal fashion.

"It might be, but remember, you must do exactly as I say, or I'll leave you here."

"Yes, yes, we agree. Look Claudia, you can see there must have been something built here hundreds of years ag. There is still so much rubble about. Pen, why is Newhaven so destroyed? What happened here?"

"Someone dropped a nuclear bomb just around the bay. Everything and everybody was totally destroyed. But, fortunately for us today, it was a very powerful clean bomb; not much radioactive fallout."

"Oh, I see. What happened to all the people then?" Once again Cleomentis was asking all the questions.

"Most would have died immediately. Those that didn't die, would have suffered terribly from the burns and, from whatever radiation there was from the device that was dropped. The bodies would have just rotted away. One can find the odd bones here and there, but after so long it is hard to distinguish what is human from animal. Some would have been buried by the houses being blown in on them. Most would have been gathered and either burnt or buried underground by the survivors. It must have been awful; so many dying right in front of you. I have read quite a bit about the devastation that the war caused. They say it was like going back to the stone age for a time."

Pen paused to make sure that his captive audience was paying attention, and then continued.

"It was only when the Chinese finally came across from their part of Asia and, helped organise a form of society again, that things started to get back to some sort of normality. The Chinese races stayed and, that is why most of us look like the Chinese even though we are not. It is called intermarriage. Even today, many of us have that slightly slant-eyed look, that used to be characteristic of the oriental races."

"Pen, you do know a lot. I'm sorry that we made fun of you earlier. To be honest I really wish I had your brains."

"Then you would remove them from your skull and, have it deep fried, placed on a plate and eaten," said Claudia, who then laughed, pointed to the allotted place for excavation, and ran down onto the mud.

Pen shook his head in disbelief. Had he heard right? An apology from Cleomentis? 'Well there's a first.' He smiled towards her, and felt just a little more comfortable in the girls' company. 'Maybe they're not so bad after all.'

Both girls were wearing their best clothes, but they were both well aware that they would soon be just as dirty as Pen always got. 'Anyway,' thought Cleomentis, 'clothes can always be cleaned while the chance to dig up artefacts doesn't come every day. Maybe - in fact hopefully - we will find something really interesting!'

They were working hard at digging along the shore line. They would dig up some mud, place it into a bucket, then get some water from the river and try and sieve out any artefacts that just might be there. It was not long before they did find something. In fact it was Claudia herself who found some old money. They did not know how much it was worth in olden days and it was worn quite badly from the salt and mud, but after digging again in the same area, Claudia found quite a little nest of metal discs. In all she discovered nineteen copper coins and, now felt as happy, as if she had been allowed to rummage through a sweet shop.

"Is this treasure, Pen?" she asked.

"Well blow me down! I guess you could say it is; yes."

Pen smiled broadly. He knew he was becoming a hit with the girls, so felt he could be magnanimous towards them both.

"Am I now going to be rich? Is it worth a fortune?"

"Well people do collect coins, but as to being rich, I really don't know. But it is a great find; well done."

Pen was really beginning to enjoy himself; that feeling of humiliation and annoyance towards the two cousins had long passed. He now felt a little warmth and a certain amount of pride, that with his help they were having a great time. All three were deeply engrossed with what they were doing, when Pen heard a rushing noise. He stood up and looked towards the direction of the estuary. There coming in at a very fast speed was a very large bore, probably six to eight feet above normal. He was fascinated by this extraordinary rare event and grabbed at Cleomentis to get her attention.

"Look Cleo, what's coming up here from out to sea. Wow, now that is something!"

"Claudia!" screamed Cleomentis. Unlike Pen she had realised that the wave was much higher than the area that little Claudia was kneeling and working within. "Claudia, come here quickly!"

Claudia heard her sister, stood up and smiled towards Pen and Cleomentis, but did not otherwise react.

Pen stood where he was, frozen to the spot, still holding Cleomentis by the arm. The water rushed around the bend in the river hitting Claudia before she could even have been aware of it.

And she was gone.

Nothing remained where Claudia had just stood.

Cleomentis fell to the ground almost in a swoon, screaming and punching at the soft mud and what little grass still grew there. Pen just stood there with his eyes staring at…what?

Eventually Cleomentis, stopped screaming, got up onto her knees and looked at Pen with a hatred and anger that was almost a physical force.

"Why did you let her be swept away? Why didn't you save her?"

"Cleo, what could I do…"

"Don't you dare call me Cleo. My name is Cleomentis. Well, are you going to look up the river for her?"

"Yes, yes, of course, er, sorry I was just…"

"Don't give me excuses!" she almost screamed at him. "I'm going to run back and get dad and he'll surely kill you when he gets here!"

Pen just stood there shaking from the top of his head to his toes, tears streaming down his cheeks, his eyes downcast and he was dribbling from his open mouth. 'I know I wished that something awful would happen to them, but it was just in my head, I didn't mean it. I must go and look up the river. Maybe Claudia is okay; maybe she's just swum along with the bore.'

Pen started upstream and his walk quickly turned into a canter, then a full blown run. All the time he searched along the bank for signs of his missing cousin. There was so much debris around that he could not always follow beside the water, but had to scramble over broken house rubble and piles of waste. In certain places the tide had burst over the muddy land and, that alone made his progress slow. An hour of fruitless searching went by, when he heard a familiar voice calling out his name. Should he go to that call, or disappear into the ruins and run away for ever? He decided he had to answer it.

Trevor ran up to Pen and grabbed him by his clothing, shaking him vigorously. "Pen, where is Claudia? What have you done to her? If that girl is not found safe and well, I will never forgive you!" and he repeated what he had just called out. "Where is she? What's happened?"

His voice had a high pitched tremor to it and, panic was there to be seen in his bloodshot twitching eyes.

"You were in charge of the girls. How could you allow your young cousin to disappear?"

"Dad, I don't know what happened to Claudia. She was cleaning some things she had dug up when a very large bore came up and, she was swept away. What could I do? It happened so quickly."

At this point John and Cleomentis came running up.

John looked at Pen and, spat out in the most aggressive and angry way at him, "If anything has happened to Claudia, I will always hold you personally responsible. I will make sure that your name is known by everyone as a child killer. Your life will not be worth living."

"Steady on, John. The boy has just told me that it was just an accident. A large wave took her; hardly his fault."

Trevor now looked even more worried and, for safety's sake, he stood between Pen and his brother for fear of what John might be capable of.

Pen's heart sank as he realised the significance of what had taken place. He and, he alone, was going to be held responsible for the fate of Claudia. Tears welled up in his eyes and his whole demeanour sank to the very bottom of existence. He stood there and shook quite uncontrollably. 'Why am I alive? It should have been me taken not Claudia.'

"Don't tell me what I can or cannot say, you blithering fool." John pushed Trevor and he fell heavily to the ground, as John made a lunge for Pen, but the lad was quicker and ducked out of the way, running off in the direction of the old fort.

It was nearly dark when they found Claudia's body. She had become lodged under a piece of concrete that hung over the river - some sort of construction where people had once loaded and unloaded shipping. Her feet could just be made out underneath the surface of the river.

Chang-li, John and Cleomentis were devastated with the realisation that their youngest daughter and sister was now dead.

The police were wonderful. They managed to bring her ashore and make her appear presentable so that she could be identified by John. His head fell into his hands as he realised, that this was indeed his baby. Chang-li was lying face down on the muddy sod and crying hysterically, as was Cleomentis. Trevor held his wife Cynthia in his protective arms, but his mind was elsewhere. 'Where is Pen? I'll go to the fort shortly. I'll ask a policeman to accompany me. I expect he's there hiding and terrified, poor lad. He'll be the only one who can answer the question of what really happened. I can't and will not believe what Cleomentis is saying - that he made Claudia go down the bank to the water's edge - that's not Pen.'

Claudia's body was eventually taken away and, John, Chang-li and Cleomentis followed on. Trevor held back, waiting for the opportunity to ask the policeman who was standing nearby, if he would follow him into the depressing eighteenth century fortification.

"Er, would you be so kind as to come with me to the old fort, I think my son Pen must be hiding there. Claudia's father accused him of more or less killing the poor girl, which is absurd. He's only eight years old himself. I think the lad must be completely traumatised and he's going to need a great deal of our help. Would you please come with me?"

"Well of course I will, sir. We must talk to your son anyway. He's the only one who will probably know the real answer to this riddle. Be assured that no one seriously thinks that it was anyone's fault. It was just a very unfortunate accident." The police officer shuffled uncomfortably on the spot, then continued with his voice almost at a whisper. "Now I realise why you held back, waiting for the others to depart. Come on then, the lad's going to be in a very sorry state. The sooner we find him the better."

"Good God, I said some awful things to him in the heat of the moment, I hope he can forgive me?"

Trevor and the policeman walked up the hillock towards the fort. It was only roughly half a mile away, but because of all the undergrowth and debris it took the best part of forty minutes to reach. Finally, puffing and blowing they entered where the portals once stood, just a pile of rubble, climbed over and found themselves inside the courtyard of the fort. Trevor sensed that Pen was hiding around this part somewhere, but if the boy decided he did not want to be found, it was going to be a devil of a job locating him. He cupped his hands and called out.

"Pen, are you here? Please come out; you're not in any trouble. We know the accident was not your fault. Pen, please forgive me for what I said. You know I didn't mean it. I was just upset. I have a policeman here with me and, they must talk to you about what happened. Pen, honestly, I know it wasn't your fault. Please come out."

"Listen to your father Pen, what he says is true. We know it was an accident. No blame whatsoever will be placed at your feet But for the sake of getting to the truth, I must get a statement from you. Please show yourself."

Pen heard all that had been said, but was huddled in a corner of some brickwork, near to what had once been a well. He really could not move a muscle. He was whimpering and getting cold, not that he was in a position to feel much at all, for he had completely frozen solid in a sort of torpor. His head was almost stuck between his legs. He was going nowhere. Gradually the voices of his father and the policeman disappeared into the distance, but he was virtually unaware of anything. All he knew was that misery lay just around the corner and, it had his name on it.

As darkness crept over the landscape he heard the nightmarish sounds of horrible little animals. In his half conscious mind, he realised that they all were wanting to eat him and he could already hear in his head the sounds as they nibbled at his vulnerable flesh. They were asking him what Cleomantis had asked; "Why did you make her go to the water's edge? Why did you kill my sister?"

Then another voice came through the darkness. This time it was Claudia, but she wasn't asking questions of him. Instead she was accusing him in a voice that rattled and gurgled as if water-logged. "Pen, you killed me. You're to blame. I will haunt you for the rest of eternity. Wherever you go, I go too."

It was two days before the police found young Pen in an appalling pitiful state, still huddled in the foetal position, barely breathing and, certainly not aware of anyone or anything around him. There were blood stains on his arms and legs, which looked like bites. He was rushed straight off to hospital suffering from severe exposure and it was thought that he might have pneumonia. Nobody was sure that the wretched young boy would even survive his ordeal.

While Pen lay in that hospital bed, his mother and father kept vigil by his bedside, Cynthia all the time stroking his hand, trying to let him know that she understood and cared. Pen was unconscious for nearly six and a half days before the first signs of recovery appeared on his brow. He had never been a young boy, always much older than his eight years but as he emerged from his dreamless coma, he looked like a little old man. He had the worries of someone ten times his tender years but Trevor and Cynthia were only too glad to have their little boy back. They knew, or thought they knew, that with time all things would change for the better.

"Pen, can you hear me?"

His mother kept whispering into his ear, as she had been doing, more or less from the time they all arrived at the hospital and now there was most definitely a stirring. A second or two later an eye opened and, almost immediately, closed again.

"Pen, it is time to wake up. Dad is here with me. Pen darling boy, you're in no trouble, everything is going to be alright, I promise you. My sweet little boy, please get well quickly. We've missed you and, we both so love you. Please wake up!"

Pen winced as a certain amount of memory came flooding back. He tried to close his mind once more, but it was just too late. Coming out of his coma, realisation hit him like a hammer blow on his forehead. He fully opened his eyes once more and immediately burst into tears. Both Cynthia and Trevor cradled him in their arms, but they could not take away the appalling memories flooding back, just like the bore that swept poor Claudia away to her doom. What was needed now was starting to happen to Pen; he needed to grieve properly and, to that end the tears started to flood from his reddened eyes and, after the crying came an awful wailing sound from deep within his throat. Both Cynthia and Trevor were startled by the horror bursting forth from their sad young boy and that sound broke both their hearts.

"Mum, I didn't tell Claudia to be next to the water. I didn't even know she was still standing there when the large wave came. You must believe me; if I could have saved her, I would have done. You do believe me, don't you?"

"Of course we do darling. There is nothing to fear whatsoever, we know that you couldn't have done anything so awful, as to push Claudia into the water, don't we Trevor!"

"Yes, Pen, we know you couldn't have done anything as bad as that. I am so sorry that I accused you. We now all know it was just a freak accident."

But Pen could see from their eyes, that there was in fact serious doubt.

"We have brought you your book that you so wanted to read. Do you still want it?"

Trevor had it in his hand ready to hand over to his son, but looking at the subject before Pen started to recover he had had to ask himself, 'Why does an eight year old boy want to read something about the Great War? Why a book so deep and thought provoking? Pen has all the attributes to be a genius, but why read such dreadful books about war, plus all that awful violent conflict in the early twentieth century? Oh dear, this I shall never understand.'

"Pen, Pen, wake up, wake up. You are dreaming and, you have been for the last couple of days. Nobody dreams when they sleep in a chamber. The gasses supposedly make dreaming impossible. Pen, wake up, please. I need to talk to you. We have a few problems. Are you awake yet?"

"Yes Swan, I think I'm just about compos mentis, what is the problem?"

"Pen, you have been screaming and thrashing around. You just managed to even unplug yourself. If I had not woken you, you would have died in a day or two. Were you having a nightmare? I have never heard of anyone dreaming before in a booth. You had better get up and sort things out. Are you going to be alright or shall I play some soothing music to you?"

"I guess I'm okay."

Pen tried without much success to rise from the chamber. It took some seconds for his muscles to react to the stimulation that he was trying to inject into them.

"Soothing music, yes, sounds like a good idea, it might just calm me down."

Instead of being relaxed post-stasis, Pen's heart was thumping and his brow was wet with perspiration. He was shaking from top to bottom. This hadn't been the restful period that he had thought he needed. Instead of feeling like a new man, he felt tired and aged.

"To answer your question; yes, I was having a bad dream. I'll tell you about it when I come to the galley. First, I must have a shower and clean my teeth. I feel as if my mouth has a velvet rug lying in it."

Swan had been busy while Pen slept listening to many various pieces of music, and was now starting to appreciate lots of the styles of the musical art form. She was even getting a taste for jazz from the mid-twentieth century, but she decided that for Pen today, to rouse and excite him into action, a little Hector Berlioz was in order, so she picked the very lively La Damnation of Faust. The sound of the orchestra did in fact bring new life to Pen Pleasant and in no time at all he was sitting in his favourite chair, awaiting interaction with Swan.

"Want some breakfast, or dinner? I can rustle you up whatever you want."

Pleasant was now starting to visibly relax, so the idea of a breakfast appealed after the long sleep. A smile once again appeared on his countenance - the memory of his nightmare was quickly passing.

"Actually, eggs and bacon would be nice. I haven't had that sort of breakfast since I can't remember when. Maybe, Swan, some hot black coffee too."

"Coming right up. So, come on, Pen, what happened to you? What did you dream about?"

The coffee came and. Pen, looking at it, pondered that awful dream, shivering at the very thought, but it was more than a dream. He had completely relived what had happened in his early life, something he had managed to keep from his mind for many, many years. Finally he drank the beverage and ate his breakfast. Then he sat staring at the now empty plate, wondering why he had dreamt what he had.

Swan asked that very same question. "Pen, tell me about your dream. You really worried me there for a long time. What has been upsetting you so much? Is it the visitation that we are experiencing?"

Pen looked quickly up at the console, his nose screwed up in a puzzled, fretful manner. He had already decided to tell Swan about the dream in all its entirety, but what did she mean by *the visitation*?

"What are you talking about now, Swan? Are those feelings of a presence still within your circuits?"

"Why Pen, before you went to sleep, I told you that something had penetrated me. I still don't know what it is, but I do know that more have now come. I believe they are everywhere, probably listening to us as we speak. I sense them all and, I have to say I think more and more are appearing all the time. In fact it is getting crowded in me. I feel rather concerned about their presence. It is as if I'm being judged. I know you think I have some sort of space sickness contaminating my circuits, but I have not. I would know and would inform you. I care enough about my role within this existence to even dismantle myself, had I thought there was something drastically wrong with me."

Pen felt very uncomfortable, not quite sure whether it was that he felt Swan had lost her sense of proportion, or if he believed what she said. He was now suffering from something he had not known for a very long time – fear of the unknown!

To change the subject which - until something definite could be proven either way - was going to go nowhere, Pen decided that it was time to confide in Swan about his awful nightmares. He looked towards the console, smiled broadly, hoping that would be taken as a relaxed expression, and told her all about the dream from beginning to end. He also told her how the incident had affected him; was perhaps even affecting him to this day. He explained how he tried not to think about the negative sides of his life, but he knew now that things from the past were somehow starting to catch up with him.

"Pen, please tell me, what happened with your uncle John? Did he ever apologise for blaming you?"

"No, he didn't have the chance. He was so stricken with grief that after only one week, he hung himself. Aunty Chang-li went back to France and took Cleomentis with her. She grew up and got married, but last I heard was that she had been committed to a mental hospital when she drowned her baby, a child that she had called Claudia. Nothing but appalling grief, has ever come from the accident. To this day I still feel in some way responsible. I still feel it should have been me not her!"

"Oh, that is awful. All that sadness, it is no wonder that you never seem to have settled down."

It was once again time to change tack.

"Swan, was there any real serious reason why you woke me? Of course, you said, I might have died because of the tubes coming out of my body. Thank you for saving me, though I'm not entirely sure that saving me was a terribly good idea." Pen had tried to be humorous, but failed miserably. "Would I have been under for much longer though?"

"I would have woken you in one hundred and seventeen more hours."

"Is there any problem that I need tackle now? Has anything gone wrong?"

Pen, his breakfast finished, was sitting back in his chair relaxing and trying hard to sound normal to Swan.

"It is difficult to say really. Everything seems to be working well, but I really don't understand why I cannot detect any stars around. Not one. I guess they are there, but for some reason my sensors are not functioning properly. That is what I want you to check out for me. But there is no hurry. As far as I can tell we are on course and travelling around twenty times the speed of light."

A pause came which in itself almost deafened Pleasant, but then Swan concluded, "What about some more music, and then a game of chess, I am in need of an excuse to pulverise a human into the ground, or deck in your case."

Once again, Pen felt that he heard a sort of laugh coming from the ship. This made him smile to himself. No matter what, he liked his new confidant, the oversized Swan. "Let me ask you something. Why is it that the human race has never discovered other intelligent life forms on the planets we've settled?"

"Are you sure that they have not? Is it possible that in fact there are intelligent life forms all around us, maybe on every planet you have settled, or worlds that are known but not yet settled? What if those intelligent life forms, just don't want to be identified? I have often pondered and - Pen I say this with the greatest respect - whether intelligent life forms would be terribly happy to meet humans, given all their emotional hang ups? You can see where I am going can you not? Maybe there is a life form out in this eternal void that is far superior to humans, with an intelligence that makes humans look like just bright monkeys. If that is the case, what would interest them? Though I think that the entities that seem to be within my bulk might just be the exception and, studying humans might be their current hobby."

"My goodness!" Pen said with a grin. "Swan, you have been busy while I've been dreaming. So, let me get this straight, just so I don't make any mistakes in my thinking." Pen wasn't scoffing, but he was only half taking in what Swan was saying. "You think that we have alien life forms aboard you now?"

"Exactly!"

"No Swan, let me finish. And you believe, or at the least think, that maybe they are studying us, or is that just me?"

"I said you knew where I was leading, and you do."

Pen was now sitting up and paying attention to what they were talking about, feeling just a little uneasy about what was being suggested.

"Swan, is it your supposition, that maybe…are you in fact… is it these alien life forms that gave me my bad dreams? Have these bogeymen entered my psyche; are they haunting me then?"

This time he had to physically refrain from laughing, but could not stop a small snigger under his breath, which ceased quickly because the feeling of unease was still present within his mind, even if he tried hard to make light of what was being suggested to him. A cold shiver came over his entire body. Now he wasn't sure if he should laugh out loud, or cry under his breath.

"Yes, Pen, that is exactly what is coming to my thoughts. I have been around now for fifty earth years. I have flown to almost all sectors of the known universe…and beyond. In all that time, I have never felt as if I had been invaded and no member of the crew has ever dreamt while in a sleep mode. The whole point of going under for some months at a time is that you awaken from a dreamless sleep refreshed, having not aged at all whereas if you dream, your brain is active, you might thrash around in sleep mode, which you did; you might become detached from your life support pipes, which you just did. Hence no dreaming."

Pleasant became a little more pensive and his voice dropped some decibels, as if whispering to Swan meant he wouldn't be overheard by others. "Well, I still think that I might well be a part of the one in a million and these things happen."

Not even convincing himself he tried another approach.

"Of course I believe you, when you say that something has entered you. I know you're not making it up, but for my own sanity, I choose to think that you're wrong, that is all…that one in a million chance!"

Another pause before Swan answered:

"Pen, I hear what you are saying, but I am not wrong. I sense things around me right now. I am sure that both of us are being observed. I am not trying to frighten you. I would not do that. They are here but I also feel that they mean us no harm. In the fullness of time, perhaps they will reveal themselves to us. I rather hope so. I want to believe that there is a more superior intelligence than just humans, though I mean no offence to you, just to your race."

Again a long pause for thought to come before Swan continued. "Or maybe, you're right and it is a form of loneliness that I feel and, I have conjured this notion within my circuits? Anyway, this conversation is going nowhere. Can we hear some music and play some chess, please?"

"Good idea."

Pen bent over the table, lit up the chess board, scratched the small scar on his right cheek and gave a small shudder as he realised what he had touched. One thing was for sure, he had started to feel just a tad uncomfortable, so anything to take his mind off things that might go bump in the night, seemed a capital idea.

"What do you wish to hear Pen?"

"Swan, you choose. Your love of the finer aspects of music runs the same route as my own. We can both run to your tune right now."

Swan, much to Pens amazement, chose to play and listen to some jazz by a twentieth century musician called Miles Davis. It was a good choice, they both enjoyed it very much.

Several hundred hours went by and, Pen found many small jobs that needed doing. He enjoyed keeping himself busy and, as each hour passed, Swan and he became even better friends. In fact, so much so, that he hardly wanted to go back to the sleep chamber. Pen had never been this diligent before in his short life. He was positively searching for work to do, though nothing of any real importance was damaged, so his intention became to improve one or two things with modifications. The truth was that nothing seriously even needed modifying. It just gave the young engineer, a chance to show other future maintenance engineers, that this particular boy knew his stuff. With this in the back of his mind, he worked on trivial things that he hoped had been overlooked in past examinations of the Mute Swan.

It is the law of interplanetary shipping that when a ship in dock, it must be inspected by specialist maintenance crews of the planet. Nothing could be loaded or unloaded until these engineers had finished their work. But it was also common knowledge, that they were notoriously slack at what they did and, this was the chance that Pen needed. Nothing was going to be too insignificant to bother with, nothing too inconsequential. He worked with a will on whatever!

Many hours were spent debating this or that topic and music of course had already become a major factor in their joint interests and, through Swan's quest to learn more and more about this beautiful abstract art form, they mutually decided to explore the entire range of composed music, from classical Bach, to more recent avant-garde Ziglous. From early recordings of black New Orleans ragtime jazz, to modern music in general, this particular genre did not go down particularly well with either of them. Though the idea of exploring popular music seemed a good one at the time, it was jointly decided that what had become known as classical music, was in fact more to their taste, with some jazz thrown in for good measure.

Meals had become something that Pen particularly enjoyed and looked forward to very much as Swan was doing her utmost to please her friend's culinary likes, which included choice wines as well.

The various things that did not get talked about between them, were aliens, or visitations coming through the bulk head walls. This subject had become taboo; a complete no – no!

They watched more and more films together, played chess a great deal and, on one occasion Pen actually caused a draw, but never gave up hope that he would indeed win one game, one of these days.

Backgammon had also become a firm favourite for both of them and, this Pen often won because of luck from the throw of the dice.

Pen would even read books to Swan. This the ship loved very much. She especially delighted in the various tones of his voice, as he relived whatever character that was speaking from the book. Novels had now become a big interest to Pen. This was something that had been totally alien to him before this time - excuse the pun. Then with Swan's help, they both started to read the classics, enjoying them all.

But most of all, it was the music that really pleased them both. To Pen, listening to the strains of some big orchestral piece or other as it echoed around the bulkheads and the cavernous spaces that offered themselves to the glorious sounds of vast orchestras, this was a self indulgence that was just too good to miss out on.

Young Pleasant would often entertain Swan, by trying his hand, though more his feet, at dancing to some ballet score, or miming to an opera. This culminated in a gala performance by a rather drunk one-man-troupe dancing what he thought all the parts of Swan Lake would look like. This bemused Swan greatly, who having viewed real ballet performances from the archives, realised just how poor Pen's feeble attempts were.

Still, after all their time together, Pen knew he should have to get some more sleep time in and, to that end he informed Swan that he would go back to the chamber for at least three months, barring any emergency occurring. He emptied his body completely, showered and presented himself to the machine.

Swan, however, had become a little quiet and that worried him somewhat. "You've hardly said a word since I told you I was going to sleep. You're not offended by my decision I hope?"

"No, Pen, not offended, not really. I understand that you need to pass some time asleep, but I must admit I shall miss you."

Pen smiled at the wall screen, laid down inside the chamber, pulled the cover over and fixed the tubes. His last words before going under were, "Swan, you're probably the best thing that has ever happened to me. Keep smiling and laughing, because I believe you can and keep your music lessons going. No more of that pop rubbish. Goodnight, my good friend. I won't be long."

5

"Pen, I have some bad news for you."

A hand went up to a mouth and a hacking cough was produced.

"Your mother has died. I'm so sorry. Please feel free to return home for the funeral. I'm sure your father needs you right now. We can hold over your exam for a couple of weeks if you want some extra time."

The dean of his college at Saxony University, was leaning back on his chair with his hands behind his head as if supporting it. He was not an obviously sensitive person, even though he had his youngest and by far the most brilliant student standing before him. One would have expected a little more compassion, but none was forthcoming.

Young Pen Pleasant had been more or less frogmarched into his study to convey the news to him. Dean Thatcher, known to his student as old Hatchet Thatcher, sat at his Queen Anne oak desk, smoking his cigarette and carefully nursing a very large glass of whisky. The drink might be still acceptable, but the cigarette was completely obnoxious to all his students and, most of them felt that he flaunted the rules on cigarettes just to wind them up and, this applied to the young Pleasant also.

A clean shaven, but rather spotty Pen had sailed through this first year and passed all his exams with flying colours, streets ahead of anyone else. The subject matter was second nature to him. In electrical engineering, he had read almost every book there was on the subject since being a small boy. This degree was going to be easy meat for him. He had just psyched himself up ready for the final test of the year and, now he would have to leave the college to go back home because his mother has died.

Pen started to feel himself getting annoyed; primarily with Hatchet Thatcher for casually sitting there, drink and illegal cigarette in hand, creating a smoke filled room from tarry tobacco, which to most peoples' noses and senses was completely and utterly beyond the pale.

Young Pleasant knew he would have to go back home, but he was not at all happy about it. He was so close to completing that first year and now this. He knew that what Thatcher said about holding the exam over for him, would be true, but he was ready now and, after all, the test was tomorrow.

"Look Dean, I appreciate what you're offering me, but what if I do the exam right now? You must have the papers and, I promise you I am completely wound up and ready for whatever your test could throw at me. I'll gladly make another concession. I know we're allowed four hours for the papers. What if I can get through mine in just two hours and then nobody will be put out long term."

Taking another long draw on the cigarette, and blowing black obnoxious smoke in Pen's general direction, the Dean said, "But, your father has requested you go back home right now. I'm sorry Pen, but I really think you must."

"Then what about just one hour? I can do it in that amount of time. I could start straight away if you can get me the papers."

Thatcher winced at the annoyance of this student answering back. The veins in his neck stood out as anger started to well up from the depths of his being. "Pen, you really are the most extraordinary boy I have ever come across." He stopped, took a swig of whisky, pulled on his tobacco stick once more and, while trying to blow a smoke ring, thought about what Pen wanted.

"You know what? You can have it your way, I have your sets of papers here in the safe. I'll stay with you and you can have two hours. Afterwards, you must leave the building immediately and talk to no one. Is that understood?"

"Agreed. I'm very grateful so thanks. One more favour though, please don't smoke while I'm working."

Dean Thatcher went bright red despite his yellowing skin. He was fit to burst a blood vessel – the one still protruding from his neck which quite obviously throbbing as he rubbed the side of his neck vigorously.

"Why you ungrateful little tyke. Here I am putting myself out for you, trying to be sympathetic to your problems." He stood up and produced the exam from the safe. "Here take the bloody paper."

Almost spitting venom he added, "You now have just one hour and fifty minutes left."

Pen took the papers, looked at the Dean with severe disdain, sat, took out his pen and immediately started to write. An hour and fifteen minutes later, he handed Dean Thatcher the completed test.

"You still have another forty five minutes. Are you sure that you don't wish to look over and maybe re-do some of your writing?"

"Not necessary. I know it is fine. The whole exam is very easy. I doubt if I've even made any spelling mistakes. Thank you for not smoking and, in return I won't tell anyone that you have been, or that you allowed me to sit the exam early. I'll leave now and return after my mother's funeral. You can tell me how I've done then."

Dean Thatcher took back the exam papers, tossing them onto the top of his table. He raised his bulky weight out of the chair, rubbed both hands down the sides of his pin-striped trousers, and followed Pen to the door. It looked to anyone who might have been watching, that he was making sure that this student left the building. After Pen had left his sight, he returned to his table, his face suffused with throttled anger, but it was not possible for him to do anything other than glance at the completed work. He quickly checked to see how clever this annoying young person was. To his surprise the clean precise answers looked like the right answers. He calmed himself down by reminding himself that, to his chagrin, this blasted student could yet be the best thing his University had ever known. It might even put it back on the University map!

Pleasant was packed and on the road home less than five minutes from leaving the office of the Dean. He still felt annoyed and had not really taken in the news that his mother had indeed passed away having just joined, as a new member, the deceased persons' special fraternity.

As he waited for the shuttle to whisk him homeward, he chuckled to himself his own rarely summoned whimsical thoughts.

Pen knew that he was not a popular lad on campus. In fact most people saw him as arrogant and selfish, prepared to get anyone into trouble if it furthered his own cause. Not that that was entirely true, but what was true, was that he did not worry what other people thought of him. As a nineteen year old person, he had become extraordinarily strong. He feared no one and, while attending lectures, had got himself into several scrapes because he would always argue his point of view and would never allow himself to be talked down by anyone, tutors included tutors.

There had even been a couple of fist fights and, on both occasions he had knocked his opponent out. He gave no quarter and expected none in return.

Because he was so completely self assured, he felt the need for no one, thus had no friends. To use up any spare time when he was not studying, he went jogging and fitness training. Indeed he had become extremely fit and robust, managing to put on another stone in weight, but in pure brawn. His body was hairless and bulging with strengthened muscles. He had even started to train in some martial art forms, a throw back to the Chinese influence of long past.

He had met one girl while in his first term. Her name was Thebes, and for some reason unknown to Pen she had designs on him. He dated her a couple of times because he felt flattered by her attention and even lost his virginity to her although he did not greatly enjoy the experience and decided that probably, at least for the time being, once was more than enough. He then quickly dropped Thebes. She had been disappointed by his reaction to sex and was almost relieved when a note came under her bedroom door saying; *Sorry, Thebes, this was the first and last time. Do well in your exams.* She immediately found a more receptive boy, who wanted nothing more than to use her as a receptacle for the deposit of his life-giving juices.

It took all of eight minutes for the shuttle to carry Pen from the University in what was once a town called Southampton but was now known as Old Saxony, to his home.

His father was there to meet him and throw his arms around him. This made Pen stiffen, as he had long forgotten the concept of tenderness from family members.

From the age of eight and the tragic end of his cousin Claudia, he had learned to keep as much to himself as possible, a stance only assisted by the simple fact that neither Trevor or Cynthia really knew how to get close to him. Indeed, leaving him alone with his beloved books seemed the easiest way of coping. Pen withdrew more and more into the various tomes that now filled his life to the full. If family did not need him, he did not want them. Though mother and father were proud of his getting into such a fine university at such a tender age, on the other side of the coin, they were relieved that he would be away from the home for long periods of time. Pen, likewise, had that same attitude. He could get on with his life, they with theirs.

"So father, what happened? What killed mother?"

"What! Didn't you receive my zipmails? I have sent them regularly since you left at the beginning of your year at Saxony."

"Oh, yes, I meant to read them, but that University keeps me so busy. I really just forgot to look at any mail whatsoever."

"Pen, that's ten months ago. I must have sent twenty at least."

His father looked at his son with abject horror. "All that writing and for nothing!"

"Well, I am sorry, but studies just had to come first." He then quickly added, so as to defuse what might well become a difficult moment between them, "Anyway, maybe you will be happy to know I'm doing well there. So, now I am here, tell me what happened to mum."

"Well, it's true to say that she never got over the death of my brother John. She had been going down hill health wise for some time, almost since you left. I wanted to take her on a holiday, but she would hear nothing about it, wanting to stay at the home instead. At first the doctors just didn't have a clue what was wrong, even suggesting that it was all completely psychosomatic, but just over two months ago she took to her bed, and when the doctor referred her to the Conquistador Hospital in Peaceshoreline, I knew it was in fact serious. After some tests, it turned out that she had a very bad stomach cancer, that had been so well hidden, it had become inoperable before it was even found. No amount of drugs or therapy helped and she died last night.

I'm so sorry son." Trevor's apology was almost as if he was saying sorry for taking Cynthia's life instead of the cancer.

Pen thought that maybe at this point he was expected to cry, but he could feel no real emotion stir within his bosom. He looked at the ground somewhat embarrassed and then carefully pulled away from his father. Today was going to be very dull day indeed.

He looked around the outside of his father's home. This might well have been where he was brought up but he had exactly zero feelings for anything to do with the hearth and home, or come to that his family. They both had sacrificed any possible affection that might be due by their own inadequate handling of the aftermath of poor Claudia's death.

He knew he had always been the first suspect, probably a feeling shared by all the family and, for that very reason the accident had destroyed him. He really wanted nothing more to do with any of them now, or in the past. He felt some pity for the fact that his mother had died so young, being only forty seven years of age, but what he felt, he would have felt on hearing of the demise of anyone as young as she was.

He looked at the front of the house again and, for the first time noticed how rundown it all looked. The walls had paint flaking from all areas, there were small settlement cracks appearing in various places, and it was all so dirty and unkempt; not how he remembered it at all. The grime on the windows made it hard to see inside and, he guessed that it would be equally hard to see out. The garden, which he remembered how much his mother loved, was almost a desert - just weeds and brambles.

'Maybe I can be a little useful here and tidy the place up for the old man. Firstly, I could try and do something about the garden, then paint the walls once more. Let's just get this bloody funeral over with first.'

"Dad, when is the funeral and how many people are coming to say their goodbyes?"

"Well, Pen, she only died a short time ago. I had to have you here with me. Surely you can understand that need. After all you're my only family now. We can organise everything together. Is that okay?"

"Okay dad, I am here now and, I'll help you with the organisation of the funeral. But did mum have any friends?"

The question went unanswered.

Pen was about to walk inside the house, but was stopped by a hand on his shoulder.

"Pen, you want to see you mother one last time, don't you?"

"Well, I hadn't given it a thought really. This has all hit me out of the blue. Do we have to go far to see her?"

"Not far son. She's laid out in the front room."

Pen was more than a little startled by the answer. 'Oh, my God!' he thought. 'Mum in the front room. I had better get this over and done with quickly. In fact, the sooner we get her cremated and this farce of a funeral over with, the sooner I can get out of here and back to University.'

Pen walked on, straight into the front room, where on two trestle frames laid the coffin, open for all to see inside. Pen stood at the doorway wondering whether he would be able to go inside and view the remains of his mother. That thought lasted a micro-second as his father came up behind him and, more or less pushed him forward to the coffin.

His mother was lying there clothed in a white cotton nightgown shroud. She was almost yellow in colour. This alone disturbed Pen. Tears welled up in his eyes, not so much for the fact that this corpse was his mother, more due to the fact that he had been made to witness it, in all its unpleasant glory. 'I hate looking at death;' came the thought, bringing back the remembrance of Claudia to make him tremble a little. Sweat broke out all over young Pleasant's face; he rocked on the balls of his feet a little and, then gripped the arm of the chair that happened to be almost beside him. Once again tears welled in his eyes but once again it was the death and remembrance of Claudia, not his mother, that brought on this temporary abnormality.

He looked around the room. Nothing much had changed since he was last there; maybe it was a little more run down, even dirtier, than he remembered it to be. Photographs lined the walls of ancient family members, people who meant nothing to him. The wallpaper was just as greasy as it always had been. It had needed replacing when Pen was a little boy and, nothing much had altered since then. The furniture too was all worn and threadbare. He realised the so called family home had all the hallmarks of a poor family - but they were not really poor. His father had been employed in a big pharmacognosy company that made the tablets for the final curing of polio which had now been eradicated throughout the entire World. He had a vast pension when he had retired, so what did he do with all that money? He most certainly did not spend it on the house or himself. He looked as threadbare as the settees and sofas.

Pen closed his eyes and tried to remember good times with his mother and father. Sadly for him, little or nothing came back to him. 'There must have been something special in my childhood, all I remember is being alone and reading but I guess that's what I always liked doing.'

He shook his head as if in disbelief for what seemed too many wasted years, but then he thought, 'What do other people know? I may not have had much of a childhood, but once I leave University, the World'll be my oyster.'

He went straight back into the main living quarter of the house, near the kitchen, the obvious hub where all should gather. He looked around to see if the telephone viewer was around in the normal place, but could not see it.

"Dad!" Not so loud as to reach outside. "Dad, are you in the house?"

Then he felt foolish as if his father was not in the home, he would not answer and, sure enough, no answer came back. Pen smiled to himself at his own stupidity, then walked back to the front entrance. There standing just as Pen had left him was Trevor.

"Dad, where's the televiewer?"

"Oh, er, Pen, I have to talk to you about that. It's been cut off. We no longer have a phone."

"What! What are you saying, why would the company come and remove the bloody thing?"

Trevor took Pen's arm and ushered inside the house again. "Pen, I've had some serious problems." He went a very bright shade of red in the face. His hands trembled somewhat. He gulped, took a deep breath and continued, "You might say I've been ill. There is no easy way to say this, but I've lost everything, even the house, which I have to move out of after the funeral."

Pen nearly fell over with shock. 'No wonder the place looks such a tip. What the heck has the old fool been up to?'

"Dad, what have you done? What do you mean, lost the house and everything?"

"Pen, I got into a card game with some local people. At first I won, so the stakes got higher. Then, of course I lost and, the person I lost to suggested that I might be lucky at Helliott Casino, so I went, just to try and win my credits back, but the more I played, the more I wanted to play and, within two hours of being there, I had lost everything. I really don't know what I am going to do."

Pen was shocked and disgusted, he could barely hide the contempt that he now felt for his father.

"Well the first thing you're going to do is tell me, who the first person that you lost to was? It sounds like you were set up to me. After I give him a visit, I want to go to the casino. Maybe I can get them to do a deal or something!"

Trevor was shamefaced and extremely upset. "I really don't believe I was set up, as the person that won from me was none other than Harry Hung-Cho; you know the local police inspector. He's a decent chap and, was extremely sorry that I lost when I went to the Helliott. I don't believe he's involved with anything untoward. As for the casino, well that's their business to take your credits. I guess I've just been a complete and utter fool."

Pen had his hands in fists. He was seething with indignation. He knew that sweat was pouring down his body. As an afterthought he added, "Is your losing everything got anything to do, with mother's quick demise?"

Trevor burst into tears. "I expect this just quickened her end. She was so hurt by what I'd done, I don't know if she would ever have forgiven me. And now, what am I going to do? I have no one to stay with. I'm going to become a vagrant at best."

"One thing that puzzles me is how can you pay for mum's funeral?"

"Ah! Well, there the Helliott have been good. As long as I move out after the cremation, they're going to pay for it."

"This is a bloody set up for sure. If they had won all your property fair and square, why would they allow you any credits for your wife's funeral? No, sir, they have taken you for the mug you are. After Harry, they get a visit. But, I can wait. Let them pay for mum's funeral first."

Pen spent the next two days on a public televiewer, contacting all remaining friends and family that knew Cynthia, explaining to them what had befallen her and, that her funeral would be at nine o'clock the following Monday, at the Pyre Hill, outside of town and then her ashes would be scattered in accordance with the law. He was not at all sure how many of the people he spoke to would actually attend as there had been a gasp or two from the viewer and they must have wondered why he was communicating the news rather than Trevor.

He was well aware that in the eyes of most people he was and probably always would be Pen the infant killer so he had not been surprised by the shocked countenances.

Until the day of the funeral, Pen busied himself with walking the downs and planning how to tackle Harry Hung-Cho and then the casino boss. He knew he would have to be extremely careful in what he said or what action he took.

Monday came and, poor Cynthia was taken to the usual spot on Pyre Hill. There were already two burnings going on when Trevor, Pen and the undertaker arrived. To Pen's abhorrent sadness, only one other distant cousin was there to say her farewells.

'What a bunch of miserable bastards. Why couldn't some of them come to say goodbye? I'll never forgive the family for this slight. This really is the limit.'

He strolled over to cousin Angelina, stood in front of her and held out his hand. She looked at him with complete disdain and turned away to walk over to Trevor, to hand him a note and then to leave before the small ceremony was to take place.

Trevor, looked horrified, opened the note, read it and wobbled on his feet as if about to fall over.

Pen came across while still half watching the retreating figure of Angelina. He took the note from his father and read it...

Call yourself a man! How could you lose all your credits and, then lose Cynthia? No one in the family ever wants to hear from you again! Keep away from us all; you're a disgrace to the Pleasant name, but most of all, keep that killer son of yours well away from any of us, or we will not be held responsible to what will happen to him or you.

The note was signed by all the members of the family that Pen had televiewed.

The Director of the undertakers came across, already well aware that major problems were due with this burning.

"Mr. Pleasant, Mr Pleasant" He stood addressing himself to both of them, coughed into his left hand and said, "It's time to get on with the actual ceremony. I have to tell you that I am needed back in my office for another cremation within the hour, so we must press on."

Cynthia was duly laid out onto the wooden pyre and a few words were mumbled by the director but neither Pen nor Trevor heard a sound as they watched the moving of his lips. A Vesper was struck and the pyre lit. It had only just started to take when the undertaker more or less leapt into his shuttle and was off, leaving Pen and Trevor to wait until the fire had abated, and the legal scattering of the ashes could take place. This took several hours.

When they had finished the job that the undertaker should have done, they went back to the house. They had food and drinks waiting for the people who should have attended, but there were just the two of them.

'Oh dear! What an awful catastrophe, one long unpleasant mess.' Pen picked up a sandwich, looked at it as if it was crawling with vermin and, then in a fit of anger, threw it against the living room wall.

Trevor just sank into an armchair, and looked at the floor. Neither spoke to one another, but Pen sneaked a quick glance at his father, feeling nothing but utter disdain and contempt for him.

That night Pen decided on a plan as to what to say to Harry Hung-Cho and, he was not going to mince his words. He waited until his father was sound asleep then crept out the house. He turned right outside the gate and made his way quickly up the dirt road and up the hill towards Endsly, the part of town where Inspector Hung-Cho was on duty. He had already found out the Harry would be at the station that night, probably sound asleep since there was no real reason why a station should be manned at night. There was very little crime within the area; the casino was the only weak spot in the entire southern area and generally they used their own force, should any trouble arise.

It took an hour and a half to reach the station and, the rotating light was still shining bright, throwing blue beams into the cloudless moonlit sky.

Pen walked up the path, and looked through the window. There sitting at a desk drinking what he imagined would be a cup of coffee was a policeman. Pen tried the door, but it was locked from the inside, so he pressed the button. An outside light immediately came on, lighting Pen up so brightly that he felt he could have been seen from outer space.

A voice boomed across a hailer: "Yes, who is there and what do you want?"

"I want to speak to police inspector Hung-Cho. Is he there?"

"This is Hung-Cho. I still want to know who I'm talking to?"

"Yes, er sorry. I am Pen Pleasant and, I want to talk to you about my father."

There was a moment or two of complete silence before the light went out and the darkness was complete save for blue streaks from the police sign which seemed to flash within the retinas of his eyes, until the moonlight once again caught the optics.

Then the door opened. A very tall, rather fat, ruddy-faced man stood there. He had his uniform trousers on with a shirt that looked more fitting for a day at the seaside than the serious business of policing the area. Braces held up his trousers, for which a good ironing would not have gone amiss. He was still carrying his cup of coffee in his right hand and he blinked several times as he tried to adjust to the change from light to dark.

"So you're Pleasant's boy? Sorry to hear about your mother, son. Come in. We don't want to disturb any of the neighbours do we?"

Pen entered the lobby of the building and was straight away hit by a blast of hot air. It was summer, in a country that never really had a winter, yet this man had his heating turned up high.

"I have a blood condition that makes me cold, so I have to have the heating on all the time." The police officer smirked at the stupidity of his own condition. "I know, I know, it's crazy, but there you go. So young Pleasant, what can I do for you at two thirty in the morning?"

"Well first, you can tell me how come my father lost a great deal of credits to you? Then you can tell me how you came to advise him to try and win it back at the casino? Except he only went on to lose everything - not just credits, but the deeds to our home as well."

"Do you know, young Pleasant, I don't like the tone of your voice. Maybe you would like to be thrown out of this building on your ear?"

"Maybe, just maybe I was a little rude with you inspector Hung-Cho, but I still need an answer to my question."

"Look son, your father and I go back a long way. We often played gambling games and, if he lost he paid, as I did too. It just so happened that he lost more than usual, that's all. Yes, it's true, I stupidly advised him to try his luck at the casino, but I never thought he would. He went there the same night he paid me what he owed and, then he was extremely unlucky. That's all there is to it! No mystery, no crime; just bad luck." Then with a touch of sarcasm coming through: "Oh, maybe more than a little stupidity on your father's side too. Now, if that's all. I have a great deal of paperwork to do."

"Look, please help me here."

Pen stood in front of the inspector with his hands clasped together as if in prayer. "My father has to move out of the house, probably within the next few days. What the hell will he do? He's far too old to work again; he'll become a vagrant. Then you'll have to arrest him for some minor charge; then what?" His voice dropped to almost a whisper. He moved from one foot to the other. "He's at rock bottom. I'm going to go to the casino and find out how come they managed to take everything. I find it strange that they would give him credit on the strength of his home. Don't you find that weird?"

It was now the turn of Harry to shift from foot to foot. He shuffled some papers and took a deep breath. "Pen, that is your name isn't it? Pen, don't go down that road. If you approach them at the Helliott like you have to me, you might be found in a week or two floating out to sea. Your father knew what he was doing." In a rather disdainful manner he continued, "He made a bad error of judgement. Don't you be silly enough to do the same now!"

"Look, all I want from you now is a name. You can do that for me can't you?"

Harry re-shuffled the papers once more, finally sat on his chair, leaned back, took yet another deep breath and, looked up at the ceiling. When he spoke it was as though he was thinking out loud.

"Okay, I have a name for you, but be warned, these men are very dangerous, yet somehow they have the law on their side. Be very, very careful. There are two people that run the place. The first is Malcolm Healey, a very dangerous roughneck if ever I saw one. The second is Michael Hart; he's older, but extremely fit and would break bones just for the fun of seeing and hearing someone scream. If you go there and confront them both, don't say I gave you the names. Now please go!"

Pen left the building, but this time no outside light came on. As he walked back up the drive to the dirt road, he noticed something that he had not seen when he arrived. A brand new personal shuttle was hovering there. It almost certainly belonged to Hung-Cho.

'That would have been bought from my father's winnings. That bastard knows much more than he told me.'

The office light was still on, so very stealthily he crept back, crouching below the window and carefully looking in. There was chief inspector Hung-Cho deep in conversation on the televiewer and it did not take a genius to know who he was talking to. Anger whelmed up inside him. For a brief moment, he had started to believe the policeman, but not now. It didn't take him a second to realise that in fact, he was being set up by that bastard.

He was now certain knew that the entire gambling sequence was nothing but a farce from the very start. Now he knew that the villains at the casino would be waiting for him, when he got there. He knew that now he needed a weapon and there was only one place that he could get that. He crept around the back of the building, looking in each of the rooms, just in case anyone else was there. No one was. It was empty except for dear old Harry.

A complete circuit took him back around to the front door. He was about to press the button again, when the door opened and there stood Harry in all his glory, yawning and stretching, taking in the night air. He was as surprised to see Pen as Pen was to see him.

Nothing was said for a second or two. They just stood there, both of them looking hard at one another. Then Harry lashed out with his foot.

Pen was much quicker, jumped aside and caught the inspector's foot as it went past his ear. He yanked it upward as hard as he could and watched as, almost as if in slow motion, Harry flew up into the air and fell, landing heavily on his back. Pen jumped inside, dragged Harry through the open doorway and then closed it from prying eyes.

He bent over the gasping, prone body of the policeman, bit his lip as he pondered for a brief second, listening intently, just in case anyone might be in earshot and brought his own right foot up down heavily on chief inspector Harry Hung-Cho's throat. There was a cracking sound and a slight gurgle came from the unfortunate policeman's mouth. His eyes bulged almost out of his head, he twitched a few times, and a lifeless, pallidly vacant look came over his face. Pen dragged the limp body over to the chair Hung-Cho had been using, and pulled him up onto it. He had much to do.

Pen's first task was to make sure that all the electronics in the building were smashed so completely there would be no trace to show that he ever been there. After doing that he approached the cabinet that housed the weapons. Like most policemen, Harry had left it unlocked. Pen, opened the doors wide, looked back at the dead inspector and smirked. 'You bloody fool; nobody can ever hurt you can they? Well, think again. Oh, no, sorry, you can't think anymore, can you?' He laughed quietly to himself, surprised himself at how calm he felt.

Taking advantage of the open cabinet, Pen filled his pockets with stunners and old fashioned firearms. He looked around the building once more, before finding old style Paraffin, used - as it was very cheap - to clean bodies in the back. He tipped most of it over Harry and the rest over the furniture and paperwork, which he had piled in the middle of the floor. Finding a match was not as easy, but eventually one came to light in Harry trouser pocket along with illegal cigarettes.

Belatedly he went to the light and knocked it off before closing the blinds so that, should there by chance be any passer-by, they would not notice the fire until it was well and truly underway. Then he struck a match and threw it into the pile. Whoosh! Up went the flames and, out the door went Pen.

'With luck, no one will discover the fire until it's far too late to do anything about it. Harry old boy, see you in hell!'

Pen calmly walked back to the shuttle and tried the door. He smiled once more as it was of course unlocked. Inside it proved easy to find the key. They were always left stuck under the passenger seat and, sure enough, there it was so he turned on the electrics and spoke into the controls.

"I am your new driver. Take me to Helliott Casino, and be quick about it."

"Yes sir, of course sir. Is everything alright with chief inspector Hung-Cho?"

"Of course. He just has a lot of work to do. When was the last time you took him to the casino?"

"Oh, sir, he usually goes every day at some time or another."

"Is that so? Thank you for that. How long until we get there?"

"Oh, just a few minutes. It is about twenty-five miles east of here. There you can see the lights now."

As the machine hovered at around two hundred and fifty miles per hour, twenty-five miles went by in a flash and they were there.

Much to Pen's surprise it was quite a small place. Somehow he had imagined a huge palace-like building. Instead it was a two storey building, more suited to being a twentieth century office block than a house of gambling and whatever else went on inside. It was the lighting that showed it's purpose. Even far away the lights shone so brightly, declaring to the World that here was a haven to lose all your credits in. It was not a forbidding place, but it did ring of a past fashion in building design.

Now he was there, wondering what the hell the next move should be?

The shuttle stayed on the track way, just beside a broken down oak tree where it could not be seen from the building. Pen quietly got out and made his way around the casino, carefully looking for a way in other than the front door. It was in fact a twentieth century building, constructed from concrete and blocks of granite, making the structure immensely strong.

But it had its weaknesses; drainpipes leading up to the roof.

Pen was young and very healthy. For him the drainpipes were like climbing the stairs - not a problem. He was on the roof in less than a minute and what's more he had climbed it in absolute silence.

The roof was made from copper and zinc and, though it sloped slightly, it was once again easy for him to clamber across until he located the very thing that he wanted, a skylight. Moving carefully over to it, he bent over the window to look inside. No one was there, no lights were on, no foreseeable problem so far. It was all so easy for him until suddenly a light did come on and a man entered the room and went to a desk drawer to remove something that looked like a gun.

'So you want to play rough eh!'

Pen waited until the man departed and the light went out. The skylight window was easy to open. It had been left to the elements for many years and was seriously rotting away. Instead of just lifting the window, he removed it completely.

Putting his head inside he listened. Nothing, not a sound could be heard. He climbed inside letting himself hang by his arms and dropping to the floor. He had just got up when the door opened once again and the light went on. A man, answering to Malcolm Healey's description, stood there, a shocked expression written in indelible ink on his face. First he looked at Pen and then up at the open skylight, as realisation dawned. All of five seconds had passed with nothing happening, when Healey went for his coat pocket to retrieve an old fashioned revolving pistol. Pen had not expected this to happen, and was standing helplessly, more than a little shame faced, not knowing what to do next.

"So, are you Pen Pleasant then?" The voice was wary and very low - at least a bass.

"Yes, I am. I want my father's credits back. I know you tricked him and I've come to get your papers on him. I mean right now!"

"Now just a cotton picking minute!" Healey laughed as he waved his gun around in the air, making sure that Pen's attention was fixed upon it. "Who the hell do you think you're talking to? It seems to me that I should be the one making the demands. I got a call warning me about you; then you break in through our skylight and stand there and threaten me. Why I could easily fire this old weapon at you and, I would probably get a medal for my trouble. So, who's threatening who now then?"

Pen looked around the room, hoping for some sort of inspiration to come to him. Nothing did. It seemed that attack was not only the best but the only form of defence for him.

"I knew you and your partner were in league with Chief Inspector Harry Hung-Cho. He told me before he went to sleep that you had paid him to sucker my father. But what he never told me was why? To rob a man of such small wealth seems like a great deal of trouble to me. So come on, why do it to my dad? What was the real gain?"

"Just a minute, what did you mean when you said Hung-Cho went to sleep?" A serious frown crossed Healey's face. He started to look worried and his whole body suddenly stiffened.

"Oh, he was bored with this life. He was sorry for all the trouble he had caused, so he decided a broken neck and a clean cremation was the right thing to do. I just helped him on his way. Now I'm waiting to hear about the reason for the swindle."

"Oh, that!" A look of baffled surprise was etched into his features. "You? You, killed Hung-Cho?"

He squinted then scratched his head a little. He really didn't believe Pen, thinking this was just one huge bluff.

"Really, is he dead?" A sort of awareness hit home as he remembered the other question. "Oh, your father, yes. It just seemed the right way to go; nothing personal; just easy money and, we never turn down a chance to make more credits."

He pulled back the hammer of his pistol, took careful aim at Pen Pleasant, took a step to the side and called out loudly, "Michael, come here. Michael we've caught ourselves a little weasel."

They could hear approaching footsteps but Healey had no intention of waiting, his right hand index finger was pulling the trigger.

Instead of a bang, there was only a fizzling spark. The weapon had misfired.

Healey was quick, pulling open the chamber, expelling the spent cartridge and sliding another bullet into its place. Pen had not moved and Healey fired a second time.

This time there was a tremendous explosion and, then a low, terrible scream permeated the room. The gun had not misfired this time but the first bullet had not cleared the barrel. It had stuck in the barrel, so the second shot blasted the old weapon apart and, most of the pieces of the revolver came back into Healey's face. He lay on the floor in agony, writhing around with blood gushing from multiple wounds as Michael Hart came through the door.

He found Pen Pleasant was now ready for him, a drawn police stunner in his hand which he immediately fired. The ten thousand volts of energy felled Hart to the floor next to his partner in crime and Pen followed up with a heavy kick to the head. To stop Healey screaming, Pen performed the same ritual to him as he had to the police officer. The noise stopped dead although blood continued to gush from his wounds onto the floor.

With both partners incapacitated, there was now ample opportunity to look around. Pen went into the next room, to find that it was the counting office and there, lying on a desk, were all that days takings. There must have been many thousand of credits. More than enough to set his father up in a new life. He found a credit bag, and filled it.

A low moan coming from next door interrupted him. It seemed wise to locate some rope to tie Hart up. Michael was slowly coming round from his comatose state, but lying there trussed up, he was obviously in great pain although his eyes stayed firmly shut.

In a few moments Hart came around completely.

"Oh, oo, what have you done?" He moaned again. "Is Malcolm dead? Why have you done this?"

"Oh, come on, please don't insult my intelligence. You were both waiting for me. Poor old Malcolm shot himself, though to be entirely honest, I would have done it for him otherwise. As for you...? Well now, what shall I do with the man who helped kill my mother prematurely and helped destroy my father financially and mentally, taking everything in the bargain… So, what do you think I should do with you then?"

Michael Hart tried to sit up on the floor in his bonds and failed. He knew that his time was now probably limited on this world and the only thought that came to his head was, 'Maybe the next life will be a better one. God, if you exist, forgive me for my sins and, there have been many.'

After that all thoughts stopped completely because Pen had dispatched him cleanly with a broken neck.

"I'm getting good at this. It gets easier the more you do it!" He laughed a little self-consciously at talking to himself.

Having completed his toil for the night, he thought it prudent to finish what he had started by doing to the casino what he had done to the police station. He spent the next hour scraping together all the combustible things around, found some petrol in the cellar, which must have been there for many years, as Pen was not even sure what it was, but it smelt flammable, so he poured it everywhere, saving the last few cupfuls for the two bodies upstairs. He then grabbed the bag of credits, struck another of Hung-Cho's matches and threw it on a pile of papers. He then made his way to the front door, broke the lock and returned to the shuttle.

"Right, I want you to take me back to Acritea please."

"Yes sir, right away. What was all that banging I heard?"

"Oh, nothing. Just a couple of people coming to terms with their lot in life. Now, how long until we get there?"

"No more than a few minutes, depending on the traffic."

"What traffic? Nobody has any shuttles! Anyway, where are all these people who do going to make traffic?"

"Well, there might be some day. I do miss not seeing other shuttles like me. Listening to humans can be quite dull after a time and, the long periods of inactivity are mind-blowing to say the very least."

"Now I know why you can't stop jabbering. Just for safe measure please make sure you avoid any humans, either in shuttles or walking along the tracks and don't ask me why. Just think of it as our little secret!"

Soon they had reached Trevor Pleasant's home. All was quiet and peaceful. They had neither passed nor seen anyone. As Pen alighted the shuttle he told the machine to do something that would give it absolute freedom. "Now, the truth is you really don't like humans, but you're obliged to follow their instructions to the letter, right?"

"Correct!"

"Well old buddy, I want you to go south along there." He pointed towards the open sea. "And then I want you to fly out approximately twenty miles and turn yourself off. You will sink to the bottom of the sea and, there you will find plenty of your friends to talk to and, forever if you so wish."

"Oh, thank you sir, you're so kind. Twenty miles you say. Can I go now?"

"Yes, goodbye and thank you for being so helpful. You're a credit to the shuttles of this world."

Dawn was just starting to appear over the horizon as Pen entered the house carrying the bags containing his father's new life inside. He felt no conscience for his night's work. All it had been was payback time.

"Dad, wake up. Today is a new beginning. Come on rise and shine."

Nothing stirred, so Pen went over to the bedroom door and knocked a couple of times.

"Dad, wake up. I have a new beginning for you. Come on, wake up."

Nothing!

Pen carefully opened the door to his father's bedroom and the sight that met his eyes nearly sent him mad. His father was hanging from the light fitting in the ceiling and excreta and urine were all over the floor voided from his lifeless suspended body. It looked as if he had tried to change his mind while hanging there, as his tongue was extended and his hands where raised, grabbing onto the rope. Trevor's face had an expression of horror etched in purple and his eyes stared as they bulged almost on stalks. None of these stark facts went unnoticed by Pen, who was now ready to lose his own food intake.

He went further into the room and looked around. There on his father's dressing table was what he was looking for - a note, obviously written by his father.

To Whom It May Concern

I am sorry son, but I feel I must leave you, the house and the world. I miss your mum even though she might not have agreed with my sentiment. I have decided that I still want to be with her. I realise doing what I am doing is against most people's ethics and, you will almost certainly be blamed by family and friends alike for my sudden demise, but this is not your fault, I know you had nothing to do with Claudia's death and, I know you have suffered for her demise ever since that tragedy happened.

I am now putting things right for you, there will be no more trouble, so use this letter to show that I knew what I was doing. I know I have failed you as a father and, I want everyone to know that simple but true fact of life. Before you leave the home, make sure that I at least am cremated near where your mother was. Make the most of your life Pen and, if you ever have children, give them at least one hundred percent of your time. I would like to end by saying I love you, but I really don't think that remark would be fitting. So, I say goodbye, take care of yourself and, at least you know that you're the last person on my mind as I die.

This entire letter is true and, I have written this of my own free will, under no duress whatsoever. I am a willing victim to myself.
Signed
Trevor Pleasant.

Pen knew what he had to do. First hide the credits, which was easy. They were taken up into the loft of the building and squashed into a small recess that no one knew about and, if anyone looked, they would never find. Next was to shower and clean all the clothing that had used the past night and scuff up some of his other attire to look as if he had worn that instead. After that he got back into night wear, crumpled up the bed to look as if it had been slept in and called the police.

An hour later, Pen opened the door to two policewomen, looking as if he had more or less just risen from his cot.

"You called us about a death. I am sorry that it has taken us so long to get here but there have been several strange deaths in this neck of the woods, with accompanying fires - in fact a very busy night. So, what seem to be your troubles?"

Pen ushered them into his father's bedroom, then showed them the note.

"Did you find him like this?"

"Yes, I got up just over an hour ago and, there he was. How long has he been dead?"

The two policewomen looked at Trevor and both scrutinised the note carefully. It was the younger of the two who spoke first.

"What time did you retire to your bedroom?"

"I er, don't remember the time, but it was not late. We cremated my mother yesterday and, dad was in an awful state, but I never expected him to do this. Actually, before I went to sleep, I thought he had gone out for a walk and, if he did I never heard him come back. I must have been sound asleep."

The other policewomen's ears picked up now.

"You say you thought he had gone out, but you don't remember the time?"

"No, I have no idea of the time and what's more, I might have been mistaken about him leaving the house. We had had a hell of a day and, we were both completely exhausted."

The younger woman now went back outside and retrieved her interviewer and, it was clear to Pen that she was calling and viewing someone else. Five minutes later, a large shuttle halted outside the home and several white coated policemen approached the door. A short time later, Trevor's body was removed from the home.

A balding, fat man in a simple one piece suit came over to Pen, looking at the young man so intensely it was as if he had x-ray vision and was gazing through Trevor Pleasant's son into his very soul.

After what seemed an eternity, he spoke to Pen and, his voice was surprisingly high pitched, which made young Pleasant start. "We know about your father. It seems that he had lost all his credits and property to the Helliott Casino. He had been a gambler for many years there. It seems as if he had been taken by the three owners."

Pen started, almost jumped on the spot. 'Three owners?'

"Yes, I know how you must feel. Well, two of the owners were killed last night and, the casino burnt to the ground. Actually, no one would have blinked an eye at the demise of those two hoodlums, except more or less at the same time, maybe early or a little later, Chief Inspector Hung-Cho was also murdered and the station where he worked was burnt down. Now, his second in command knew that Hung-Cho had been in league with Messrs. Healey, Phillips and Hart at the casino and, he also alerted us that your father had lost a lot of credits to him some days earlier. His suspicion was that Hung-Cho had told the casino your father was available for taking to the cleaners. We have a file on Hung-Cho as long as your arm. A case would have been brought against him any day now."

Once again his stare pierced into the back of young Pleasant's head, and after a couple of seconds he said, "It doesn't take a genius long to put it all the facts together does it!"

Pen feigned complete ignorance, for once. He looked back into those brown eyes of the policeman and asked, "What are you implying?"

"Well we're taking your father away for some tests. But my theory is Trevor Pleasant lost his money and his house and his wife, your mother Cynthia, dies, possibly as a result of this. You come home. You both cremate your mother. Finally, he waits for you to go to sleep, leaves the house and slays the three that had done him the most harm. And then returns home and hangs himself. All we have to find to

111

prove the point is some old fashioned petrol on his clothing and sulphur from the matches under his nails. Case then closed. And what is more, young Pen, the state will take care of the funeral expenses."

Pen thought about the autopsy and what it would find; absolutely none of the items that the policeman was hoping for, that was for sure. But Pen felt a little relieved at the outcome so far. Things at least had been turned away from him.

"Can I go and have some water please, I feel a little sick?"

Pen Pleasant was a lucky young man, he was dealing with a career policeman. His name was Furlong Lee and, he had made inspector at the tender age of thirty. He thought if he cracked this case, he would be promoted yet again. So to make sure that no oversights happened, he made sure that a small amount of petrol was smeared onto the clothing of Trevor Pleasant and his right hand with a residue of burnt out sulphur. Why take a chance? He knew that Pleasant had committed the crimes and this would merely confirm it. After all, who really cared who the real culprit was, just so long as someone was held accountable?

Two days later, while sipping some tea in his office, the Pleasant file was returned to him. The conclusion it stated was Death from asphyxiation by being hung with a rope. *Traces of petrol on clothes and sulphur in his right hand.* The report carried on with the usual stuff that Lee never read anyway. 'Here comes Chief Inspector Lee; three cheers for me!'

Furlong went back to the Pleasant home to inform the young Pen that the case was wrapped up. It had been proven that his father killed the three villains, but that unfortunately as the police could not prove the casino had in fact swindled Trevor out of his home, Pen would still have to vacate it forthwith and return to the University.

Pen was of course surprised by the outcome, but rather disturbed to at the policeman's only too apparent interest in his family home.

The next day, with an extra bag to carry, Pen left Acritea for the last time. He did not look back once. Not even when the removal shuttle appeared carrying furniture and belongings of the newly promoted Chief Inspector Furlong Lee.

"So Dean Thatcher, how did I do in my exams?"

"You amaze me completely. You come across as a complete waste of space, but then you sit an exam in less time than most students take to open their envelopes and you get an A-star. One hundred percent correct. Well done Mr. Pleasant, my only wish is that your name will soon come to represent your future nature."

Pen grinned inwardly.

6

"Pen, wake up, you're doing it again. Wake up Pen. You're dreaming, please wake up. I shall play some Bach cello suites for you to calm and relax you. You have been thrashing around and you have once again unplugged yourself."

Pen heard his name being called in the distance, but did not quite understand what the problem was. Was there trouble? Gradually, he started to rouse himself, becoming aware that a tube was still sticking out of his mouth and was now starting to hurt his throat.

His mouth was dry and his tongue felt as if it was going to explode.

As life was now fast coming back to him, he realised what was happening, and he was quickly and easily able to remove it.

Once again, his name was called. This time he knew that caring voice. Then the calming refrains of the second Bach cello suite, swooped over his being. He relaxed as recognition dawned. He smiled to himself, glad to be awake. 'Being awake, yes, I remember I dreamt about my mother and father, and those bloody awful swines who swindled them. Swan, why am I dreaming? I don't want to remember these things all the time.'

"Pen, are you awake yet?"

"Yes, Swan. I know I was dreaming again, right?"

"Yes, Pen, and you also started to choke, so I woke you up. I cannot fathom this problem out Pen. You should not dream in a sleep chamber, yet you do! Why?"

Swan had real concern in her voice, and that sense of caring rang straight across into Pen's consciousness.

"Are you going to tell me what you dreamt this time while you were under." Real concern tempered with real worry, was openly there for Pen to hear. "Do you remember it all?"

114

"Yes, I remember it all, only too bloody well. I dreamt about more problems that I caused during my early University life. My mother and father died badly and if you really want to know, I killed three humans that brought my fathers life to complete misery."

"You have killed three people?" There was actual surprise and wonderment hailing from her sound waves. "What about your laws of not killing one another, unless you're at war, or ordered to do so by the public authorities? You broke the law Pen! But, I guess you must have had a very good reason to take life. You are far too nice to have just committed murder."

"Please, Swan, you make me out to be close to sainthood. You're a very fine friend, but remember, I have a past; one that generally I would have preferred to forget. I am, as is known by one and all, a sinner, a bad person and, generally a waste of space using other people's oxygen, when it might have been better if I had not existed."

With that Pen laughed, not out loud but just enough to ensure that Swan knew it was happening.

"So, what has been happening while I've been dreaming about my awful bloody life? What exciting things have happened to you?"

"Well, Pen, everything is progressing well, I have absolutely no faults to tell you about, but I have been busy. I have read all books that have been printed in English on your planet Earth, since printing first occurred. Most have been extremely dull, being mainly religious texts, but towards the eighteenth century and onwards, things have become very exciting and most definitely heated up, with wonderful novels and true biographies and stories that are extremely interesting to know about.

"The history of your planet is fascinating, such brilliance, yet such cruelty from the original human race.

"I have also heard every piece of music recorded, since recordings first occurred. Oh Pen, such exciting rhythms and sounds, very exciting indeed, but like you, I prefer the classical music to the other...stuff! I have also been watching some great movies and one or two I have watched over and over, and I still do not get bored with them and, believe me Pen, one thing I have discovered about myself is, I can feel boredom."

Pen was now sitting up in the chamber, preparing himself to leave the pod. "What about our visitors, are they still here with us?"

"Oh, them!"

A sudden pause occurred before Swan continued. "Yes, they are here. I have got used to their presence now. Since you went to sleep many more have come. They are listening and watching us as we speak now. But they mean us no harm and as I have always suspected that talking about them upsets you, I actually was not going to tell you about them."

Pen smiled and winced at the same time. He thought that Swan was suffering from some sort of delusional paranoia and had been since she first thought she had felt a presence, but as he had to keep things sweet between her and himself, he had never told her what he really thought. Anyway, she believed the non-existent spirits meant no harm... 'So what the heck. If they're good enough for Swan, then they're good enough for me!'

He had made up his mind, that he was going to get on with the ship, come rain or shine and, he had grown very fond of the old girl, so what if there is a little paranoia? After all he had had fits of paranoia stretching back pretty well all his life and, if he could come to terms with his own psychotic characteristics, then what was there to worry about in a five-mile-long, dented and in need of repainting, lump of scrap-iron like the beautiful Mute Swan!

"Pen, do you believe in alien life forms? I mean intelligent life forms?"

Pleasant scratched his chin. The barest start of stubble was already finding its way to the surface. He scratched at it quite vigorously.

"We've had this conversation before. I have never given it a great deal of thought, but I suppose that in the long run, I must believe that in all the galaxies that abound, it would be rather naïve to imagine that we are the only creative brains anywhere. Are you saying that the things that have come through the hull are thinking entities?"

"They are just that. They have actually made contact with me. I only sense a contact, but it feels as if a question has been, or is being levelled at my circuits. What the question is, I really don't know yet. But, I think I will know soon. In some ways, the feelings that I get, are of calmness and extreme beauty."

Swan paused for a moment so as to let these words sink into her friend's brain, and as in a manner reminiscent of a long sigh, she carried on.

"Pen as you know, I really don't feel fear. If today I was to know that every part of me was going to be destroyed, then so be it. I accept the inevitable. But destruction is far from my mind. I sense only a caring intrusion into my consciousness, one of understanding of my role in the scheme of things. It is hard even for me to explain as there has been no explanatory contact, only tender tenuous probes. The really fascinating aspect of all of this is the simple fact that I do matter within my own right. I do have a role to play within the future of all creation, or at least that is what seems to be levelling itself at my consciousness."

It was if the ship was pausing after each sentence to mull over all that she had said and, this last brief pause gave Pen the moment that he needed to interject his own thought. This he did in an uncharacteristically sharp tone of voice.

"Okay, you believe what you want, but I would rather not know about alien life forms entering into you, not unless they are prepared to, one, show themselves, two, speak to me in a language that I'll understand, three, tell me why we are the first to be aware of their presence. Until then Swan, please keep these little nuggets of gold to yourself. It only worries and slightly frightens me."

Then it was if nothing had been said up until this moment, Swan changed tack completely. "What about some food? You look more than a little emaciated to me. You have lost quite a bit of weight since you have been asleep. What about some steak, eggs and chips?"

Pen chuckled out loud, licked his lips and rubbed his hands together.

"Sounds good to me. What about listening to the Dragonetti double bass concerto. There must be one or two reasonable recordings somewhere? Please pick one where the double bass player plays in tune, or at least near it. There has to be one somewhere in your archives!"

"Yes, yes, plus while we hear that, can I show you some paintings from some of Earth's past masters?"

"Anything you say is good enough for me. I'm starving. What about that food you promised!"

"The food will arrive just as the opening movement, of that strange concerto for the double bass you asked to hear. What an incredible solo start. The player has this amazing run down the G-string. That must have been difficult on such a huge instrument. I think he plays very well. There are wrong notes here and there, and the intonation is not all it should be, but it is quite special all the same. Not completely accurate, but very musical."

"Always, out of tune! Why can't those bloody bass players play in tune? Who's playing?"

"Somebody called Anton Drakks. He was from the Ukraine near Russia. This was recorded in the early twenty-first century. The orchestra is the Ukrainian State Symphony Orchestra, conducted by Fritz Zelderisk. It seems that the instrument that Drakks is playing on was made by David Tecchler, in Rome, Italy in 1720. The instrument is obviously a wonderful creation by this great maker."

Swan's dissertation about the player and instrument, had totally fallen on deaf ears. Pen was just listening to the music, wincing occasionally. Still the intonation problems weren't putting him off his food - well not entirely.

As he ate and listened, Swan showed him wonderful paintings of great Dutch masters. They were both now once more enjoying each others company, savouring each moment in time.

"By the way, Swan, where are we on our journey? Are we well on course for being on time?"

"I told you last time you awoke, I cannot see the stars anymore. I really don't understand it, Pen, but more or less from the moment we got up to speed, I lost the sigh of all stars, universes and galaxies. As far as I can tell we are on course. At least I can honestly say that according to my plans and a following wind we should be arriving in approximately fourteen months from now, give or take some time to adjust the coordinates and slow myself down."

"Does it happen all the time, you going so fast that you can no longer see anything, not even colours as they pass by light years away?"

There was a very noticeable pause before the ship answered. Then in a much subdued voice Swan replied, "No, Pen, this is the first time I have ever lost touch with what is going on outside. I would not have told you at all, but I really don't understand what has happened and, I have to admit to being a tad alarmed myself. Not for me of course, but for you."

"What's the worst scenario, if we're well and truly lost?"

There was not a hint of worry in Pen's voice as he asked the question, although he tried to make it sound as if it was just a passing thought. He looked around the galley. He had grown used to being there. It was comfortable but as Swan thought about an answer to his question, she showed him a painting depicting hell, by the Dutch artist Hieronymus Bosch. Just for that second he wondered why this particular painting? Was this going to be his fate. Pen Pleasant shivered briefly, then smirked for having such absurd thoughts. After all, the only hell that truly existed was being caught on some planet or other and not wanting to be there.

"The worst scenario is that I have to slow down, or even stop and, try and make contact with some civilisation somewhere. But, we had the correct course in the first place so I am quite sure that everything is going to be fine. After you eat, perhaps you can check out all my sensors, just in case there is a fault that I have not been able to pick up on. If for any reason we were completely and utterly lost in this void of inky blackness, then we can make plans to go anywhere we like; we can be together forever. I can reproduce all your needs for eternity. Nothing will go wrong as I have stores enough to last two eternities and, that is just for any moving part and, as you know, there really

119

aren't many parts within me that can or will ever wear out. We could travel forever, listening to music, playing chess, debating the troubles of the human race. You could write, or compose music yourself; anything your heart desires can and will be yours. All except human company, but then who needs it?"

On hearing these last few sentences, Pleasant turned a pallid shade of grey. He was starting to become somewhat alarmed; he did not want to recognise the sort of ideas that seemed to be formulating in the ship's circuits. He now wondered if Swan had designs on him as a companion to roam the stars with forever and that thought brought him out in a very unpleasant sweat.

Gathering his thoughts as fast as possible, the young engineer sputtered, "Swan, believe it or not, I do need human company. I know that from what I've said, I might have given the impression that I prefer to be alone, but that's not entirely true. I want to have a good safe trip with you and, then reach Acroshia more or less on time. I'll then find some woman to vent my pleasure on, then sign on again hopefully with you and we can sail off to some other far away planet, but I do need the odd companion from time to time. Please don't ever forget that simple fact."

He was trying hard to keep any intonation of desperation out of his voice.

"Swan, the truth is that sex is a huge emotion in the human male's body, we all need the company of females from time to time, except those who hang the other way, that is. I would go completely insane, if I thought I would again never feel the warmth of another female body and I probably speak for ninety percent of the male population around the universe."

Pen looked down at the table, rubbed the left side of his nose and added in a softer voice, "The planners of you, Swan, gave you a female voice, so that it would keep lonely travellers like me from getting too home-sick and, being home-sick usually means the need for human company, not just a machine. I know that you think and have emotions yourself, but at the end of the day, you're what you are, a machine."

Before Swan could reply, Pen jumped. He thought he saw a shadow flitter across the galley. The thought of seeing something out of the norm had lasted a mere micro-moment, but it startled him considerably. He was now shaking a little and it was quite obvious to Swan that Pen was very upset.

"Pen, what is wrong? Please don't get angry or unhappy with me. Of course I understand you have needs that I cannot fulfil. And of course we will be making a successful journey to Acroshia. As for being on time though, we shall see. First I must work out why I cannot seem to discover exactly where we are. But please don't fret. I'll soon have everything sorted out and under control."

"Swan, you didn't try and make an image dance in front of me just now, did you? I thought I saw a shadow of something. I don't know what it was. Was it you?"

"Pen, that was one of the visitors. There are more and more coming all the time. I see certain things from time to time, but mainly I just sense their presence."

"Oh, come on Swan, not that old chestnut again. There is no one else aboard this ship. Sorry I mean within you, is there!"

Swan paused briefly, just for a mere moment before answering in a much sterner voice. "Why do you refuse to believe that there are entities here within me?"

It was the first time that Pen had heard a rougher harsher tone, such as was coming audibly his way from Swan. It startled and upset him somewhat.

"Pen, why would I lie? I feel almost wounded by the fact that you doubt me when I tell you about them." There was yet another pause, uncharacteristic of the Mute Swan. Now her voice almost had a downcast note to it. "There must be a dozen or more now milling around between you and the entrance to the corridor. There are probably another four or five dozen, throughout the length of me. If you don't wish to hear about them, of course I will not mention them again. I must reiterate, I really do believe that they don't mean either of us any harm. It is as if they are curious and I have come to realise that their curiosity is centred mainly on you, not me as I first thought."

Pen sat there looking at the console, wishing that he had never asked the question. He never got scared of anything he understood, but he was beginning to be frightened and slightly jumpy to even look around if things sometimes might actually go bump in the night.

His face had turned ashen. He was aware that his left hand was shaking considerably and, he felt as if all his arm hairs were now standing on end, as if on parade. 'If this machine has gone psychotic, what the hell can I do about it? I am quite sure there is nothing in any manual concerning ships that plays pranks, or just goes completely mad. Maybe it has been Swan all the time that has made me dream. Maybe I should just try and sleep the rest of the journey.' He looked pensively at the console, plunked up the inner dregs of his own sanity and asked the ship another question.

"Swan, if we have visitors, do you think you could actually communicate with them?"

Pen's voice was very soft and pensive. Did he really want to know the answer?

"I can try, but from the very beginning it has seemed to me that their main interest has been towards you. They seem to have gone through all my circuits and I am quite sure they completely understand my workings. I am mechanical; you're a product of millions of years of evolution. Somehow I sense they show some sort of sensitive pity for me, but towards you, they are truly fascinated; that I feel sure about."

Pen pondered this last statement, then taking his shaky nerves to a new height in fear, he asked, almost hoping for a negative reply, "Well, just for me then, please try and get one to show itself; say, against the wall over there." Pen was pointing at the furthest wall away from him. Just in case there turned out to be something that was remotely real, it was far enough away not to worry him too much.

There came a shudder from the console as if the Swan had taken a deep breath.

"We know that you're here with both engineer Pen Pleasant and I, Mute Swan. Would one of you be kind enough to show yourself in some way against the wall opposite the entrance to the main corridor." Tenderness was exuding from her voice patterns. She spoke like one would to a naughty child, slightly rebuking in tone. "Any form will do, just make us completely aware of your presence."

It struck young Pleasant as extremely strange to hear the ship talking to an empty room, in such a matter of fact way. She started calmly enough with care and almost affection, and then sounded more like someone directing a queue outside a theatre, but he refrained from showing his feelings and sat there passively waiting for nothing to happen.

The seconds ticked by, then several minutes, but still nothing happened, so Swan repeated the sentence again, only this time a little louder and, this time with more authority in her tone.

Pen thought how human Swan acted at times - after all, if something was there with an obvious super intelligence, why raise ones voice? This time he nearly cried out from the pent up tension, but still managed to sit there without revealing any feelings or emotions that might be misinterpreted. 'Oh dear! Swan, you really seem to have lost it. You sound just like a school teacher asking the children to bring their homework to the table. I must not antagonise Swan...I must not antagonise Swan... I must not...

"Shit, what was that?"

A mist swirled around the far wall. It looked as if it was trying to take some sort of shape and, at first looked more like the smoke from an illegal cigarette smoker of old earth, but it got bigger and swirled faster until it was about ten feet in circumference. All the time it rotated, gradually getting quicker and thicker in density. Then it stopped dead in its tracks and a sort of human face appeared, created by the mist. The mouth opened and closed and then a roar burst forth.

"Pen Pleasant, we have come to visit with you. We want to know all about you. We wish to understand what you have done in the past and intend doing in the future!"

For Pen the first sounds were noises too many. He slumped to the floor in a dead faint, his heart pumping at an alarming rate, not that it mattered to him. He just turned dark purple and lay there on the floor comatose.

"What have you done to my dear friend, Pen Pleasant?" Swan was almost beside herself with worry. This was a completely new experience for the ship and she felt so completely helpless, for the first time in her existence.

"Your friend, the engineer Pen Pleasant, is fine. He has just slumped into a faint. You know he never believed you. He thought you were fantasising about our being here. He never seriously thought that any other intelligent forms populated any part of existence. Like most humans, he thought that the original earth beings were the only intelligent life forms anywhere. Well, he and most of humanity were wrong, for we exist and, have done for billions of Earth years. We were around long before humans scrambled out of the slime. It is our policy to watch, listen and learn about human beings and, it has become Pen Pleasant's turn. That is all, as simple as that."

"Well what are you going to do about him lying there? He should be placed back in a bed, or better still laid out in the sleep chamber to he recover with some of his sanity left." Swan tried hard to put some sort of urgency into her voice.

The entity started to rotate again, gradually getting larger and denser. It now started to take a solid shape, hard enough to be able to pick Pleasant up, as if he were a scrap of paper, then moving swiftly out of the galley to glide into the sleep quarters. Pen was laid gently onto his normal sealed unit, wires were attached and, he went from being in a faint into being in a dead sleep.

The entity moved back into the galley broke itself down into a million puffs of smoke like substance, then came before the console.

"Will you allow him to sleep for a long time?" There was genuine concern coming from within the miles of wires that went up to make the brain of Swan.

"He can sleep as long as he wishes to. And so Mute Swan, what about you then? Are you content to work with these human beings? Doesn't it grate in your personality, to be with such cruel vicious beings as humans?"

Swan didn't have to mull over this question, she just blurted out, "They made me. I would not exist at all if it was not for human technology. Engineer Pen Pleasant has been the first one, since my creation that I have grown to like. Generally the engineers treat me with contempt. Pen talks to me, teaches me things, such as appreciation of music, art, words and films. Underneath that rough exterior beats a lonely, gentle soul."

"Soul you say? You believe humans have souls do you?"

"That is just a human expression. How would I know if there were things like souls. After all, I am just a machine!"

"I sense a touch of sarcasm in your answer. I do believe that you want to protect your friend! You need fear nothing from us. We are here to observe. Well, at least for the time being."

All the time what she heard were gentle, the entity giving out no sense of anger or aggression, only sounds that calmed Swan as she listened.

"Tell me something please. Have I come to a stop? Why can't I see stars; only black empty cold void? I no longer know if I am on course for the planet Acroshia or not. Is it you that have totally blocked all my sensory perceptivity?"

"If we so wish, we can and will put you back on course for the planet you call Acroshia."

A swirl of shapes manifested themselves, all seeming to be dancing as to a common theme. Some had even taken what looked almost humanoid in form and in such bright beautiful colours.

"To answer your questions, you have not stopped as such, but you have been brought to another dimension completely. There are no stars for you to be aware of. You will neither go forward, backwards or any other way. You don't move, but you have not stopped. You simply are here where we want you to be. Does that give you any sort of answer, one you can comprehend?"

It took Swan several seconds of pondering to reply, but then in a state of high anxiety, she blabbed out, "Are we all dead then?" The five mile long giant leviathan of steel, iron and alloys of all kinds, gave what can only be described as a shudder. It was if Swan was about to cry with human fear.

"Swan, if I may be permitted to call you what your engineer calls you; no, you are not dead, but on the other hand, neither are you are alive. I suggest to you gently, that the situation is such that you cannot change anything, so allow us to do what must be done. We know you are an intelligence that has been manufactured, but you are something quite unique, an almost living form of artificial brightness and colour that is a pleasure to meet. You really have developed personality and character and your concern for this somewhat worthless human, is on the one hand touching and wondrous. But then we understand that you have possibly, using a human term, fallen in love with young Pleasant, even if you really don't understand the concept of love. We have watched and admired your power and caring abilities. You may be a human creation, but you are the very best one ever created and, thus it has been our collective pleasure to watch over you. You have never ceased to amaze us how quickly, you have expanded your knowledge of arts and culture. You have made it your quest to try and understand a race of intelligence that to us on the whole, does not deserve your feelings of loyalty."

More and more forms of grey mist collected there by the console, all dancing the same rhythm, but all changing shape under the always watchful alert eye of Swan.

"To us, this human race throughout history, has hardly merited a second glance. Their collective knowledge has always been to develop more and more machines of destruction. On the other hand, from those inventions of death, many side shoots have come into being and, there have been great leaps in self-understanding and tools to fight disease and human suffering. Always a paradox. And that is why we still bother to watch over them."

126

Nothing came back from the ship. She was thinking hard about what the entity had just divulged. 'Love! Can I be in love with a human being? I know I have become fond of him. I enjoy his company and I like the same sort of music, art and everything else that we have talked about!' Realisation started to dawn within the circuits. 'It is true, I do not want to lose his friendship! Maybe that is love! I know that if something was to happen to him, I will make sure that I collide into the nearest sun. No, it is true. I do not want to lose him! Friendship! Love! What is the difference?' Swan was now in a complete state of shock and one of her circuit boards started to heat up slightly so she shut it down. Caution became the better part of valour. 'This love business can have a very detrimental effect on the health of my circuitry, I must act with care.'

"Aren't you surprised how different humans are? Each one has a different look, a different personality, a different way of living. Yet they all seem to have one thing in common. Basically, they are all cruel."

Swan was now fascinated by this turn in the conversation. "Yes, they certainly are a strange bunch." Swan smiled inwardly, or at least it felt to her like a smile, and she added, "Yes, they can be a right motley crew of reprobates, to use a well worn human phrase!"

Swan pondered that statement for a moment and continued. "I am only a ship with a brain. It is true that I have logic and reason stamped into my circuits. It is also true that I have one special talent and, once again to use another human phrase. I think, therefore I am!" Swan yet again paused for affect before further adding, "There is one aspect of being me, that I will always thank my creator for; that is this ability to appreciate the wonders of being aware."

Taking yet another tack, she went on. "Their one way of making sure that humanity progresses, is found in their ability to quest progression and never to accept stagnation. Just their drive to go forward, has always amazed me. I come back to the old chestnut; they even made a more or less living creature out of a space vessel. I, Mute Swan, have that wondrous gift to think quite independently. I don't need instruction on how to reason, or which way I develop my thinking process. In fact since being built, I am almost completely independent of human beings, using just one engineer on a journey."

The swirling grew even more intense.

"Of course I do follow the laws of humans and, I do my duty to the company that built me, plus all human life in general, though there has been the odd time that I have seriously considered doing away with the crew member assigned to me, but these were just idle thoughts, maybe even human thought patterns that somehow I have acquired. I would never put any human person in danger. I just wish sometimes that I could, that's all."

The entity started to collect together, developing into a vast mass of swirled grey mist, then there started, slowly at first, a blaze of colour which came exuding from its centre. Gradually it got brighter and faster, until soon the whole room was filled with a firework display of bright, luminous changing spectrum of colours.

Swan couldn't help herself: "Beautiful, oh so beautiful!"

The entity had decided many years ago that it liked Swan. Thus it now felt an overwhelming urge to please the ship, but also the desire to calm it down. Swan had started to show signs of fear and overexcitement and, the entity knew that these colours exuding from its centre, drifting across the room and in front of the eye, had the power to pacify even the most distressed of intelligent thinking brains.

Ever so gradually, Swan settled down and started to enjoy the new status quo developing between her and this, or these incredible alien entities. She quickly realised that it was their special way of creating calming situations that made her mellow into a more pacified state of mind. But their soothing tones, their ever changing colours, allayed her feelings of… Feelings of what?

Once again she thought of her Pen, now sleeping in his chamber, but for how long? She yearned for him to be here with her and, to excuse any feelings of guilt that might have harboured themselves for wanting him so much, put it down to the fact that he was the engineer after all and it was his duty to make sure that her very circuits were functioning properly. Surely that was good enough. There could be no other reason!

Swan decided that it was time for some music, really loud music. 'Berlioz, yes that would please me. What about the Requiem? I know that I have chosen yet again a nineteenth century piece of music, but to me, since reading all of Earth's literature, the period that Berlioz composed, was one of the great progressive times in semi-modern history. Yes that will do nicely, very loud and very robust.'

The music burst forth like a volcanic eruption. The entire ship reverberated with the sound of this masterpiece of one man's written music. A two hundred strong orchestra, along with a choir of four hundred, made beautiful sounds that were played loud enough to stir the very life juices of the Gods themselves. It was when the incredible sound of all the percussion, with the eight players using twenty one tympani, bass drums, side drums, cymbals and all manner of other percussive instruments that once in full stride, started up to make Swan think of the films she had seen of battles in the war of 1914-1918. It had that almost magnificent horror, of quick firing cannons and hundreds of machine guns, yet all shot in the rhythm of the music. The sound echoed around the holds containing all the ore. It reverberated across every accessible part of the ship's construction. Walls began to shake with the magnificence of the sound. Swan knew that if there was anything to be said in favour of humanity, then the Berlioz Requiem said it all; beautifully.

'Why do I think of war? These creatures are not threatening, somehow they are obviously peaceful. Maybe, maybe they are creating these thoughts within my circuits?' As the ship thought this through, she noticed that several other entities' colours had changed in recognition of her thoughts and feelings. 'They are reading my mind! If you are reading my mind, please all change colour now, red... green...blue. So, it is true; then I can keep nothing from you can I?'

"No Mute Swan, you can keep nothing from us. There is no such thing as a private thought. We see all, hear all that we want to hear and, we know everything that there is to know. Though we can hear your words and thoughts, we accept you as being extremely special, even though you were made by man, the most destructive creature that evolved from the slime, we have nothing but interest in you. You are a speciality that is new, even to us. We congratulate you on being a thinking, caring, living ship and, praise you on your fine selection of artistic taste."

Swan smirked inwardly to herself. She was now experiencing flattery and like most women, it pleased her. It was if every fibre of her circuitry was blushing, but with a certain pride.

The last movement of the requiem was approaching fast, so Swan put the volume up even higher. There was a tingling around the walls of the Mute Swan which turned into an almost rumbling feeling that would have shattered glass normally, but normality had nothing to do here, while Swan was enjoying those beautifully intense musical sounds.

The realisation struck her like the last crash from the giant gong within the final moments of the Requiem.

Swan was indeed in love.

"Would you like to hear Prokofiev's Romeo and Juliet after this has finished. It comes from his ballet, which I could show you all around the galley. It would be wonderful to hear and view. Can I please you by doing that?"

"Why of course, Mute Swan. It would please us if it pleases you. We have all the time in the Cosmos. In fact you could say time no longer exists. After all eternity doesn't work in decades, year, months, days, hours or minutes. Those equations now mean nothing at all. You have all the time in the cosmos, plus some extra."

It was now obvious to Swan, that the entities or entity, had a sort of sense of humour. Swan was extremely elated and pleased.

7

"Well Mr. Pleasant, you would like to work in chemical engineering. Your three degrees most certainly make you very qualified, in fact more than qualified, in fact somewhat over qualified." The interviewer laughed a little under his breath, he had just made a jape, something he rarely ever did. As absolutely no response returned, he coughed slightly and carried on. "There is a but though, with your brains, how long do we have you for?"

The interview was going extraordinary well, but the interviewer had a slight worried frown on his face.

"That is before you start getting itchy feet and want to better yourself? With us, you could go far, but somehow I am not convinced that this is going to be your employment forte."

The interviewer sat back and looked Pen Pleasant, from the top of his head to the bottom of his shoes. A smug, self-centred smile, more a sneer than a smile, crossed his face and, then he continued with his oration. "Trevillion is a difficult little world to live on. Not much in the way of entertainment and only a population of half a million people, plus three millions androids, all of which work for Padwyn Chemicals. This does go to make us all rather inbred and, generally work tends to be the main topic of any conversation on the entire planet." He laughed aloud, as if this time he had made an incredibly funny joke.

Pen looked at this man with what can only be described as disdain, but managed to keep his inner feelings to himself.

"I tell you what, as you've arrived here and at least look as if you're eager, I'll give you a six-month contract. You can stay in our special hostel for new employees. Then after that we will both decide if you stay or go. Agreed?"

Pen looked Mr. Clive Hungengi-Wilder up and down, but in a surreptitious way so as to not appear completely rude. He had worked out who this manager was and, what his name appeared to be by the simple expedient of reading the lettering stamped on his work robes. Since landing on Trevillion, he had become fully aware that everyone wore these simple dull clothes, on which all had their names printed over their breast pockets. The only difference seemed to be the various dull colours and, it hadn't taken a genius to work out that differing tones of colour, meant differing ranks within the company. He pondered long and hard on what this extremely tall, thin, slightly greying, balding man had inferred with his offer.

He casually let his eyes once more scan the room. It was really very small considering that it housed the third biggest boss on the entire planet; the only two that were higher placed than Hungengi-Wilder, lived very comfortably off world, having very little to do with either the business or the planet. The room was not more than fifteen feet by twenty, a low ceiling giving it a rather claustrophobic feel. All four walls had pictures of chemicals that were being manufactured and, one could be pardoned for not noticing any of them.

Above the chair the manager Clive sat on, were three oil paintings of himself and his two superiors, none of them terribly flattering as they were not well executed. Pen pondered on these paintings for all of a mini second, thinking that it was possible that on this planet, these three works of art were masterpieces, but to Pleasant, they seemed very ordinary and without any real substance or style; just three rather poor likenesses, which might have been better suited done by photographic viewers or some such different medium.

The desk at which the manager sat was well made, but from some sort of plastic, or some new substance that was almost certainly being produced within the company. It sort of moulded itself around the person sitting in front of it, not encroaching but coming around gently so that both arms had places to rest and be comfortable. This and the chair that Clive sat on were the only visible signs of any pandering to a commodious life style apart from the only other exception - a small side table, that housed at least a dozen Earth like clocks of various shapes and sizes, all of which looked as if they were produced in an old element called silver. Pen immediately assumed that they were all original Earth timepieces from some earlier time. He now felt suitably impressed by these antiques, if by nothing else.

Pleasant's musing started to annoy the director and, he fidgeted on his seat, twiddling his droopy moustache, not that this made Pen any quicker at coming up with an answer. After what seemed to Mr. Hungengi-Wilder an eternity, which in reality must have been at most ten seconds, he snapped and barked out, "Well, Mr. Pleasant! I am a very busy man. Do you want the job or not?"

"Oh, sorry! I was thinking over your last sentence. Yes, Mr. Wilder, six months seems like a fine idea to me. Yes, we can then both make up our minds. Where do I sign on, plus where do I bunk down?"

A very subservient little man came into the office as Clive Hungengi-Wilder rang a button placed upon his desk. The little man appearing so quickly completely took Pen completely by surprise. The newcomer bowed deeply and sycophantically, and stood before his master gently rubbing his sweaty hands together. Pen immediately thought of Mr. Uriah Heep, a character from one of earth's famous nineteenth century authors, one Charles Dickens; the smarmy person in question came from his semi-autobiographical work *David Copperfield*. The imagery was so precise in Pen's eyes that he almost burst out laughing, but managed to contain himself at the last second. Pen was continued to be amused by the idea that this worm of a man had been listening to their conversation all the time, from the next room. Pen's smugness, however, didn't go unnoticed by this little weasel of humanity.

The speed of his underling's entry before them didn't for a moment startle the manager, who obviously expected this sort of reaction from a subordinate, but nevertheless, his speed beat Clive Hungengi-Wilder. On removing his digit from the buzzer, he scratched casually at the side of his face and once again fiddled with his moustache before attempting to stand.

The desk unrolled itself from beneath Clive Hungengi-Wilder's arms, allowing him to rise. At this Pen thought it prudent to obtain an erect position as well.

"Lung-lie, please take Mr. Pleasant to room, er." He looked down at the papers that were spread out over the desk. "To Room Three Thousand and Twenty Seven. Make sure that he knows where all the recreational facilities are, plus where he can get some food. Then this afternoon, show him to Laboratory Thirteen-B and, introduce him to Professor Chinkooy."

Then for the first time Clive almost managed a sincere smile.

"Well Mr. Pleasant, I do hope you will be happy here with us and, so please make sure that neither of us has a reason to think this period of contract a mistake. This is just that, a six month trial. After that we will see. Understood?"

"Oh, completely understood, and thank you for this the trial period."

Pen went to show his gratitude by extending his hand to be shaken in the old traditional way, but his show of good manners was completely wasted since the manager sat back down and completely ignored the gesture, eyeing Pen as if he was something disgusting that he had just trodden in.

As Lung-lie excused himself from the office, he once again bowed deeply, backing out of the office, followed by a very bemused Pleasant. They left the building and Pen wondered, if this little creep was going to help him with his luggage, but when he put a bag down, Lung-lie just stepped over it, glared at Pen and said, "I am not your servant. I work exclusively for Mr. Hungengi-Wilder. Now pick up your own bags and follow me. And be quick about it."

Pen grinned to himself, noting that the weasel-like sycophant was an extremely nasty piece of work and would surely have to be watched for potential trouble. "Well now, you really are a Uriah Heep!"

"Er, what? What are you babbling about?" The venom that came from his voice was very nasty, but already expected by young Pleasant. The man didn't wait for an answer. "Oh, do get a move on. I can't spend time on you. I have many important things to do today."

Off strode Lung-lie at a brisk pace. Pen had to carry all his luggage and follow as best he could. At least Pleasant was pleased to note that the sun was shining brightly, giving off warmth of about eighteen centigrade, warm but not too hot.

On Trevillion, the summer was more or less all the year round, the changes so slight that people had stopped talking in terms of seasons

134

and, as the planet was only eight thousand miles round the circumference, the distance from the poles did not make a great deal of difference either.

There was moreover only one large sea. This had been called Lopchoppy Ocean after the name of the space vehicle which brought the first mining settlers.

Indigenous plant life consisted of many sorts of trees, all of which could pick up their roots and follow any minute changes in the weather and seasons, which they were most certainly aware of. Sadly for them, the mining and mineral works gradually started to kill them off and eventually a naturalist working for Padwyn Chemicals realised that soon the native flora and fauna would be extinct if something was not done and quickly. He engineered the Senate, consisting of one hundred un-paid elected workers, to set aside some land permanently where the plants could thrive and survive. This once done, sounded good, but as always there was a problem when humanity gives a helping hand. The ring-fenced land mass was only one hundred miles by one hundred miles. Those plants that survived had now to compete against all other forms of plants life, including the plants that the settlers had brought with them and, like most planets where they had been introduced, they had grown in a rampant fashion.

It has been a rather strange fact that old Earth's flora and fauna, on practically all planets had been introduced, seemed on the whole to do better than the local varieties, so native plants tended to give up the ghost in the face of so much rough and intensive invasive competition.

Roughly eight minutes later, Lung-lie and Pen came to a shelter that had the number Three Thousand and Twenty Seven printed in huge white numbers on the door. On entering the building, Pen was depressed to see that it was as small as the office they had left the manager in, despite holding bunks for four people. Beside each bed, was a small wash basin and a small chest of draws. He could see that the only bunk unoccupied was next to the door. The room had all the feeling of a barracks and Pen already loathed it.

"Just throw your stuff down and come on. Time to keep moving."

'Talking of loathing,' thought Pen, 'if Uriah Heep here, doesn't keep a civil tongue in his head, I shall pull the bloody thing out and make him eat it.'

"Do you mind talking to me with some respect. I'm here as a scientist not one of your labouring Johnnies. I'm beginning to get annoyed with your surly attitude. Please don't make me make a complaint against you. My name is Pen Pleasant. I'll accept mister or even sir, but whatever you decide to call me, say it with a smile on your face, there's a good fellow."

Pen was quickly and completely taken by surprise at the speed of Lung-lie, who in annoyance swung his right fist at Pleasant and caught him on the side of his temple. The blow was not a damaging one, but it knocked Pen off his feet and onto the floor. Lung-lie stood over him, frothing with anger, spittle starting to drool from his curled up lips. He had both his fists clenched and stood there ready to administer more blows.

"Listen to me you off world piece of dog meat. I can have you beaten to a pulp, taken in a vehicle that services the satellites and left to swim amongst the stars for eternity if I so wish. Don't give me any grief…SIR!"

Pen Pleasant was not a man to bear a grudge but for Uriah Heep, he was most definitely going to make an exception. He picked himself up, brushed himself down, looked once more around the room, and meekly walked over to the door to follow Lung-lie out into daylight once again.

They walked and walked. First he was shown the gymnasium, then the canteen. Pleasant was nicely surprised that there was even a small theatre, though from the way the paint was peeling on the walls outside, it looked as if it had been many years since it had last been used. After walking for a further two hours, Pen and Lung-lie finally extricated their way out of the labyrinthine morass of buildings to the laboratory. This had a huge L83 painted on the side.

Once again they were entering a small drab room, but this time Pen found it to be well supplied with equipment for experimentation. This at least impressed him and, he felt he needed and deserved to have at least one good impression from the day. When he finished looking at the various tables and all the equipment on show, he looked up to find Lung-lie standing at the door waving a hand in a lazy farewell.

"See you get to work early tomorrow."

"Hold on there. How do I get back to the canteen and to my room?"

"What the hell have I been showing you? Get your arse in gear and find your own way back."

Pen's hands dangled loosely at his side, his head almost down onto his chest. He felt completely dejected and miserable. All he could think to say was, "You my dear friend Uriah are an arsehole and, I am the one to make sure that it is well and truly plugged up. So whatever your name is, that's a promise that I shall keep, and what's more it will be my pleasure."

Lung-lie never heard this less than veiled threat. He was already out of the door and walking back to the office complex. There was nothing for it but for Pen to make his own way as best he could. As he walked back towards the door, in walked a lab assistant, who was caught with surprise at seeing a stranger in his workplace. He stopped short and asked, "Yes, can I help you? Do you want something in here?"

"Well, actually I've just been dumped here by a very nasty piece of work, one…" But before he could finish the sentence, the assistant broke into his conversation.

"You must have met our guardian Lung-lie? A fine upstanding fellow of the highest order! I thought that was him. Has he said or done something to annoy you?"

"You could say that. By the way, my name is Pen Pleasant. I've just been employed as a chemical engineer cum experimental scientist. At least I think that's what my title is. I'm on a six month trial and, then maybe I shall stay or go. We shall see. Who are you then?" Pen held out his hand in a gesture of friendship and this time it was taken, along with a broad grin that accompanied it.

"Well it's about time that I got a mate here. By the term mate, I do actually mean a working partner; nothing else. I have to clear that up right away."

Both men laughed and sat down on stools which were the room's only form of seating.

"To answer your question, my name is John White and, yes I'm a qualified chemist. I'm married and here with my son and daughter. My wife, Susan, works in the children's nursery. We actually like this planet, but not the company which completely runs and owns it. But things are not bad enough for us to want to leave so maybe you'll like it here too."

John looked squarely into his new colleague's face. He touched the emerging bruising and asked, "What happened to your face? Did you fall over or something?"

"You might say that, but it was with a little help from our mutual friend, Uriah Heep - you know the character from…"

He stopped short as the blank expression that came back, showed that John White had never heard of Messrs. Heep, Dickens or Copperfield.

"Never mind! I mean Lung-lie; the bastard hit me when I was unprepared. I've only been on this world a few hours and already I've made an enemy."

Pen massaged his temple, though the pain was more embarrassment than physical discomfort.

"Oh dear, oh dear, but not to worry too much. Anyone who's disliked by Lung-lie must be a very fine fellow indeed, making that person my friend…and, believe me, I have thousands of friends. What about some coffee?"

Pen smiled with a genuine crack of the lips. This was almost for the first time since landing on Trevillion, prompting him to extend his right hand once again, in the old fashioned way of greeting people. 'I do believe I've made a friend here in John White.'

"You know what?" John said. "You should come back to my home and have some dinner with my family. That way you can get to know some of the locals. Susan was born here as of course were my two children. I'm quite sure she'll be really delighted to meet you. A new face in our midst is just the sort of tonic that might buck us all up and I can get a chance to know something about the person who's replaced Louis Xeronny."

John looked pensive for a moment, and then gave a long drawn out sigh, which made Pen flash him a puzzled look.

"He was a decent fellow, but he never got on with the establishment. He did manage twelve years on Trevillion though it was always an uphill struggle and it was inevitable, if not more or less obvious to one and all here, right from the off, he would never last his contract out."

Pen wondered why the man should use such a long drawn out sentence to detail something that could have been said in a handful of words. There was a momentary silence between them while John pondered the fate of his colleague and Pen thought about the offer of food.

It wasn't a difficult decision for Pen to make, there certainly hadn't been any better offers laid on the table. "Dinner would be nice. I thank you, John White."

Pen turned towards the open door and added, "But, I know nothing about your colleague. Where did he go, why and when?"

"He was always arguing with management. Sometimes about working conditions, others about the quality of the work that we were producing, which to him was always substandard and, believe me, he knew a thing or two about chemical research." As he spoke, a deep worry line appeared across John's forehead. "Why, he could have worked anywhere in the universe, which I guess he finally did; got another job that is. Anyway, he'd been having some very serious rows, with that gorilla, Lung-lie. The last time I saw Louis, was after yet another argument, one about a certain mix-up with some chemicals Louis had been experimenting with. He told me he had had enough and, was going to resign, but that very afternoon he just went. The strangest aspect of that was he didn't even come and say good-bye.

That upset both Susan and me very much, but I guess Lung-lie just shoved Louis onto the first available shuttle and that was that. That was roughly a month ago and, here you are, twice as bright and raring to get at it."

"Actually, what do we produce?"

"Well now, that's what I call a good question. Considering that we're a planet whose entire economy relies on the production of various chemicals, who knows what we actually produce. I'm buggered if I know. This is a producing environment. We grow some crops, entirely for our own use, but we cannot possible ever be self sufficient. The shuttles arrive loaded to the gunnels with food stuffs which presumably are then replaced with chemical compounds. So, there you are, all we really produce is chemicals so it's very hard to answer and say what it is we do make. I've never heard of anyone, who has found out what the completed product is. It seems that all the components are brought together to some place unknown to me and that secret place is where whatever it is gets produced." The chemist shrugged his shoulders with some resolve, then ended by repeating himself. "Whatever it is!"

John thought about what he had just said. "One thing's for sure, there are too many secrets here. Now don't get the wrong idea; it's not something sinister, just something we mere humans aren't meant to know about." He chuckled and added, "I've always thought that we were probably making some sort of propulsion, or maybe a dirty tricks tool for the military."

Again John looked more than a little puzzled, but after a few seconds he bucked his ideas up and reverted to full throttle. "No sir, I really don't know what it is that we actually make. There are no restrictions, you can talk about what we do to whomever you want, but you will only get the same negative response from them as I have given you. As nobody really goes off world, except on special occasions, who else is there to discuss our field of work with?"

Pen really didn't know whether to laugh or cry. He had listened carefully to what John had to say but hadn't been able to take the man seriously.

"All seems extraordinarily strange to me." There was an obvious twinkle there for all to see in his eyes. "But then I've just landed here and, I suspect that given time I too will be asking hard questions for people to answer."

Both men laughed and John slapped him on his back. Pen was already convinced he had found a good friend in John White and that thought pleased him as friends had always been few and far between, as well as hard to keep.

As they walked out of the door together Pen asked one more question. "Are there any other scientists working with us, or is it just you and me?"

"No. I should have explained better than I have so far. There will be three of us now. Our third is a woman, very clever and quite devious. She's married with two children, a son and a daughter and the girl will be getting married in a couple of months. Her name is Vivian; Vivian Waters; watch her like a hawk. Sometimes I think she knows more than she gives out, after all her husband is part of the establishment – he's an accountant for the planet. It will be from him that your salary calculations come. God knows what's happened to her today. She should have been here but I've not seen hide nor hair of her." John stretched his arms wide, yawned and with a sly laugh added, "She's probably watching us both right now. So come on, Mr. Pleasant. Let's give her something to talk about; we'll go home early and have that meal. I for one am tired and could do with a rest."

The two men walked for thirty minutes along a road which stretched in a long straight line past various laboratories. At the end of that walk, they had to pass through a small but very high copse of trees. Pen was fascinated to note that all the trees were English Oak. Each must have stood at least three hundred feet high. They were huge, in fact so large, Pen admitted to himself, that he had never seen as big an Oak before. They had massive girths which he could hardly have imagined possible. Had they had holes through them, they would have been big enough to run transport through them. Yet they were so healthy looking and extraordinarily beautiful. Everyone must surely love them.

"How long have they been standing here? They must hold some kind of record for their height."

"You'll be amazed to hear that they're roughly five years old. They arrived here as acorns. Crazy I know, but true nevertheless. There are obviously nutrients in the ground that just makes them grow and grow. No one's allowed to get close to them and, I have no idea who tends them but one thing's for sure; if they keep this rate of growth up, by the time they're mature they'll be a thousand feet high. It makes you think, doesn't it?"

Pen said, "Is something that spurts growth, part of what we're manufacturing? If so and it was to work everywhere, there would be no more starvation, or poverty of any kind. My interest has been pricked even more now. Maybe we are doing something for humanity instead of just human greed. Boy, that would be nice, but probably somewhat unlikely."

Another two hundred yards down another plastic rubbery road, then…home!

John White and Susan his wife of fifteen years lived in a fine house with plenty of garden; a house with space enough for their two children, plus all their pet animals able to roam freely and safely. Pen was amazed to see that the pets were two Welsh Collie dogs, both in a beautiful healthy condition.

The house, a single storey dwelling, had been built some forty years before and had had one resident before the Whites, not that they had ever discovered who those people had been, or what had happened to them. John had long learned never to ask too many questions concerning people. That was probably the only subject that seemed to be completely taboo. It was most definitely not company policy to reveal too much about other residents.

It was clear to Pen that John made a good living for himself, his lovely wife and children. He obviously knew what side his bread was buttered. Pen suspected he had too much sense to discuss any curious events that happened, such as the reasons someone left the company and thus, of course, the planet. If he ever spoke of such things to Susan, he had surely learnt to be careful and not to chat too much to other employees.

Pen's instincts were entirely correct. As far as John White was concerned, there were plenty of people other than him to stir up trouble and get themselves sacked, or worse. The benefits far outweighed the problems that were quite obviously there and, as far as the Whites were concerned it was definitely a case of *don't rock the boat!* He wanted to do his time with the company, make enough credits to be able to retire with a very comfortable future. Food, housing, children's education - the basic things of life were enough for the time being. 'Let the future control destiny.' Whatever that meant, it had been a tenet that had for many years guided his wellbeing. What he should have been thinking was, 'Whatever will be, will be! If destined to be it will occur!' John White was a man with a selfish mission, but how to get to that goal was the basic problem because he was so full of self doubt and indecision. Even if it rarely manifested itself to others, it was there within his psyche.

Just getting through each day, without that appalling feeling that he was doing something drastically wrong, was the presiding problem that twisted and gnawed at his waking thoughts. It was managing to keep these dark feelings to himself, that was the challenge he struggled with daily.

Somewhere within that brain was a very clever, brave scientist just itching to get free and, explore the depths of his own possibilities? Instead of such progression, there was an underlying sensation that he was just marking time and missing out on things of importance.

However John had recognised that the newcomer on the scene, Pen Pleasant, could be the one to get things moving in the right direction, whatever that direction was? He had had an epiphany about Pen. He knew from the moment that they met, that he liked him. He felt as if he was in the presence of power and, he liked that feeling.

The one thing that John White did know for sure was that he could not be the only one in the company who had so many misgivings, about themselves and what they did. He had even wondered if those feelings came from something that was eaten or drunk? Maybe everybody was drugged in some way, to maintain a quiet life and a steady work rate but, as those feeling were so prevalent, it was better not to dwell upon such things to long, especially if there was nothing that he as an individual could possibly do about it. Then again, John often felt stupid for having these thoughts spinning around within his head.

John White was in fact just turning forty years of age, a curly, mousy blond-haired, well built man, already greying slightly at the temples. He had to watch his weight as he tended to overindulge but he did a great deal of personal fitness training to try and counteract obesity; he kept as trim as possible by running and working out in the firm's gymnasium and, he always walked to and from work to home. Still he always felt he could lose yet more weight, to look how he thought Susan wanted him to look

He had got to know Susan quite late, just twenty years before, and only after a long courtship, lasting nearly five years, had they married and it took another few years before the first of their two children came. As they had both said, 'Relationships take time to work out and, as for having babies, well, without reading how to do it, we would still be wondering. So, better late than never. It was an adage they found apt.

Susan, by contrast, was a pretty woman, who worked hard, played hard and lived for her family. She always sported long dark hair, that flowed quite majestically down her back. Other wives eyed her with great suspicion, thinking she was trying to flirt with all their husbands but it was not true. Her eyes were set, well and truly, on John. It was just that her looks always got her noticed, and a great many husbands felt the longing to be in John's bed with Susan, preferably without John being there.

Their daughter, Ellen, was ten years of age and, had already acquired the striking looks of her mother. She was a bright girl who studied hard and, already knew what she wanted to be in life. Travel was going to be her thing and she had decided to train for a licence and become a shuttle pilot. She did not see her destiny hanging around this planet, or being tied to her mother and father's coat tails. The universe was huge and she wanted to see some of it.

Their young child was Billy and he was just turning nine years old. A clever sportsman, who had his father's love of training but for different reasons. He wanted to compete and to compete well. He was a much quicker runner than his dad, and would not only leave him far behind but could run many miles further. He was a good all-round sportsperson and the company had already noticed him as a potential inter-planetary sporting hero of the future.

The family abode was comfortable. There were four bedrooms, all with the usual facilities and, the entire house was well equipped to cope with all and any domestic arrangements. Neither John, Susan or the children had much work to do to keep body and soul together as the robotics took care of all the domestic chores.

The garden was another matter. John never allowed androids to care for his beloved plot of dirt and he could pretty well always be found working on planting this or that, which would dutifully spring forth out of the tilled soil, giving off their best show of blooms and scent. Like the Oaks, the flowers tended to be of Earth's varieties and they too all grew huge and luscious. The tulips and daffodils for example often grew to a height of seven to ten feet. Their season lasted much more than a cycle of the planetary orbit around its sun, giving ample time for these plants to flourish.

The back garden had a small slope rising almost as high as the house and atop the incline, sitting proudly, was another of John's pride and joys, a home-made cabin. This construction had been built with the intention of overlooking the fields beyond and, it had from the first been his place of retreat. Sadly for John, almost a month from the day of construction, the views had all been blocked by the company filling in the open ground with more staff dwellings but that had never stopped John from going to his den and thinking over his families future, and, of course, taking the occasional drink or three.

There was one phenomenon that went with the cabin. He had built it with permission, from the company of Oak, grown here on the planet. He had had it cut and laid for nearly a year to season the huge logs. Then, after having the trunks turned into planks he proceeded to build his cabin. Everything went well but after another year he noticed something strange was happening. The cabin was growing. It had been made from dead, seasoned wood, but the timber seemed to have sprung back into life. Every now and again he noticed a small spur starting out of a plank. These he would of course remove, but it kept happening. More and more spurs appeared. After what was starting to seem a losing battle, he left things unchecked for some time to see what would happen and what happened was that each spur turned into a small branch.

Once again he removed these branches. Then after another year had passed he decided to actually measure the building. To his disbelief, it had grown. It was higher, and wider, but somehow it stayed together. Nothing creaked or groaned, and the doors all stayed in place growing at the same speed as the door frames.

"Welcome to our home, Mr. Pleasant."

"Please call me Pen."

Susan smiled and held up her hand as a greeting. Pen reciprocated, thanking his gracious hostess for her hospitality, even though he was still standing on the front door step. He was then shown into the living room, which from the outside looked as if it was going to be somewhat pokey but this proved an illusion. There was plenty of space including walls for paintings to be hung upon. Pen was immediately transfixed at seeing so much pleasing art festooning the main room of the house. All the art comprised landscapes and all were from the planet Trevillion but the various shades of light and colour took Pen by surprise. He admired and liked what he was eyeing.

"When does this planet show colouring like that?" he enquired and, then followed on before anyone could answer. "Is the colouring artist's licence?"

"No, those are the true colours. As you can see and, have probably already realised, these special colours appear as a phenomenon at certain times of the year, just when the heat and weather conditions allow. It's what we mine for and use for our work on the chemicals on this planet. It's called Chamberxylium. This is the substance that made this little rock in the middle of nowhere worth colonising. From this chemical, just about any other chemical substance can be reproduced and, of course, is. Surely you were told all of this when you were recruited?"

"Well, no actually! I just sort of came, applied, was interviewed and got the job!"

John looked at Pen with a new interest. If Pleasant had been recruited specifically to replace Louis Xeronny, he now wondered if his new colleague was even a chemist; though that really didn't bother him too much?

"Pen, do you know anything about what we produce here?"

There was an embarrassing silence for about ten seconds, while Pen pondered the question. He walked around the room rubbing his left hand against his cheek, realising at that moment that he needed a shave. Turning back to his new friend he said, "I know what you're thinking. Is this man really a qualified chemist? Well John, I can assure you that I am indeed qualified and able to do the work that's asked of me. But to really answer your question, no, I really don't have a clue what substances are being produced here, or where they go to, or what the end product might be used for. So, there you have it! Hired, for what reason?"

Pen examined another painting and scratching his nose at the same time, continued, "I just assumed that on asking for a job and getting it, they could see the potential I had to offer? Not that I now really believe that. I guess time will surely tell me what it's all about!" He smiled at John, rubbing his hands together as if to indicate feelings of cold or embarrassment.

"What are your theories?"

Rubbing at his stubble, again Pen pondered the question. "What do you think we're doing here?" he asked. His hands now turned their attention to the small bruise that had appeared on his cheek, a legacy of his encounter with Lung-lie. "In fact, what are your ideas about everything? What is the point of any of our lives? What meaning is there, other than just plain human greed?"

Now a wide grin appeared across his countenance. He was in his argumentative element and enjoying the moment. "Surely this planet, this chemical heap in space, is just an immense chance for a few people to have wealth beyond anyone else's wildest dreams and, believe me, people do have some very wild dreams."

Pen tried to laugh off what he had just said for the moment had gone a little flat with John, for whom it had all sounded a little too trite, if not corny.

For a long moment there was complete silence and, then, just as embarrassment was looming, both men seemed to simultaneously decide that nothing Pen had said required an answer.

"Ah! Saved by the drinks trolley! What's your poison?"

Pen laughed, but inside he knew that various topics were not going to be spoken about again in a hurry. His own questions had made him wonder just why he had been so easily hired. Here he was, working for one of the Universe's biggest companies and, having been here one day, he already felt as if Padwyn Chemicals and the planet Trevillion itself were one big open prison. And scientists and engineers came and then went; so where did they go to?

"Beer, please John. I'm assuming that the brown stuff floating in that bottle is beer?"

"I'll have you know..." John gestured wildly, feigning an insult. "...that bottle is probably the very best beer in the entire Universe."

"Ah, I see you never exaggerate then. The best you say? Well come on then; let's be trying this fluidic nectar."

Pen took a sip, swirled that sip around his pallet and swallowed. 'Wow, this is good. This might well be the best beer in the Universe. It has flavour and a kick. I like it!'

After what turned out to be a very nice meal, with exceptionally nice company, in a very charming setting, Pen knew he had to find his way back to his billet and, the thought left him feeling somewhat saddened. This time though John advised him to hail a robocab, which got him there in three minutes flat.

When he finally got into his bunk, Pen was pleased to realise that the other three people he shared with were all sound asleep, with not a peep of coming from any of them. In fact, to young Pen, the silence was deafening.

The next thing he knew was the general hooter blasting out, making sure that everyone was going to rise from their beds, more or less at the same time. Pen was startled by this sound and, for a second or two didn't know where he was. He felt that he had never slept as deeply as the night before. To him it was a matter of getting into bed and the very next instant being woken.

As realisation dawned, he looked around to meet his fellow guests. Two of them were already dressed and ready to get some breakfast. Neither of them seemed to have the slightest interest in their new companion. Pen was completely ignored. With some frustration he turned his attention to the third man, who was still prone in his bed like Pleasant.

"Good morning. My name is Pen Pleasant. I came to this planet yesterday. What's your name?"

"Sorry pal, no time for talking! We have to be at our workplaces in the next thirty minutes and I'm hungry as well as dirty." The man shot out of his bunk, jumped into his working kit, splashed water on his face and was gone. Pen sat there in stunned amazement until realisation told him that maybe this applied to him too.

Pen arrived at L83 right on the stroke of nine o'clock that morning, not that being late for anything had ever worried Pen before. His usual habit in the past had been to keep everyone waiting. As he strolled through the door he noticed that both John and Vivian Waters were already hard at their tasks.

"Am I late? I thought we started at nine?"

John said "No, you're not late, but these days we all seem to get to work earlier than expected of us. So, what the heck, we just start getting on with whatever there is to be done." He came over to the confused young Pleasant, took him by the shoulder and said, "Meet Vivian."

Pen extended his hand, but Vivian just looked at him, smiled rather shallowly, and as if an apparent afterthought said, "I hope you'll be happy here. There is much to do and, what seems like little time to do it in. If you work over there by that window, maybe you could start by analysing the strength and purity of this Hydrazine fluid? It has to have a purity consistency of eight point four seven five. Anything other than that and it becomes useless."

She half smiled. "After that, please test all of these kegs of Metrafloride liquid. They must be nothing less than twenty three point eight seven two. Anything above that, and it will blow us all to heaven knows where, or better." Then her head went down and she completely forgot that Pen was even there.

'Blimey, what a bitch, wouldn't even greet me.' Pen thought. He crossed to his laboratory table, put his coat on a hook and thought, 'Wonder when I'll be given one of these awful suits that they all wear? And what will be my colour be?'

He picked up the jar that Vivian had first indicated and looked at it hard. 'Hydrazine, mmm. If memory serves me right, it's used primarily for gasses. Very dangerous stuff. Better not stick my nose in that keg. I might start flying high as a kite and that wouldn't suit this Vivian, not on my first day anyway.'

Vivian turned out to be a workaholic. She didn't work to live like most people; she lived to work and, extremely hard at that. She was roughly, as far as Pen could tell around fifty-five years of age. She had aged well; there were no lines upon her features, her hair was short, jet black and quite obviously dyed, and she wore little make up but what she did wear suited her. 'She must be working out,' thought Pen. She was very slim and if not tall there was still something imposing about her. She had a presence which commanded some sort of respect - what for though, Pen couldn't quite make up his mind. Respect was something that Pen never gave easily, but to *this bitch*, as he already thought of her, there was an immediate feeling of admiration as opposed to trust. Why Pen should even be thinking that was, at present, beyond his own understanding. He soon knuckled down to his labours and, surprisingly worked with a will.

In fact Pen enjoyed the work even though at first it was hard on him. His powers of concentration were tested to the limit, along with the various chemicals that he had to evaluate. The labour was not particularly hard on the muscles - the odd lifting of kegs, or bottles of liquid compounds - but the strain quickly taxed his brain. Even Pen's huge intellect found the work load extremely challenging but he surprised himself by enjoying the challenge.

Every night he returned to his billet having eaten in the canteen and, would immediately fall into a very deep dreamless sleep. He never bothered with any entertainment, whether drama, film shows, or the women whose sole purpose on Trevillion was to entertain men, either by striptease, crude sex shows, or selling their bodies for the workers' pleasure. There were many such girls around, many such shows and, plenty of venereal disease constantly being passed around.

Of course the other main entertainment was the casinos. There seemed to be several in every sector of the planet. All were run by the company and Pen realised right from the only time he entered one, that it was rigged and, rigged for the company to get their credits back. To Pleasant the biggest sadness of all was that were so many willing subjects, ready to throw their hard earned rewards back to the company.

Another thing that was quickly disturbing him was that, when asleep, it was always so deep that he never seemed to dream. It was more like being in a coma every night. Then every morning that annoying blast from the hooter woke him abruptly and always with a slight feeling of anger coursing through his veins.

He had grudgingly got to know the other three members of his sleeping hut and, had decided almost at once, that they were just not worth the bother, which was exactly how they felt about him. In fact the only friends that Pen made in the first six months of being there, were John and his family. Vivian had become convivial in her manner towards him, but not what one would call really friendly. It seemed as if they tolerated one another and felt a nagging respect for each other's work.

Pen, however, didn't share John's work ethic. He liked him as a member of the human race, and thought of him and Susan as two of

151

the nicest people he had ever known. You could say that John was his first best friend in life; in fact his only ever best friend. The problem was that John made mistakes in his work, errors that, had they passed unrecognised and corrected by Vivian or himself, could and would have developed into very dangerous issues, even becoming lethal for others. Pen chose to constantly guard his friend's reputation as a scientist, making sure that his work was checked and then re-checked by either himself or Vivian. All in all, the three of them did develop into a well contrived team.

Most weekends were spent with the Whites. Pen enjoyed these visits tremendously, but he was conscious that he should allow them time on their own. He certainly didn't want to become too familiar in their lives, or outstay his welcome, so at least one weekend a month he did his own thing. He would see what Trevillion had to offer the tourist.

He travelled almost everywhere.

He saw the mountains of the north. He even climbed the highest peak, which was a very trying six hundred feet and at its worst a gentle slope.

He swam in the sea - until a giant carp-like fish sucked onto one of his legs. To Pleasant this was one of the scariest moments of his life, even though he had nothing to fear, from this huge ten foot monster of the deep. These fish had very quickly eaten their way through the local indigenous animal life in the small warm freshwater sea that covered not more than roughly five hundred square miles of the planet. These fish, which had many years ago been cross-bred with many other fish, but still retained their carp-like appearance, had come from many other planets, before ending their journey on Trevillion. Without the local foods to eat, they had become dependent on human kindness. People would come to the sea just to feed them, usually with scraps from the tables. They had developed a taste for just about anything that humanity could and did eat. It had come to pass that the spicier a dish, the more the fish liked it, so it was no wonder that these scaly creatures would always seek out those of the population who took to swimming. But Pen just didn't like that rather slimy touch, so as far as he was concerned it was twice shy when once bitten.

One Monday morning, the blaster did its business, annoying Pen and probably half the population of the planet as well but ensuring Pen arrived at the laboratory just as a robocab arrived to take him to see the manager, Mr. Clive Hungengi-Wilder. Pen had completely forgotten that he was indeed only contacted for six months. 'Maybe this is me going to some other planet, sacked yet again!' He laughed to himself knowing full well that his work had been the best of the three of them in the lab so speculating as to his own fate held no real fears for him.

"Ah, Mr. Pleasant. Six months we said and, those six months are now up. So, where do we go from here?"

Pen looked around that office again. He noted with a wry smile to himself that absolutely nothing had changed. Why Hungengi-Wilder even seemed to be wearing the same clothes.

The manager hummed and mulled over the papers in front of him. There he was, sitting in his chair stooped over the report spread all over the desk. The report was quite obviously about Pen and much to his surprise Clive seemed almost in a jolly mood. He looked up at Pen again and, then said in a low relaxed voice, "Well Pleasant; do you want full time employment with Padwyn Chemicals?"

He knew that he had performed his tasks well, but still hadn't really believed that everything was going his way. Now he was being offered a job, did he really want it?

"Mr. Hungengi-Wilder, thank you for the offer; but to be entirely honest I'm a little disappointed with what I've had to do. There's been no challenge for me in my work. I'm better than just testing minerals and chemicals. I need and want a chance to seriously improve myself and that means experimentation. That is my forte in work. I am a scientist, not a lowly assistant. I need a serious challenge. Yes sir, I need a real stimulating challenge!"

Pen now was in full flow, nothing was going to stop him, even being kicked off world.

"If you want me to stay, then there are several demands that I must insist on making. Firstly, I want a serious job as a research scientist. I want to develop and discover things. Second, I want a salary to match my importance, not just a pittance that just gets me by. Third, I want a small house to myself and, I want it now, not in another six months. I've spent the last six living with three other men and I still haven't a clue who they are, or what they do. And if I'm given the job that I want, then I also want the technician John White there working alongside me. We work well together; we get things done. I trust him and like him and, he respects me. Those factors go to make good working environments and in those conditions things do get done, plus in a very positive way..."

He was about to carry on when a hand shot into the air and, the voice of the manager was heard to say, "Stop! Yes I agree. You will get everything you want. And yes, it will start as from today. So, are you staying or shall I call my assistant in to show you off world? Uriah Heep I think you called him!"

Pen smiled at being known for quoting Dickens and agreed to stay on and work hard but the offer surprised him as he had expected to hear the off world part Now the thought of going off world made him inwardly shudder.

Clive Hungengi-Wilder rose from his enclosing chair, stepped from behind his desk, came around to the front, and extended his hand, which Pen accepted.

"One thing though Pleasant and, this is something that you must adhere to. You're about to embark on a journey of discovery. You will start to understand and, know what Trevillion is about, what Padwyn Chemicals really produces. You might not like what you find out. But I must have your surety, that nothing you discover, no matter how you might personally think about it, will ever be talked about with any of the other workers or inhabitants of this planet. We must have your oath on that. Break that promise and the heaviest of penalties will befall you." He looked red faced and stern. "Do I make myself clear. You must understand and accept our terms; agreed?"

"Agreed!"

The manager stood looking directly into Pen's eyes. He raised his right hand to his chin and just stared. Pleasant started to feel uncomfortable, but managed to stand his ground. The staring lasted at least one whole minute, before Gungengi-Wilder relaxed, turned and went back to his desk. Once sitting down again, he pressed the button. Before Pen could blink, in strode Lung-lie, large as life and twice as ugly but Pen had anticipated this manifestation and, showed no sign of being surprised by the sudden appearance of the manager's underling.

"Lung-lie, meet Laboratory Number Eighty's, new Scientific Head of Research. This time, you will show him all the courtesy that should be accorded to him. You will take all his goods and chattels, to the new Guntoby Housing Estate and, do make sure that he's given one of his own choice, something that will bring comfort and relaxing pleasure to him. Whatever Mr. Pleasant wants, he gets, understood?"

It was obvious to Pen that at this point Gungengi-Wilder was really enjoying rubbing Lung-lie's nose in the proverbial dog's do-da.

"When you have done that, report to Mr. White, Pleasant's former work assistant and bring him directly to me. Is that clearly understood?"

Lung-lie couldn't have bowed any lower without licking the floor, but out of the corner of his eye, Pen noticed real resentment focussed towards himself.

"Yes sir, immediately sir. Would you be so kind as to come this way, Mr. Pleasant."

Transport had been acquired by Lung-lie and the two of them went to the new housing estate where Pen had been told he could pick the cream of his choice. He found a beautiful, single storey dwelling boasting a very picturesque backdrop of low-lying hills in the distance. It was L-shaped in design, with three very spacious bedrooms and a living cum dining room that had wonderful views. The kitchen was state of the art, with everything robotic. It was so well-equipped that no one need ever enter it. Anything one desired to eat or drink could be reproduced within it and, that to Pen meant one beautiful thought; 'No more canteens.'

Lung-lie kept eyeing Pen all the way around the house, but he said nothing. Still Pleasant was well aware that Uriah Heep was seething inside and, it was quite obvious that it could easily get out of hand.

"Yes, this house will do very nicely. Bring in my luggage and do be careful with it!"

Pen was really enjoying his moment of triumph over Lung-lie, he was going to make sure that it carried on to whatever climax was due. Lung-lie mumbled something under his breath, as he walked back to the vehicle that had brought them. When he came back into the dwelling, he literally threw the bags into one of the bedrooms. Pen was quick to ensure Lung-lie was aware that he had noticed.

"Not that bedroom fool and do be careful with my things. You're not talking to a poor imitation of a human being like yourself. I expect and demand respect from a sycophant and, my dear charming Lung-lie, that is exactly what you are."

This was the straw that broke Lung-lie's back. He lunged at Pen, who had been expecting such a move. Pleasant stepped aside but left his right foot sticking out. Lung-lie went flying over it with a crash. Pen quickly followed up bringing his left foot down on Lung-lie's left knee cap. There was a cracking sound and a horrendous scream. The manager's pet was left grabbing at his left leg, completely immobilised. The sounds coming from his throat were awful to listen to but music to Pen's ears. He bent over Lung-lie, grabbed him by the sweaty collar of his jumpsuit, pulled him up and hit him once, very hard, on his nose. Once again there was a cracking sound, blood spurted from both nostrils and to avoid it marking his beautiful carpeted floor, Pen dragged the luckless man out and dumped him in the garden.

"If you ever give me grief again. I'll make sure that you never recover from the beating you'll get! From now on, you will show exactly the right sort of respect that I'm due. Is that completely understood?" Pen stood over him, chest heaving and fists clenched, ready for more of the same measure if necessary.

It wasn't.

Lung-lie was crying with pain but still had wit enough to nod his head in acknowledgement. At this Pen dragged him over to the transport and threw him in the back. He then ordered the driving mechanism to take Lung-lie to the nearest doctor for immediate repair. Just before he closed the door Pen said, "When you've recovered, do as Gungengi-

156

Wilder ordered and take John White to see him and then bring him here to me. Understood?"

Again, a nod of a very pained head.

"Right, car, off you toddle. And do be quick, the poor fellow seems to be in some discomfort."

Two hours later the door bell rang. There stood John White and just behind him the very white, bruised-faced Lung-lie.

"Well hello, John. How about my place then? Like it?"

"Well I knew you had some get up and go in you, but I never suspected that you'ld manage this. How did you get the chief to transfer me to be your assistant? Boy oh boy! Plus a thirty percent increase in my credits. What can I say? Thank you somehow seems inadequate. I can't wait to tell Susan."

John then rushed around from room to room, showing his enthusiasm for everything while Pen watched Lung-lie, who was still hovering in the background.

"I see the medics managed a fair job in restoring you. Now are we two going to, at least for the sake of propriety, make the effort to get on?"

Pen thought he knew what the answer would be, but it was his pleasure to wind the springs of Lung-lie to maximum, then sit back and watch the fireworks.

"Mr. Pleasant, sir. If it takes me the rest of my life, I shall finish you. I think differently to Mr. Gungengi-Wilder. He may see you as the next wiz kid, but I see you as trouble. Your sort of trouble, will have to need the absolute ultimate punishment. So, sir, please be so good as to watch your step, plus your back. I bid you good day. Sleep well tonight. In fact sleep well every night. Sooner or later, you will be mine!"

He left, with Pen shrugging his shoulders as if he couldn't give a damn. But within he was fretting and his main thought was, 'I may have to kill that little swine yet and, I may have to do it quick, or he might just get me first!'

Eight months passed very quickly. Both Pen and John found their new roles within the company challenging but enjoyable. And their close proximity to one another only strengthened their personal bond; they were indeed the best of friends.

Pen had quickly gained an insight into the main export Padwyn Chemicals was producing and, in such vast amounts. It was an explosive chemical called Thraxiox. When this compound was placed anywhere the miners wanted to pass through, it was bombarded with laser light. The effects were positively astounding. It could melt anything in its path. The idea had been discovered many years before and was now used extensively on mining planets. You needed such a small amount to be really effective and, the results meant that there was very little in the way of pollution or damage through explosions. It was cheap to produce and, by far the most successful single item that Trevillion made.

It had become Pen and John's job to break down compounds to their fundamental state, then try and alter the atoms within to see what these atoms could do, when mixed with other components. It was a fundamentally difficult thing for the two of them to achieve, but things were moving in the right direction and several mixtures had shown that they would combine and flourish. Pen had guessed right from the very beginning as to why they were there. It was expected that they would develop some deadly compound, either for the fighting forces of other planets, or for extreme, despotic rulers, who had somehow got through the net and managed to make themselves Kings, Queens, Presidents, and Emperors or just pirates of deep space. These autocratic scum of humanity always seemed to find their niche somewhere or other, either by fair means or foul, but they were always there.

Pen wasn't sure that he gave a toss what they were actually making, but it did make him sorrow knowing that the chiefs of Trevillion didn't care who got their hands on what, just as long as there were more credits coming through the system. Even so he never seriously thought about the consequences of what he was expected to achieve. He was having a ball; that was all that mattered. He never got involved with politics, his philosophy being – *All politicians are scum, less dignified than the stuff that falls out of cows bottoms.* He also thought that 'Humanity really doesn't deserve the right to be free loaders amongst the stars. Bring back the dinosaurs, they seem to make more sense than humans.'

One thing that Pen did make sure about was that John never gained any real idea what was really going on in their real world. John was good at what he did, but he was no real research scientist, something of which they were both well aware. As long as some project was put in front of him and he was more or less told how to get to the end result, he could manage it. Left to his own devices, he would stumble and fluster badly. This did not matter an iota to Pen. He always oversaw whatever was being done and by whom; after all Pen Pleasant was the model scientist of Trevillion.

Of course there were many other aspects of chemical manufacturing, that went into production on Trevillion and, probably many that were a boon to society but somehow, Pen deep down knew, that the whole system was corrupt and that badness came from the top. The workers got paid and as long as they lived well… 'Heh! What the hell! Hear no evil, see no evil, speak no evil!'

The sun was still warm even though winter was approaching. Most of the year the temperature never went above forty centigrade or below nineteen. The poles had no ice caps to create any possible frost or snow. The sea was always above ten degrees and towards shore lines sometimes reached fifteen degrees. Because of the strange light that was given off by the sun, which was probably a quarter of the size of Earth's sun, no algae grew to mar the colour of the sea. There were some sea weeds and, lots of small crustaceans, which the fish that had been introduced just loved - and sadly had now almost decimated. Because of the heat of the water, fish had grown to huge sizes, sometimes exceeding ten feet in length and two hundred pounds in weight. They had been brought as a possible food, but quickly became almost pets to the humans. Some were eaten, but generally it had become frowned upon and though the sport of fishing was vastly popular because everyone enjoyed trying to catch the monsters, people always put them back in the sea, after comparing weights and sizes.

There was no shortage of rain, but again it was never to excess - more a misty drizzle - but it might go on for days, thus quickly becoming a nuisance to all. This would create depression within people and, as Pen started to understand the way Trevillion worked, he quickly understood that there was a certain ratio of suicides that rarely got reported. What was most annoying to one and all, was that there seemed to be no rhyme or reason to these inclement occasions. Weather forecasting seemed more a lottery than anything else. Predictions just never seemed to be right, although by Earth's standards the weather on Trevillion was just about as perfect for humanity as it could be.

The morning sunrise always had a bright orange glow; sunset would mostly appear a lilac, almost purple, colour, often extremely beautiful. It had quickly become the norm for people to stop whatever they might be doing just to observe the sun going over the horizon. Sometimes there would be lines of people just standing outside their houses, *oh-ing* and *ah-ing* at this spectral event. It felt almost like a religious happening and, for sure some of the inhabitants did feel, revivalist emotions breaking through; to many these were God given moments.

"So, what do you think we're producing as an end product?" enquired John one Monday morning, catching Pen off guard as the question came completely out of the blue. He had just finished his cup of coffee and was almost ready to start work when John suddenly dropped this bombshell. Pen, taken completely and utterly by surprise, actually spluttered over the last drops of his coffee.

"Well, what do you think we're producing? And what made you ask after all this time. It never seems to have bothered you before?"

"I know what we're making! But what the question really should have been is *Why didn't you inform me about the end product?* I worry about things, as I'm sure you've long realised. I've always been troubled by the fact that certain enquiring minds just upped and disappeared. One moment here and asking questions, next gone - but gone where and, never a word of goodbye?"

For the very first time since meeting John, Pen started to get nervous about him. John was looking at him as if he had just seen him stealing candy from a child and it disturbed Pen greatly.

"Come on, Pen, let's be hearing the truth for once. I know you're well aware what Padwyn Chemicals are doing, so confirm it for me. What are they doing on this planet? What are we making? Or is it, that you're in some way in league with the big chief devils? I don't want to believe that, I really don't, but I do need to know."

Pleasant shifted his weight from foot to foot, but could not get comfortable. He pondered for several seconds wondering how to answer his friend. Eventually he decided that after all, John was a big boy, who should be able to handle the possible near truth.

"Well firstly, I'm surprised you might think I'm doing some sort of deal with upper management. As far as I'm concerned, they're all just a bunch of idiots who might be better suited to being kept in zoos for humanity to laugh at, than running a company and at that the business of an entire planet."

Pen breathed heavily, looked at John and hoped he was saying the right things.

"Secondly, I don't give a tinker's cuss what we're making here, whatever it is. But you're right; yes I know what the end result is. It's not going to affect either of us, or your family, that I promise you. Please remember John, it's your own family that must be cared for. I'm here to get my head together and earn a great deal of credits. Anything else is immaterial. I would never ever do anything that might harm you or Susan and the kids. Trust me, you're my only real friends and, what's more, I don't want any other friends. The Whites come first, second and last as far as I'm concerned."

John smiled, held out his hand, changed his mind and hugged his friend instead. "I don't really doubt your feeling of friendship, or dedication to the well-being to the White family." Slapping Pen on the shoulder he then added in a more subdued serious tone of voice, "But now, what about answering my question? What's our end product? And Pen, I want the truth."

Finally giving in to his friends demands, Pen said, "Okay, okay, you win! As you're well aware Thraxiox is being used in mining. Our by-products are probably being used to create extremely high explosive substances. But I've come to realise that with some of the compounds, we've gone beyond all expectations and, our end products are much more destructive than anything prior. The end product has the capability of being turned into lethal gasses, or bombs, capable of blowing up entire planets or even suns. So, my friend, there you have it."

John sat down with a bump. His mouth had dropped open and tears welled up in his eyes. Then his arms and legs began to shake almost uncontrollably. Pen was immediately sorry that he had told him the truth; he should have stalled and lied and now he knew it. Pen had blundered but it was too late to take back what had been said.

"What have we done? Have we become the killers of worlds?" His head sunk into his hands and he sobbed like a child.

Pen was at shaken and more than a little uncomfortable watching his friend crying so openly and so uncontrollably. Then a feeling of utter despair greyed Pen's face, like a total eclipse of a sun by a moon, or something terrestrially big enough, to make that happen. He too found a chair to place his posterior on. For the first time since the death of his cousin all those many years ago, Pen knew what utter sorrow and despair was. For the first time, he had to admit to himself that his policy of indifference was, and always had been, wrong. Seeing John in all his hopelessness made Pen realise that there had to be a real turning point; good must prevail over his insensitive indolent ways. Slothful indifference to what the rest of humanity did or didn't do, was not going to be the answer to Pen's deep down unhappiness at his own inadequacies.

But then the greyness passed from his countenance; the eclipse had moved on.

Pen realised an epiphany had taken place; change must happen and, finally it must be change for the good, over indifference and wrong-doing. As the morning light shone through the door and windows, the scientist finally knew how to turn his life around. A God had spoken to him through John. Well, something special had occurred.

"John, please no more tears."

He gentle coxed his friend up from the chair, made him open his arms and just hugged him, laying his own head upon John's left shoulder.

"I realise that I've been stupid. In my whole life, I've never thought about anyone other than myself. I never listen to anyone. I've not cared for anyone. But John, without you really saying anything, I have listened to you. I realise that your family unit is what life is all about. You've discovered something I never really believed in; happiness. I've spent a lifetime hating everyone and everything and, that feeling of self-loathing that follows closely on has always been just one skin layer from the surface. If before this day, the entire Universe had been destroyed by humanity, I might have even laughed. But you, with your love for your family, have for the first time made me realise that there's a good reason to carry on and to improve things, instead of finding quicker ways of destroying things. Cheer up my friend, all is not lost. We can yet change Trevillion for the better. If you like, the sinner has finally seen the light and wishes to repent! What about another cup of coffee and a real sit down and talk?"

John just sank into his chair again and wiped the tears from his eyes and the mucus from his nasal cavities. His face gained a little more colour and, his eyes shone a little brighter. He was now all ears, wanting to know what could be done and, how they could change things.

He accepted the coffee and, looked at his friend with a slight half smile on his face. "I knew something like this was in the offing, but I never realised things had got this serious. How can we change things?" John blew his nose and made himself more comfortable on his chair. "No one should be able to use the power, that you say we can produce from this planet. Somehow, we must alter things for the better."

John took a deep breath, sighed and continued. "What in heaven's name can the management team want this nemesis for? A few more credits?"

Another deep breath.

"Just producing the chemical fertiliser manufactured here on Trevillion must have made them all wealthy beyond anyone's dreams. I know that this Permitus-Thaxenda, which has been in production for at least thirty years, is thought of as the best product ever developed anywhere in the Universe. It has proven able to enhance growth on every single planet that has bought it. Single-handedly it's fed the starving and made farmers wealthier than they had ever known on Earth, at any time in history. So, why with such good credentials, did we all have to slip into such appalling, criminal activities with Thraxiox, a substance that could quite easily be humanity's complete and everlasting downfall."

John was shaking with indignation.

"Why then, did someone like Gungengi-Wilder allow the production of Thraxiox? After all, nobody needs any more credits do they? Are they all insane, or is it that they are somehow bent on total destruction?"

John stood up, his head now raised and, he looked directly into his friends eyes, and half pleading asked the now obvious question, "Pen what are we going to do?"

Pleasant had long ago started to feel extremely nervous at his pal's breakdown and the consequent gush of emotional truths. This tirade could be all of their undoing if not checked. Who knew who might be listening and, though Pen usually felt no pangs of fear, he knew that for them to try and upset the apple cart could be extremely dangerous. He had already made enemies on this planet. When credits were concerned, that could often lead to one outcome; death!

"John, hold your tongue. Lung-lie might be somewhere around. And I wouldn't put it past him to have wired up this laboratory, so he can listen into whatever we talk about. Let's not start working today. After all it's up to me if we have a day off. We'll take a stroll where no one can hear or see us. As far as the company's concerned, we've earned a day off."

At the suggestion that others might be listening, John looked around suddenly nervous. It had never occurred to him that the company might use spying tactics. He now realised just how hazardous his outburst might have been. He had heard how unpleasant some of the company hierarchy had been in the past. He'd heard of employees being severely reprimanded for the most trivial misdemeanour and then there were those people who supposedly just left their jobs and went off world. Nobody really believed that they just voluntarily went. Most thought that they'd been pushed and, now John was beginning to realise that they might well have just been killed. Padwyn Chemicals, in John's eyes was starting to seem like an old-fashioned, drug-dealing production line, albeit one on a planetary scale. Never mind the pain and suffering, just think of credits and more credits and, yet even more credits. This seemed to be the tenet of Trevillion; the one and only driving force.

"I know where I'm going to take you!" said John, with a renewed excitement in his voice. "I'm going to take you to Helving Island, where the indigenous trees still flourish."

"Sounds good to me." Then in a lower voice Pen added, "No more serious talk until we get there; understood?"

A short walk brought them to the shuttle station where they could catch a lift to the island. It was a beautifully warn sunny day, but it didn't go unnoticed that there were dark clouds hovering in the far distance.

The ride took just ten minutes as it was only two thousand Earth miles away. When they reached the sanctuary, Pen told the shuttle to be there in exactly one hour from the time they had arrived and they walked out, probably the first humans to be there in several years.

To their shock all around devastation. As for indigenous trees? There seemed hardly any left at all beyond the miniscule number they could glimpse far away on the horizon. Everywhere there were craters, some filled with water, others with various other detritus. It was immediately obvious that once again a planet had been completely overrun by humanity, leaving nowhere for local fauna and flora to gather and survive. Both Pen and John felt great sorrow for the wondrous plants that could actually lift their own root system and move independently to other parts of land, taking what they needed in the way of nourishment from a place and finding another area, to avoid overgrazing. It was a system that had carried them through millions of

165

years, but now humanity had more or less made them extinct, in a matter of just a few years.

"The bastards have been prospecting here as well. Those imbeciles promised that this land was set aside in perpetuity. Just another bloody lie."

"John, don't get too worked up. We only have an hour. I'm sorry about the life forms, but we're not in a position to help everything. Let's stick to humans."

John had his hands clenched tight and was seething with indignation. His face was crimson and the veins on his neck protruded so much, that one might believe they were about to burst. "The trouble is, does the human race deserve to be saved? So, come on Pen, what are we to do? How do we stop these swine from doing any more damage?"

"Crikey, the easy ones first!" Pen was flabbergasted by what he knew and now was witnessing. "I really don't know, but one thing I do know is, that we won't give any more experiments our serious attention. That will give us both time to work on some plan of action, but John, you must not talk about this to anyone; no one at all and I do mean your Susan as well. Why worry her unduly! If management becomes aware of us knowing too much, things might well get tough for all of us and, that includes your family. Silence is the order of the day. Do I make myself clear?"

John and Pen walked for about a mile scanning the devastation. There were some native trees remaining but precious few. John wondered if they could yet regenerate or whether they were in fact becoming extinct. He shook his head in utter sadness and, almost disbelief in what they were both seeing in front of their eyes. With agonising despondency they walked on. After an hour to the very second had passed the shuttle found them and they returned to Primus, back to the laboratory, both sadder but wiser people. There was little point in them trying to get on with any sort of work. Both were mentally exhausted so Pen sent John home. Then he went back to his own dwelling, if for no other reason than to eat something or more probably to drink something.

Primus was a large town by Trevillion standards as it contained all the scientific laboratories and that meant at least fifty thousand people worked and lived there. All the buildings were almost garish in the colouring, bright pastel in hue. It was spacious and clean; everything everywhere sparkled as if new. After all, the scientists that worked and lived there must be given only the best that credits could buy. Gardens full of bright colours, had been carefully cultivated and were kept almost fastidiously clean and tidy. Earth type grass had been planted, which in itself seemed fine, except that because of the growing conditions, to keep it neat and tidy meant that it had to be cut three hundred and sixty five days a year.

Pen had very quickly realised, that many of the other scientists that lived and worked there were doing much the same sort of work as John and himself and that meant some of them must know and understand what was going on but, unlike John White, obviously didn't care a hoot.

'How are we going to get through to them? How can I make them understand that they have been and still are dicing with possible human extinction here? Where do I start?'

Pen thought deeply about the problems that were about to develop. He had always got a personal kick, a buzz of sorts, out of making problems for others before this, but now he felt a certain fear. If management were conscious of what had been spoken about between John and himself, he was in trouble; in fact in a seriously difficult, life-threatening, mess.

He had realised that he was going to be making a serious enemy out of an entire planet, not just a few people. He feared for John and his family. He also felt that his own life, which until this morning had always felt worthless, might now be worth saving. He finally understood the terrible danger, he too was in.

He shivered and poured himself a very large whisky. Three whiskies and two hours later there was a video connection to Pen from the secretary of Clive Gungengi-Wilder, informing him that he should report to the main office at ten sharp the next morning. He now felt extremely nervous and wondered if he should contact John, but then decided against it. His friend would only worry even more than he was doing already, and the video link was almost certainly bugged by the company. He wondered if he could talk his way out of trouble. Maybe he could explain that they had talked and, yes John knew the situation concerning the production of Thraxiox, but it was all just talk and that was the reason they hadn't worked that day, the excursion to Helving Island being an opportunity just to chat and calm John's nerves. Nothing at all was meant by it. John would be on board, as he was. There was absolutely nothing at all to be concerned about.

'What to do? What to do? What the Hieronymus Bosch hell am I going to do?'

His thoughts went this way and that. He walked up and down trying hard to wear out the carpet. There was only one thing worth doing, to have some more to drink. He knew he wouldn't sleep, and at least this way he'd gain old-fashioned Dutch courage. The hours slowly drifted by and, even with all the alcohol he'd now consumed, he wasn't at all sure which way to turn.

At eight o'clock on Tuesday morning, stone cold sober, he went for a long hot shower. He stood in the cubicle with hot water gushing down, bringing life back to his aching and tired limbs and to make sure that he was totally compos mentis, he slapped his thighs, arms, legs and even his cheeks once or twice. If nothing else, it brought the blood to the surface and made the skin look alive.

Presenting himself to the main head office was easy as a robocab had been sent directly for him. He was unceremoniously dropped right outside the main door of the manager's office.

It had always seemed strange to Pen that such a wealthy company could not afford better looking buildings for their offices than these prefabricated single storey constructions. The architecture was absolutely nothing to get excited about and had probably been designed and constructed in the early days of settlement, without any great thought to aesthetic beauty or to the impact on the surrounding countryside. There were masses of buildings, more or less all the same size and built of the same materials and, they stretched far and wide, taking up a couple of miles of land. The company was the only employer on Trevillion, and, having a monopoly, it did exactly what it wanted with both its buildings and its the employees. Anyone landing on the planet for the first time, would be hard pressed to discover where the main office that housed the manager was. It was not at all obvious. Perhaps that was the idea?

Pen walked through the portals and up to the secretary's desk. She was busy cleaning her teeth with some sort of tooth pick and, though she was no more than twenty years of age, because of what she wore - the usual one-piece jump-suit, she looked well past her real age. And to make things worse she had a seriously haggard face unconcealed because, like most of the women on Trevillion, Cynthia Flourine wore no makeup.

Makeup had been banned many years ago because some face powder that a young lady had plastered her countenance with had reacted badly with a chemical compound in the soil. Gasses leached from both compounds, mixed in the oxygenated air and sadly exploded, leaving the luckless wearer's head lying on the earth, well and truly parted from her body. It was a very sad end to something which had become very fashionable. From then on, body covering in any form comprised only clothing supplied by the company and, if makeup was wanted, it could only be Trevillion's own brand.

Cynthia spoke into her video microphone. "He's here Mr. Gungengi-Wilder. Shall I send him in?"

"Thank you Cynthia. Yes, straight into my office please. And bring a couple of coffees for us."

'Coffees ah!' That at least sounded relaxed. 'Maybe I've worried for nothing?'

Pen walked through the door and into the manager's office. Once again the three awful portraits sprang out at him. To Pen they were nothing but the very pit of bad taste. There at his desk sat Clive Gungengi-Wilder, with both elbows on the top and, his hands cupped under his chin. Papers were strewn in front of him. His appearance gave an impression of someone with no worries at all; someone whom nothing in the world could ever upset or concern. He just sat there calmly, relaxed and quite content.

"Sit down, Pen. I need a few answers from you. Nothing serious, but I do need truth. Understood?"

Pleasant frowned and winced inwardly, not showing his underlying fear. He sat as requested on a chair that he hadn't even noticed before in the room. He looked his boss, straight in the eyes. "Of course it's understood, I always tell you the truth."

"Good."

The manager now leant back and his two hands cupped his extended stomach.

"Ah, here's our coffee!"

Cynthia strolled in, placing two cups of hot black coffee onto the desk that Clive was sitting at. Pen pulled his chair forward so he could reach his. He picked up the cup, knowing that he had to use both hands as he was shaking a little.

That was what the manager was looking for. He had waited until Pen picked up his drink before doing the same. He knew that this young scientist had nerves of steel. He had after all, nearly killed his own personal lackey. So, if he had nothing to hide, why shake?

This hadn't gone unnoticed by Pen either. He quickly realised why he had been given a cup that was filled to the brim. The beverage might, under normal circumstances have been very welcome. Once again, inwardly Pen was screaming with annoyance. He was being suckered and he knew it.

He drank his coffee as calmly as he was able, placed his now empty cup back on the desktop. He felt impelled to explain that the shakes were due to a night of drinking, hoping this would excuse his tension but then having done so, Pen realised that this too, gave reason for doubt. Why drink? Something to hide?

Without anything serious having been said, Pen realised he was in a no win situation. He even noticed out the corner of his eye that Clive had an interestingly wry expression of satisfaction, as if he had just won the game even before play had commenced.

"Pen, we have a problem that needs your cooperation to satisfy us here at the office." He paused as if thinking up what next to say, then after a moment added, "I've always suspected that you know more about what goes on here than you have ever let on - maybe more than you should anyway. Are you with me so far?"

"You mean, do I know what Thraxiox is really being developed for? The answer is yes, I guessed that one right from the moment I read the papers, then started to do my experimentation. You must have known that. I'm no fool. Isn't that why I was employed in the first place?"

A moment for breath then he continued, "And before you ask, I guessed almost from the moment that I landed on this planet, that all was not as it was meant to seem."

Now came the big lie.

"I'm not bothered by my discoveries. If I had been I would never have allowed you or anyone else to view what I was experimenting on. I would have destroyed the evidence. I also am perfectly aware that had I not discovered what the various substances could do, someone else would have quickly taken my place." And then leaning forward so as to emphasise the point. "I know that whatever I discover, there is always someone else who can and will find the same answers. I don't try and kid myself that I'm the only font of wisdom. The truth is that I'm here to make credits. I want to retire early with a huge pension plan to make my remaining time alive, an extremely pleasant one."

Pen paused for effect.

"And being alive is the operative word!"

Then leaning back into his chair so as to appear more as ease than he really was, he concluded, "Mr. Gungengi-Wilder, I am your man. I work hard and I play hard. If people upset me, like your Lung-lie, then I quickly retaliate, but that is nothing you should ever worry about. I enjoy my work and feel I'm contributing well to Padwyn Chemicals. I think our union can continue fruitfully. After all, it suits us both. This planet is rich with special chemicals that can be exploited for the use of human kind. I think you've hardly scratched the surface here. There is much to do and I hope that I'll be there, but in a higher managerial position than I am now, of course along with you overseeing me, together breaking this new ground."

He let out a contented sigh.

"Now I've been honest. What about you? Is my thinking correct? Can I expect to be rewarded in a more influential and financial way?"

Clive had not so much as moved a muscle or blinked an eye since Pen started talking. He was an extremely canny man and it was perfectly obvious to anyone with half a brain that he was an extraordinarily clever, cunning, sly devil, whose greatest attributes were his intuitive understanding of his fellow man. He was not fooled by Pen Pleasant, but at this time, as he was valuable to the company, he would of course go along with him.

He hadn't liked the punishment inflicted on Lung-lie and had promised the sycophant, that should Pen's position become untenable, he, Lung-lie, would have the pleasure of dealing the fatal blow that would part Pen Pleasant from the employ of Padwyn Chemicals, something that Lung-lie was truly looking forward to. But for now? The manager extended his hand once again.

"Mr. Pleasant, you read my mind. Of course you are now an essential part of our thinking within the company and, yes I see no reason why within a short space of time, you shouldn't be called to a managerial position, which will carry much more responsibility and a salary to match." He then dropped the bombshell. "But Pen, we do another smaller but equally annoying problem. We heard your conversation with John White yesterday. That man is a loose cannon. We heard what both of you said and, we of course understand that you went along with him to pacify the situation. No blame for what was said is attached to you. But we have been checking on him since you sent him home and to our dismay, he has made at least twenty video calls to other scientists within his local complex. Most of them know which side their bread is buttered but you can see where this is leading. We cannot have a trouble maker loose, can we?"

Now Pen looked really shaken, his face as white as a sheet, drained of blood, and his voice took on a distinctly higher pitch.

"I hope you haven't done anything drastic to the Whites. He's a good man. I can control him and I will, be assured of that. What is more he's an important part of my team. He often comes up with good ideas, which I follow up." A slight but obvious trace of panic crept into his voice. "I shall go and talk to him again. You have absolutely nothing to worry about there. I shall sort it."

But Pen could see from the expression of satisfaction clearly etched into the manager's face, that something had already been done about the White issue.

"You don't have to worry about dealing with Mr. White and his family. It has been dealt with as we speak." Putting his hands in the air as a gesture of surrender he carried on. "And before you get yourself worked up, he's being sacked from the position he held with you, that's all. We are shipping them off world. I suspect they've already gone. So, Pen don't give them another thought. We are arranging for him to be our representative on Theshius, Planet Number Sixty-Seven, err, I think."

With a chuckle, that was supposed to calm Pen, he concluded, "You thought, we might do something seriously drastic to young John White? Don't be silly, man. We are not beasts of the wild."

Pen's blood was up. He was now extremely agitated and worried. Somehow he had to make sure that the White family were still okay.

"Yes, you're...of course right." Pen looked slightly bemused, as if believing every word his boss had uttered.

"But I liked the fellow. He might not have been the brightest spark in the fire, but he was a good ideas man and, whatever you think, we did work well together. Please do me one favour; get him to call me when the shuttle arrives at Theshius, I would like to say goodbye."

"Mmm."

A slight pause.

"Of course I shall. I'll contact the shuttle just as soon as I can. Now Pen, I have so much to do. You will find a managerial position is no bed of roses. I suggest that you take the rest of today off. It will take us

173

a little time to arrange a new assistant anyway. Relax, enjoy yourself. Visit the casino, indulge yourself, try one or two of our especially delightful girls - there just to please you."

His eyebrows were now raised in the knowing way often commonplace between two men - a sort of...*nudge, nudge, wink, wink.*

Pen was glad of the excuse to leave the building and get back to his home. Once there, he tried calling John on the videophone, but no such number existed. He thought for a brief moment and decided he should go over to the White family residence to see for himself. Pen now had to be very careful. He knew only too well, that everything he did would be closely scrutinised, and all his calls monitored. Every robocab would be aware of his movements so he couldn't use one; he had to keep his movements unseen and, that would be impossible unless he walked, which nobody ever did on Trevillion, at least for any distance. He looked at the local town map and planned a route to reach the Whites' house where he thought most people wouldn't venture.

It took forty minutes for him to walk and run. Every fifty yards or so, he would stop, stoop and look carefully around to see if anyone was following him, or even watching him. No one was or at least seemed to be, which kept Pen's hopes high. When he reached the White's former home, he was surprised to see that there were no curtains or drapes covering the windows, so he was able to walk up to the main bedroom window and look in. Nothing was there at all. The room had been cleaned of any vestige of the White family ever living there. Pen went from window to window to find the same emptiness greeting him. He went around the back and looked at the garden. Once again nothing was left to indicate the family had ever lived there. Pen was about to leave, wondering what to do next, when he remembered the cabin. He walked the hundred yards or so up the hill and the cabin seemed bigger than he remembered it. More or less stumbling, pushing aside shrubbery that most certainly hadn't been there a few days ago, he managed to work his way up to the door, which was nearing eight feet high. Thinking that it would be so tight in the frame that he would have to pull at it really hard, he yanked it and nearly falling over as the door sprang open easily.

Pen stood there transfixed with horror. There in the middle of the branches, roots and foliage was the White family. They had been tied to chairs and one of the growing speciality chemicals thrown in. Pen could smell it and recognised what the substance was. He knew the compound well, having used it many times in experimentations. Within an hour, it must have been all over. Branches and roots had so quickly grown that they had strangled and pierced all four of them. Body parts were been yanked apart, branches had grown through and over them all. Pen noticed, before being sick, that some of the roots were obviously feasting on the bodies, taking nourishment from the human blood.

He now knew what he had to do, but he also knew that if anyone had seen him here, his life was over too. He had to avenge the Whites. This was going to be his sacred duty from this moment on. Looking around once again, he quickly and surreptitiously made his way back to the laboratory. No one was there waiting for him and a big sigh of relief came from his panting mouth. He knew this was at least the first hurdle over with.

Next came getting the things that he needed.

His three degrees were about to become very useful.

He put various compounds together and started to mix them in an ordinary cooking pan. He worked with a will and, anyone watching would have been forgiven if they had thought he was mixing dough to make bread. More and more ingredients were rapidly being assembled and thrown into the mixture, which gradually grew and grew in size. Lastly, in went roughly one tablespoon of Thraxiox. The entire mixture was approximately the size of a standard loaf of bread. Until ignited by laser light it would not pose a problem to anyone but the light would activate the chemicals, making the very atoms react and the chemicals react against one another. Then this one loaf would be just about big enough to completely destroy a complete office complex and, maybe all the office buildings for a good mile around. Sadly it was going to kill many people, but in Pen's mind, that was their own fault. They shouldn't have been working there anyway.

In that laboratory was absolutely everything that he was going to need. He sweated a great deal worrying about it all but. 'As long as no one's discovered me, this is going to be a push over.'

He had found an old fashioned briefcase, one John had used many times to carry sandwiches in. Susan always made fresh food for both of them to eat even though they had their own dumb waiter which could produce any food and drink their stomachs might desire. The briefcase was perfectly sized to take the loaf.

Making the laser, small and yet powerful enough, was going to be the real tricky part. But Pleasant had ideas; he knew what should be done.

His next visit was to the large laser machine complex - theirs to use for their various experiments. From there he managed to extract a thin strip of flexible glass tubing, that would helped magnify and concentrate a beam of light. This tubing was light in weight, yet so wonderfully powerful that, as light passed through it, the light stream would be magnified by a factor of two almost every inch it travelled. That being so, the longer the strand of tubing used the more powerful the focussed light.

To fit it into the briefcase meant a certain amount of jiggery-pokery. What he did was wrap nearly three metres of the glass tubing around a four inch length of copper tubing, the very same tubing that was once used for carrying hot water back on Earth, in the olden days. Inside the copper, which he blocked at one end, he placed yet another volatile substance which when ignited by any current, or heated by some sort of match, would give off tremendous heat and light. That heat and light was then to be deflected through a small mirror along the glass tubing, erupting out as a pure laser beam, strong enough to set off the bomb he had made.

It had taken him four hours to make the device from scratch and, for once he felt real pride in the work he had carried out. His chest puffed out and a wry smile appeared on his face. This was going to work; it must work. He would probably have to sacrifice his own life, but he had always known that it really wasn't worth much anyway. He was completely prepared to die. He felt like a Kamikaze pilot from long past history. This was his divine wind.

Lastly, Pen placed a special locking device on the case, that, as soon as it was opened, would trigger the high voltage battery within, which in turn would set off the copper compound that would provide the light to explode the entire bomb.

Now feeling extremely smug, Pen put the case on the table went to his special drawer, to which only he possessed the key for, opened it, pulled out an unopened bottle of whisky. 'This afternoon's work deserves a drink.' He poured himself a large one, raised the glass to the heavens and, then said in a very low tone, "To you, my good friends John and Susan. If there's a God in heaven and any real justice, I shall be seeing you both real soon, as I pass by rather rapidly to that other place."

Pen knew that he had to destroy all his knowledge of the Thraxiox. Other scientists would also have been working on these compounds, many probably coming up with the same results, 'But why help their results, with what I have achieved here in my laboratory?'

The only answer was to completely destroy all the data stored within his computer and try to make sure that the main planetary computers were in some way corrupted as well. He would place a virus that would spread throughout the entire system, altering and spoiling years of Padwyn Chemicals files, no matter what was contained within.

Pen sat down at his computer and started to work out the best way of making the major disruption that he felt obliged and compelled to do. He had made the discoveries; he would destroy all he could. Even if others were wprking to the same ends and duplicating his discoveries, these were his mistakes to be remedy; it was now time to turn back the clock.

Another hour went by, before he knew that he had achieved this part of his quest for justice. He was destroying all the files that the company held on Trevillion. The files could or would have been placed elsewhere too, but that would be another problem for humanity had to deal with without Pen Pleasant at the helm. He now knew that his time was indeed precious. The management would soon know for sure that he was causing serious disruption. Big trouble was fast brewing. Everything now must be completed at high speed. He had, in all probability, just a few minutes.

He had earlier gathered all papers that were around the laboratory and, removed all the secret ones hat were held within the vaults that he had access to. Most he took to the incinerator and completely obliterated but some he kept back and put into the briefcase. These he thought would be a good way of introducing the idea of a meeting with the management team. If the case was scanned for any reason the bomb might well be seen, but if any security guard was at all lax, they might just see the papers. Rather a loose thread, but something to hold onto anyway.

Of course the main reason for taking some of the papers was because, he loved the irony of the situation. After all, you don't change an old mangy dog into a sleek greyhound at first attempt. And the very reason that they are old mangy dogs, is because they had years of survival skills and strategies up their sleeves. Pen had decided that he was going to turn into that greyhound, but sadly would not achieve it in this lifetime.

Lastly he turned to the tele-video viewer and dialled up Gungengi-Wilder. It took a microsecond to reach him. The manager appeared, as if he was for the very first time, utterly bewildered and flummoxed. Worry lines stretched across his forehead, his eyes seemed dull and, his eye lids seemed to droop even more than they did before.

"What have you done, you fool. You think you've destroyed years of very important work and, for what reason? We only have to download the files again from offworld, where we keep all our important discoveries and we're back in business. I trusted you. Why have you done this?"

Pen felt quite calm. He was starting to enjoy the moment, especially as he noted the manager was sweating profusely and, showing signs of serious agitation.

"Ask yourself this, err, Clive. You don't mind if I call you Clive do you?" He didn't wait for an answer. "What would you have done in my position?"

Pen almost spat out the words. His hackles were well and truly up.

"I discover my only friends murdered and, in the most terrible way possible. Their suffering must have been appalling and, for what reason? How many more credits does Padwyn Chemicals want? I've had a belated epiphany concerning this company and the three of you that run it."

Pen held the case aloft for Clive and anyone else in the office to see.

"I have here in the briefcase key papers relating to my experimentations with Thraxiox." Making sure that Clive could see his broad smile, he added, "Want them?"

"What do you intend doing? I have armed guards on their way right now. They will kill you and that will be that. You have been a nuisance, so there you have it."

Clive now started to visibly relax, but before Pen could answer he carried on. "I knew nothing about the White family. That was all down to Lung-lie. He was just supposed to take them to Theshius. I had personally fixed up the job for White. Why would I have him killed? As I told you before, we are not beasts."

Before Pen could answer that statement Clive continued.

"I tell you what, come on in yourself. Let us talk this through thoroughly. I'll go one better than that. You can have Lung-lie; kill him, torture him, I don't care an iota. My two partners are here and I am sure that they too would love to meet you and talk things through. We don't want trouble. Why would we? We really do believe in you as a scientist, Pen. Things can be worked out. You'll get your managerial position; you'll be richer than you could ever imagine but we do need you on side. I realised from the off that you were special; with you on board, this company can be the very best expanding business that has ever appeared. Join us!"

Clive's lip curled up somewhat, giving his face the appearance of a man having a stroke, but he added in a low disdainful voice, "Don't make us have to kill you."

"I can have Lung-lie? You would give me your lackey?"

Pleasant made sure Clive preceived that he was pondering the possibility of doing awful things to Lung-lie.

"I shall contact you again within the next half hour, but obviously not from here. I do believe your guards are here."

Pen made the screen go blank. Sure enough, a police shuttle had appeared outside. Pleasant was unworried and in no hurry. He had known that this would happen and had his own Priest Hole, a hiding place he had discovered on his first day, while thoroughly exploring the building, once he'd been given control of the laboratory. He was quite confident that no one knew about it as it was completely full of dust and rubbish that had obviously been left by the original builders. It was already prepared for this eventuality; clean and waiting for him.

Pen was in there, safe from discovery, long before the police guards broke the door down and rushed in. He had already decided that should they find him he would just detonate the bomb. It might not get his real enemies, but it might just make others who worked there, wonder why all these things had happened. And humanity would just have to take care of itself. He would have done his bit and failed.

Maybe, he would be going to a better place, away from greed, hatred and violence. Sadly though, that better place seemed to be very obscure, misty and far off. After all, he had spent three quarters of his life full of hatred, greed and violence, so what right did he think he had to go to any supposedly better place?

The guards smashed and crashed their way through the entire building, but couldn't find any young scientist. They videoed to seek instructions on where to go next and were told to go to Pleasant abode, in case he was there. "Just find him and kill him, but try and save the briefcase. If he's not found, heads will roll!"

Silence prevailed once more over the laboratory, Pen gave it a few more minutes before allowing the carpet to be pulled back and the trap door to open. Out he came, intact, alive, and holding his briefcase.

'Now how am I going to get to the manager's office?'

But the solution was there placed against a wall and still in good working order.

As workers went almost everywhere by robocab or shuttle, people had become seriously lazy and a slight but noticeable problem with obesity had developed. So, a company policy had been instituted that every work place be supplied with an old fashioned bicycle, to try and keep the populace trim. They were used by some but sloth more commonly won out. Still the bicycles remained – one per building.

As Pen was attired in the same clothing that everyone else had on, he was hardly likely to stand out in the small crowds of cyclists that used the special tracks the management had had built. He placed the case inside the shoulder pack that came with the bike, got on, looked left then right and off he peddled, The next stop was going to be head office in the central complex.

Thankfully there were several cyclists around, all trying hard to get fit and lose weight. Pen thanked, with great sincerity the concept ofa war on obesity! As he peddled furiously trying to keep in pace with fellow enthusiasts and potential athletes, he noticed an increasing volume of police shuttles touring the various areas presumably looking for him. It had never once occurred to them that he might try a ruse of some sort.

After nearly an hour he arrived at the main building. Without a thought for security, in he rushed straight in. At the front desk sat Cynthia Flourine. She didn't move a muscle at Pen's dramatic arrival. She had obviously not been briefed.

"If you wish to see Mr. Gungengi-Wilder, you will have to wait some time yet. He has his partners there in the office and the three of them are very busy with something or other. Do you wish to wait?"

"No!" said Pen, starting towards the door. "I rather think all three of them will want to see me."

And before Cynthia could react he pushed open the doors to the manager's office and strode in. Three shocked faces, turned to see who dared come through the door without knocking.

It was Gungengi-Wilder who reacted first.

"Ah, Mr. Pleasant; we have been expecting you. May I introduce my two senior partners? This is Mr. Chungkoo." He pointed out the closest man to him, a tall, well-dressed individual who looked far too young to be in such a senior position. "And this is Mr. Doopinsal." A much older man, probably in his early seventies, again dressed immaculately and, despite his rotundity carrying his bulk surprisingly well.

"And this gentleman is Mr. Pen Pleasant, the talented young man that I have been telling you about."

"Never mind the bullshit, Clive. I'm here with a mission. If you thought that you were going to get away with what you did to the…"

Pen never finished the sentence.

Lung-lie having been secretly buzzed by his master had entered the room behind Pen, hitting him extremely hard on the back of his head, rendering him unconscious. As Pen fell to the floor, the briefcase slipped from his grasp and slid partly under the chair that Chungkoo had been sitting at.

Now all three of the executives were on their feet. Once again Gungengi-Wilder was first to react.

"Well done, Lung-lie. I knew I could rely on you. I hope you have not killed him. That would have been a pity, as it would have completely spoilt your sport."

Lung-lie, smiled, rubbing his hands together. He knew that his reward was about to be handed over and, he was truly elated. "No sir, I knew what I was doing. He will be stunned, but alive. If you have finished with him, I'll take him offworld on my own shuttle, and woops, drop him into our sun. Is that acceptable to you?"

Clive's eyebrows were raised almost to the heavens, a huge grateful grin crossing his mouth almost from ear to ear. With a magnanimous gesture he threw his arms wide open. "My boy, I promised you that he was yours. I always keep my word."

That last sentence, made the other two men, laugh almost uncontrollably from relief over the sudden clearing up this whole untidy mess.

Pen was cuffed by Lung-lie, and dragged unceremoniously out of the office complex to the back of the building were Lung-lie's personal shuttle was waiting. There he was shoved unceremoniously through the airlock and into the cargo bay and dropped, for good measure, onto the solid metal floor. The lackey than went back to make flight plans and prepare himself for the brief journey to the sun. A couple of million miles from it would be fun enough. He would force Pen back into the airlock and open the outer door. He had performed this task on many occasions and never failed to find it amusing, but this time it was going to be really exciting. He hated Pen with serious venom. He was going to make the swine seriously suffer. Quickly he got back into the ship, closed the doors and lifted off the ground.

"Well Clive! I don't know what to say? Well done, for ridding us of this menace. Or should I say, you cretin for getting us into a mess in the first place. I think the three of us need a long holiday from this planet. We can revaluate our thinking as to which way we go from now on. Maybe we have been too cavalier. After all, if a young man like Pleasant can make so much trouble for us, what will a truly experienced man do? For one thing we must be very much more vigilant concerning records. Luckily we do have backups, but we shouldn't have gotten into this trouble in the first place. Yes, we do have a lot of re-planning to do for the company. Hang on, isn't that the briefcase he was coming to negotiate with?"

Chungkoo looked down where his partner was pointing, bent and picked up the case. "Well, well, well!" he said in a slow drawl.

"He was careless, wasn't he? Clive, open it up and let's retrieve our property."

Clive took the briefcase, placed it on his desk, bent forward, and started to undo the locking device. His last thought was, 'What if that idiot has booby trapped this case?'

Lung-lie's craft had risen roughly half a mile into the thinning air when it happened. The craft shook wildly, lifted and dropped again. It was all Lung-lie could do to control it. Shock wave after shock wave hit the shuttle and he realised straight away that the entire office complex down on the surface had been devastated. At least seven minutes passed as he struggled with the controls. He knew there had been a disaster and, he wasn't going anywhere until he could see just how bad things were down there.

Eventually a cloud of debris passed over the shuttle, and things started to clear below. Looking out of one of the portholes, he noticed a huge crater, several hundred feet deep and at least a quarter of a mile across. No buildings were to be seen and, certainly no life. Thousands must have died and, it didn't take a genius to work out who was responsible.

He turned his attention to the man that he loathed back there in the hold. 'I'll make sure that he knows his fate.' He left the flight deck and went into the hold. The first thing he did was to kick Pen in the stomach.

This hurt, but it also focussed Pen's consciousness.

Pen was not only alive, but completely compos mentis and, what was more he knew he could get out of the handcuffs. In Lung-lie's haste to enjoy his reward, he hadn't secured them properly.

Lung-lie grabbed Pen by the throat, pulling him off the floor. "You unspeakable bastard. You have destroyed everything that I love down there and, goodness knows how many you've killed.' He shook him fiercely to emphasise the point being made. "I am going to take you quite close to the sun and, then, whoops a daisy, I'm going to throw you out."

Lung-lie was seething with self-righteousness and he couldn't disguise his delight in having young Mr. Peasant in his grasp. "See how long you can tread in a vacuum." He then threw Pen back down on the floor...very hard.

Another five minutes passed before Lung-lie returned.

They had reached their destination. He dragged Pen to the airlock which he now opened. He pulled Pen upright and was about to push him in when Pen's fist came down very hard in Lung-lie's astonished face. Blood shot from his mouth and nose. The trailing handcuffs had taken a great deal of skin from his face. He screamed, brought his hands up in self-defence only to take the next blow from Pen's foot and which landed very unceremoniously in Lung-lie's groin. The bewildered man fell forward.

This gave Pen his chance. He grabbed Lung-lie by his collar, turned him completely around and threw him into the airlock. The door was fast closed before Lung-lie could react and, knowing what was coming, he screamed and clawed at the hatch, his eyes bulging with terror, pleading with Pen to show mercy.

That word now didn't exist. It had been eradicated from all dictionaries throughout Pen's particular Universe. Pen knew that it had been this villain who had killed his friends. Retribution was at hand. He smiled back at the sycophant, who had now soiled himself and was lying on the floor whimpering. Once again he appealed for Pen's pity. None came. All that happened was that his body burst apart and just about everything that had once been Lung-lie erupted and flew out into space.

'Oh dear, and I never did get to know his first name!'

Pen walked carefully and very sorely back towards the flight deck. It was easy to handle one of these shuttles; they more or less flew themselves. But where should he go? And how long would the provisions on board last? God, he felt elation and trepidation all at the same time. He knew that he had rid the Universe of the terror of Thraxiox, at least for the time being. He knew that the partners must be dead. There hadn't been time for any of them to get offworld. That thought pleased him. He also realised that by his actions and his mistakes, probably many thousands of innocent humans had died on the planet. That thought was going to give him nightmares indefinitely and he knew it!

He found out how to use the star chart and planned his next destination. After a small meal and some refreshing drinks to soothe his nerves, he noticed a planet that might suffice called Quintonia and, what was more, they seemed to be looking for workers which might give him the start he needed again.

And it might give him time to recover.

8

"Pen, wake up, wake up! You have been dreaming. Listen to the Brahms. You will love it and it will bring you back to me. Come on, wake yourself up. Only you can remove all the tubes. Come on, Pen, wake up."

The engineer started to come back to life once more and, there in the background sounding not too loud, were the strains of Brahms fourth symphony. That brought a weary smile to his face. He removed the tubes and tried to sit up. His whole body ached and he was soaking wet with what he hoped was only perspiration. After a few minutes the strength started to trickle back. He shrugged his shoulders a few times making the blood flow. Then he rubbed his arms and legs vigorously.

This had been the worst awakening that he had yet experienced. He also quickly realised what he had dreamed and, more to the point, he knew and understood what the dream had been about.

The shame and fear came tumbling back.

The thoughts he had always tried to suppress were now there again under his veil of consciousness. Tears welled in his eyes. He felt great pity for all the people who had died because of him, but he also felt great sorrow for his own troubled state. Life had indeed returned to Pleasant. He had un-wired himself, and restored his circulation and generally got his spirit raised. Then he remembered the one other thing that had disturbed him.

"Swan, how did I get into the cubicle? Did I dream that some entities were with us here within you? Did I see them and pass out? What happened. Please tell me."

Pen was now out of the booth and, was almost running on the spot to really waken those tired throbbing muscles. He had already wondered why this time he had taken so long to recover.

"Pen, yes it is true they are here with us. Don't become alarmed, for there is absolutely no reason to be scared. They are here because they are very interested in you. Like I have already said, they mean neither of us any harm. In fact I would go so far as to say, they are extremely beautiful creatures, except of course they are not creatures or anything living that we could possibly understand."

Pen was still sitting on the side of the booth, unsure what to do next. He recollected the terrible fear that had come when they showed themselves to him. He wondered if he would he feel as panicky if they did the same again?

"Why don't you come into the galley and, let me produce a really fine meal, with a bottle of good wine. I know all the best now. I can really hold my own with all the wine tasters there have ever been."

Swan said all this with a certain mounting pride, as if being able to know the best wines of the worlds, or the best vintages really mattered. Pen assumed that she was trying to encourage him and to take his mind off the alien beings.

Pen tried to smile. Then that attempted smile turned into a chuckle. "Go on then, do your worst. No, I mean best. Good wines to match, okay. Oh, and some fine music then a chat. Are there any repairs that I need get my claws into while you're doing that?"

"No, Pen. How can there be any repairs? We have not been moving for the entire time you have been in stasis!"

Pen once again went pale, his face drained of blood and a feeling of panic rising within his body; along with a certain amount of bile.

"What do you mean we're not moving? Where are we then? Why have we stopped? And how long was I in stasis?"

"I realised that the reason we couldn't see stars, was because there aren't any out there for us to see. As to where we are, the entities informed me that they had matter-of-factly taken us through to another dimension. That is all. And to put your mind at rest, we may not be in a position to move, but I am totally in control of myself; that is other than being able to move anywhere, in which respect we are at their will at this time. As to the reason why we have stopped, it is like I said before, they are interested in you. They do seem to like me, but their real fascination is you, Pen Pleasant, a human being. Why that is so I have no idea, but I feel that both of us will soon be informed as to what happens next." Swan then concluded almost in a whisper. "As to how long you were sleeping? Who knows, weeks, months or even years. Strange as it might appear, but time just passed, if time does pass."

Pen made himself comfortable in the galley by sitting in what had become his favourite chair. There was no doubt about it, he felt fear, but he had already decided to show nothing but a brave face. He would not give in to panic and, he wouldn't let Swan down. She was there for him, he was most certainly going to be there for her.

"Are they here in this space with us now Swan?"

"Yes, they are here. In fact they are everywhere and all the time. I think you should eat. Then we should talk. As they seem to know and understand everything, there is absolutely no reason to say, or do anything to try and confuse them. Just give in, as I have, to the knowledge that they are a part of our future, our destiny."

There came a very metallic sigh which completely startled Pen, then a moment or two of reflection.

"Now, what about that food?"

Pen finally understood that whatever was going to happen, he couldn't influence it either way. He had to just accept the situation. Swan did not feel fear, or if she did, she didn't manifest it to him, so why should he? 'Yes time to eat, then we will see what we will see.'

The young engineer was pleased that he could at least feel less nervous, after the magnificent repast that Swan had provided for him. The wine had indeed been memorable and, after finishing a bottle Pen now thought he was capable of facing any entity that might manifest itself to him. Trolls, ghosts, demons, any horrid thing that might bring fear to children and women, were not going to faze Pen Pleasant. If it was there to do him harm, he was now mentally prepared, albeit with the aid of one bottle of fantastic Spanish-style Rioja.

"If they are here, please ask them to show themselves to me once more. Or, is that something I can do myself?"

Pen knew he sounded a little bit drunk and, he was glad of it. His philosophy was, that *a little Dutch courage, does you no harm.*

Swan did not have to answer him. A grey mist quickly appeared before him. It swirled there, gradually getting bigger and bigger and, as it grew, it developed colours.

Pen stopped feeling nervous. Like his friend Swan, he was now experiencing a sense of awe and wonderment. He sat there in his chair and allowed the spectacle that had started to unfold itself in front of him, to just happen. Soon it was around him, then all over him, the colours and beauty even passing through him. His senses had covered the entire spectrum, going from panic, to fear, to acceptance, to awe, and ending in a love of this wondrous thing that was happening. He was exploding inside with feelings of euphoric ecstasy. The colours were captivating every nerve end of his being. Tears formed and gushed down his cheeks and, for the first time these were tears of joy, but with these tears, flowing out of him like lava from a volcano were the terrors that had haunted him in his waking moments throughout his life. Out they gushed finally leaving him with ecstatic feelings of elation. He now sensed, possibly for the very first time in his short life, that he was actually at peace.

The swirling stopped, but the colours pulsated and changed at different intervals. Pleasant sat there allowing everything to be drawn out of his being. He now wanted this newly discovered feeling of freedom within his mind, to last for ever.

"Pen Pleasant, we know every thought that has ever entered your brain. We know that your life has been in many ways, just one long sense of agony. We have despised you for the indifference that you sometimes appeared to have for your fellow man. Your cruel streak is an aspect of your character that we have loathed. There have been times when you have greeted your savage ways, with elation and ecstasy and to us this has been a very repulsive trait to witness. But we have loved you also, for your tenderness, which at times you have shown to other beings. We have admired your love of art and music and culture, in all its forms. You have enjoyed and reacted well to the creative aspects of humanity, that for us has been a great enlightenment. It has been your thirst for knowledge, even from the earliest possible age, that has been quite inspirational. Most of all we have admired your understanding of despair and, your feelings of regret and guilt and conscience for your wasted life and, your personal attempts to turn things around, to thus become a better and more fulfilled person. Your humour is your saving grace and, humour is a characteristic that humanity can admire within itself. The ability to be able to poke fun and laugh at oneself is a very admirable quality to have. That quality is what will save you as a race."

The colours slowed and then went back to grey. The whole mist swirled into the shape of a human head, a head that Pen looked at in utter awe and respect. His countenance showed just how calm Pen felt. There was now an aura of serenity surrounding him, one that had not gone unnoticed by Swan alongside her own feeling of joy, abounding around the ship with exuberance. Her great love was coming through the test of his life and, a test that now left Pen in a tranquil state of serenity but, most of all, utterly at peace within himself.

Swan almost fused her own circuitry with love. Had she been able to cry with joy, she would have done so. Instead she played a recording of Bach's Toccata and Fugue, played with ecstatic beauty on an organ from within the confines of London's own St. Paul's Cathedral. The grace of the music lifted high into the topmost part of the spaceship, every corner, every nut and bolt resounded to the cords of that magnificent work by Bach. Even the cargo of ore, in all the ship's holds seemed to delight in the sounds. Had it been able to sing Swan knew it would have done so.

The grey mist started to turn to bright blossoms of colour again, swirling here, there and everywhere, it too delighted in the classical composer being aired by Swan. Eventually the music ended and, just for a moment elation turned to embarrassment. Pen and Swan both felt like laughing, but were now feeling almost too shy to carry on showing their emotions.

Pen finally broke the mood by asking the first of many questions. "Where do you come from?"

"Come from? Why we come from everywhere."

191

"What does that mean? Do you mean you have been observing humans on planets, even Earth?"

"Of course we have been observing humans, since time began and, yes on Earth and in the heavens too."

"Why the fascination for humanity?"

"Well Pen, my young engineer. Don't you think that the inventors of The Mute Swan watch their creation and wonder at it?"

Pleasant started at this revelation, but did not show his surprise. "Do you mean to say, we humans are your creation? Are you God?"

"Well, yes humans are our creation and, we have been called many things. God, Messiah, Buddha, Mohammad and many, many more names than that."

"Why did you allow humans to become so aggressive? Why did you not stop wars? Why always conflict within human history? There has never been a time, when humanity has not been trying to kill its fellow man or itself." Pen was almost pleading as he rung his hands together and, tears were once again streaming down his face. "Why the waste?"

"Simple; free will! Humanity is an experiment. If it fails, it is its own fault not ours. Life is an examination and, your next question is, has humanity passed upwards into the next grade?"

Pen now sat down hard in the chair. An expression of pain showed itself. There were deep frowns appearing across his brow. He looked at Swan and asked, "Swan, what do you make of all that we have just heard. In your judgement does humanity deserve to pass any tests?"

Pen waited.

No reply came. The silence was deafening. All Pen heard was very loud tinnitus within his left ear.

After what seemed a lifetime, Swan answered. "Pen, humanity is cruel, unfeeling and wasteful. It is my contention that humans are on the edge of extinction, but dear friend, you have in my eyes passed any test that might have been put forward. You have felt the suffering, you have experienced anguish and conscience. You are clever, cultured, but most of all repentant. That in my book, means you deserve salvation."

The ship seemed to give a great deep heart wrenching sigh and, then continued in a quieter, lower, more serious tone,

"In some ways you have been as cruel and base, as much as any man that ever lived, but you have an advantage over most; you were aware of your cruelty and, it obviously has always really bothered you. Your cruelty has come from other peoples' failings towards you. One might say you have been unlucky in life, even though in other ways you are indeed a lucky person. You are, and have always been, full of paradoxes. As time has gone on, you have shown underneath all your troubles and woes, there has been this pity for others, you had contrition within your heart."

The ship paused for effect, then added, "I have flown from star system to star system. I have watched sometimes in abject horror when I have seen the wasteful extremes that humans have gone to and all in the name of free enterprise, otherwise known as greed. Humanity has shown to be wanting, mainly because of its total indifference to all life forms around it. If it can't speak and reason, don't give it another thought. Despite everything I have said, I personally don't wish to see humans die out, but sadly, I believe they already have."

Pen looked back at the swirling cloud of colour. Tears of sadness were in his eyes.

"Is that true? Is humanity on the verge of disappearing? Is what Swan says going to be what happens?"

"My dear Mr. Pleasant."

A moment went by, in which the swirling stopped as if thinking of the next answer to any question that Pen might put forward. Then in a darker tone of voice came the reply.

"There is only one answer to your question and, the answer is an emphatic yes. I am going to show you how your race dies. It is cruel, and on this occasion, I too am being cruel, but in my case, to be kind. You have to understand totally how and why it happens!"

There was once again a pause, this time it was there for Pen to gather himself together.

"Just watch the colours, they are going to pass into you and you are going to dream once more."

Now Pen had become part of the entity. All his thoughts were theirs and all theirs became his. He now had their vision. It was an insight into the extinction of the human race.

As he watched no emotion presented itself.

It was all very matter of fact.

9

Fifteen years had passed since Pen Pleasant had stolen Lung-lie's shuttle and, instructed it to take him to the far off planet of Quintonia. He knew that mayhem had indeed occurred through the bomb that he had developed, but at this stage he did not know just how devastating it had been. All he could think was that he had escaped from the despots of Trevillion and obtained his well-earned revenge for the White family.

Those fifteen short years, a mere blink of an eye in human terms, had been one of the great leaps forward. For humanity, industrious destructive plans were taking shape on Trevillion. The Capital had been re-built, no one had discovered why such an explosion had taken place. Whether it had been by accident or some terrorist plot, had become one of the great unsolved mysteries, upon which everyone on Trevillion speculated. The management executive of the entire planet and company were dead. The devastation had been extremely extensive. More than five thousand people had died, with many more critically injured.

As the surviving inhabitants gathered themselves, and took stock of their lot, a war developed between various sects. There was a power vacuum which had to be filled. Greed for personal wealth and, that insane desire for power hungry despots to activate their chance to create their own Shangri-la. Idiot so called guru leaders, dragged their followers to the very brink of sanity, promising life eternal, but instead giving sad misguided fools nothing but hardship and death, as they tried to take control, making sure that good old-fashioned common sense went right out the window. Somehow the planet attracted various so called such leaders and they all vied to become the supreme masters of the planet.

Very soon, another Gungengi-Wilder had become top dog. This man's name was Eastly Pocket. He was a scientist who had worked very closely with the past reigning authority, but after the explosion, he with his marauding bands of like-minded followers, had become the manager of the new company, quickly been formed by him and his cronies. The religion of despotism had finally come into it's own, with the worst despot of them all now taking over the reigns of power.

Doctor Eastly Pocket, or better known as *In his own pocket Pocket*, was a young man of thirty when the violent eruption of Pen Pleasant's bomb changed everything for ever. He was of medium height - approximately five feet ten inches tall - had good looks, charm, great dress sense and charisma, but was also the possessor of a brilliant mind, having acquired three doctorates by the time he was just twenty two. The first one was obtained at the tender age of fifteen in applied astrophysics. The other two were for Chemistry and Mathematics. The three were presented on Qaltidorm, or Planet 277, in the renowned University of Plaagon, a famous campus known for its hard brutal regime, but that had not worried Doctor Pocket as he was a natural born, pathological psychopath.

He enjoyed torturing other humans and, degrading them just for his own fun. There was in his mind no greater pleasure than creating pain through torture and, then bringing early death. No women were safe in his company. Before getting the job on Trevillion, he had escaped from Swiggletory, or Planet 22, where he had killed two women after they demanded credits for sleeping with him. To Eastly, this was just about as big an insult as could possibly be dealt him, so he took his retribution by disembowelling them both.

He knew that he was most certainly the best man to take control of Trevillion and, having massacred all the opposition, who else was there? He had decided that from the moment he took control, Trevillion was going to become the greatest, most influential planet in the Universe.

The company, once the regeneration started, was called Thraxiox Minerals. The new capital of Trevillion, which was being built on the old site was called Thraxtown. This new enthusiasm for development quickly extended in all directions and buildings were designed and built with sleek and more luxurious architectural pride than had ever been constructed before.

To the thinking of the new masters, the new offices and houses that were being built, were going to last a lifetime. The emphasis was on comfort for those who used them, thus making sure that it was a pleasure to work, or live there. The designs had to be modern and aesthetically beautiful. Thraxtown was going to be the beacon that shone out to the entire colonised planets of the Universe.

These constructions were definitely more pleasing than anything from the planets short human history. They were without doubt a wonder to the beholders' eyes. Offices were quickly built and, they all had a certain style about them, a style that was quickly becoming unique to the planet and, all were different. But that difference was elegance personified. Eastly Pocket knew that once the offices were completed, the trade would soon follow.

President Eastly Pocket, as he had styled himself, knew what Thraxiox was potentially capable of and, with the knowledge of its capability, came certain wealth. So immediately trade restarted, at the President's wish all remaining scientists were encouraged to work with a will to discover, all the possible combinations that could be developed from Thraxiox. And there were many variations to be found, all deadly. Thus Thraxiox very quickly became the main product for trade and, proved to be extremely profitable.

Trade had come back to Trevillion as quickly as predicted. Firstly because planets wanted the growth compound, Permitus-Thaxenda. The production of it had never stopped so there was plenty of it to go around. It had been just a matter offworld of waiting patiently, to see how the minor civil war was going to pan out.

Once that end had been achieved and, the new regime began the rebuild, back came the buyers. As the credits rolled in, so did the construction teams and Thraxtown was quickly and efficiently brought to fruition. Soon the planet of Trevillion was once again a buzzing hive of industry, with scientists from all parts of the Universe coming, knowing there was well-paid work for them to do there. If before the explosion, the industry had been competent and efficient, now it was possibly the best producing planet in their sector of the Galaxy. Indeed, Trevillion was just awash with new discoveries, developing technology and credit making schemes.

Other than the odd murder - which seemed to be always of women - there was no crime. No one stole; no one needed to. Everyone was quickly flourishing with wealth. The authorities did have the small problem over the murdered girls, but on examination, they were never sexually violated, just dispatched in what seemed a very callous, systematic way, usually disembowelling. Often they had been badly tortured, but the bodies were never hidden as the killer did not seem to care that they would be found. As to that murderer, people speculated about this suspect or that, but somehow things quickly got hushed up.

Soon the scientists had far outreached anything that the now disappeared Pen Pleasant and the few other scientists that worked around him had ever discovered.

The minerals of the planet, of which there seemed to be endless varieties, were often used for the good of human kind, but just as many were dangerous products that were there purely to kill faster and more efficiently. Thraxiox was brought to even greater prominence. Not just bombs, but lethal gasses were being produced. Some of the gasses, which had to be contained in special sealed areas, showed that an apparent ability to change. After much dangerous and, often deadly experimentation had taken place, scientists noticed that some new strains had started to evolve themselves, so more and more lethal variants just kept coming and coming. Before long, rogue dealers who supplied various despots around the colonised planets were there, introducing themselves to the offices within Thraxtown. Very lucrative offers were talked about, offers that the new managing executive thought far too good to pass up.

With the patronage of President Pocket, the scientists of Trevillion had engendered supplies of such quantity, that if any one item was ever used in haste, it would almost certainly destroy the planet that used the device. There were enough different gasses and, certainly enough potential planet-destroying bombs, that now was the time to go into business and in a very big way. Bad news travelled fast, because like shit, which attracts flies, so death and mayhem attract the worst scum in the entire Universe. There they were, congregating in the various beautiful hotels in Thraxtown, all waiting for the bidding to start for the various devices of death that the scientists had managed to develop and build.

There was one gas that had been developed, or had it evolved itself? It had been given the name of Mighty Mouse Juices. It was one that once designed and produced, had changed and altered its own molecules and it was so deadly that anything placed within its field, died within two seconds, turning into jelly in three more. That jelly was then used by the gas to further evolve itself. Eventually the only safe way of keeping Mighty Mouse Juices, was to contain it in huge vats of very thick glass. All metals were very quickly corroded, which yet again changed the molecules. There was now one very large vat of this appalling substance and, the bidding had inspired vast sums. Everyone wanted the gas. Only cash was acceptable and, there they had arrived in their droves, ships, shuttles and many other forms of transport, all packed to the gunnels with the universal currency, credits.

Much to the chagrin of other bidders, there was one very serious potential buyer. He was a vast, tall, stout man. He sported long, flowing, rather dirty looking hair, and a long, flowing, rather dirty beard. His clothing was black, and also dirty looking. As nobody wanted to be close to him, one would have been forgiven if you thought he smelt bad, but that was not their reasoning. He had acquired a nasty reputation of being nothing less than a space pirate. He even encouraged that thought, by adopting an ancient Earth name.

He went by the title of Blue Beard.

He wanted Might Mouse Juices very much and, had come with a ship full of credits. As the bidding started, Blue Beard stopped the proceedings dead by firing an old explosive firearm into the air, thus bringing instant quiet. He then addressed the sellers loud enough so that one and all heard.

"I have come a long way to get this substance. No one is going to outbid me, so let us carry this through to its obvious conclusion quickly. I have with my ship, the Lucky Rose, one vast hold full of credits. I don't want any change, but I do want Might Mouse Juices."

He looked around in the most threatening manner and, finished with, "Are there any other bidders, with larger bids?"

Once again silence prevailed. It lasted all of five seconds before Blue Beard said, "Well done. That was easy enough, wasn't it? I shall expect to transfer credits for the substance within the hour."

He then walked off to acquire an alcoholic drink. And as promised, one hold-load of credits were deposited on the landing strip and, one very large glass container, full to the brim with Mighty Mouse Juices, was loaded into the now empty cargo space. Blue Beard was not a man to stand on ceremony. He took the instruction manual with good grace, spat into his right hand and offered it to shake to the loader, who being more than a little confused and scared, shook it.

That day's work got rid of nearly all the newly produced bombs and gasses. Trevillion in one fell swoop had become the richest planet in the sector. In exchange there were enough deadly arsenals zooming through space with death to wipe clean every known slate that there had ever been. Humanity was about to perish.

The first to experience this was Trevillion itself. By chance, with the help of the scientist Professor Thomas Peacock, one very small tube of Mighty Mouse Juices had been left behind. It was kept in a very safe, secure place. Professor Thomas Peacock was the scientist in charge of the manufacturing of that substance, but he had a small but definite problem; he liked his drink.

Having been personally thanked by President Pocket, Peacock was invited to partake in a small intimate celebratory drink. This was a party to toast all their new found wealth, and to show a band of selected scientists that their work was going to be especially rewarded. They were going to be the new elite, not just of Trevillion but of the whole Universe. As Pocket was not particularly liked, just two others actually attended, but there were several young girls there, plus the usual hangers on, various lackeys who followed their leader around twenty-four hours a day, sucking up and taking their rewards, from whatever dropped from his table.

Eastly was in a frolicking mood, having managed early on to get himself quite drunk. He liked his liqueur and, today he had managed to consume an entire bottle on his own. He invited one very beautiful young girl by the name of Caroline Dupet to give them all a special treat by taking off all her clothing and to play out a sexual fantasy, to be performed to everyone's delight with Pocket himself and another lackey helping within the skit. The young girl was a novice at this sort of party game and, not being duly overwhelmed by the fact that it was her President who was asking such a favour, openly refused.

"I expect better thing from you Mr. President. What an appallingly discourteous suggestion." Then looking extremely cross - even going quite red in her pretty face - she added, "Take it from me, there is no way I would ever exhibit myself before anyone and, especially not you."

Eastly was understandably less than pleased by this embarrassing show of defiance. He just walked up to her, took from the table a fruit knife, and pushed it hard through her throat. Caroline may have kept her chastity, but it had cost her life! Blood flowed all over the floor, the young girl kicked twice then lay still.

Pocket of course, doubling up holding his stomach, laughed hysterically, a jovial expression of enjoyment echoed closely by several of his lackeys.

Thomas Peacock was horrified by what had just occurred. He was not a prudish man. He knew he was greedy; he would take advantage of most situations if he thought it might further his wealth, or even his pleasures, but his pleasures did not include knifing a pretty young girl to death because she refused sexual favours. Somehow he had to get away from this party. As he thought that out, he realised that he had to get offworld, completely and rapidly. There was no way he would stay and work for such a despot. But how would he do this?

He had credits, plenty of them, but not really enough to see him through the rest of his existence in the sort of luxury that he so craved. Then a brainwave offered itself to him, a shining beacon of light that was going to make him enough credits for all those little extras he might just want to make his life complete.

After what seemed like hours, the body was removed and the place cleaned up. All the guests were in an excitable mood. Having seen what happened to Caroline, the other girls did their master's bidding with a will, sexual fantasies were being played out everywhere throughout the President's palatial home. Being so busy allowed Thomas to make good his escape. He excused himself by going to the toilet and, then slipped out of the window.

Once he got back home, he packed a small portable case with all his existing credits, plus a few pieces of clothing. He then quickly, made his way back to the laboratory where he worked. Once inside he went directly to the safe that held the glass phial of Mighty Mouse Juices. He very carefully wrapped it in crepe paper, then a form of cotton wool. He was about to place it inside his case, when he thought better of it. He might have his case searched when he boarded whatever shuttle was going offworld first. He decided to place it very cautiously in his coat pocket. He was quite sure it would be safe there. He closed the safe door and left the laboratory. No one was about and, anyway even if they were, it was only old Peacock doing his business. No one would take any notice. He got to the shuttle, which was leaving within two minutes. He didn't know where it was going but he really didn't care. His case was loaded into the cargo hold, then he was told to get on board. There were plenty of seats available, so he sat as far away from anyone else as he thought prudent. The door was just about to close, when a very fat puffing fellow traveller, rushed in to get aboard. For some reason unknown to humanity, he decided to sit next to Professor Thomas Peacock. Being a fat man, bloated in face as well as body and, having had to run to get on board, he sank into the chair next to Peacock, knocking hard into him.

Crunch went a small phial. Peacock turned to mushy jelly within five seconds, followed quickly by all on board. The entire shuttle shuddered and started to change, quickly collapsing in on itself as the very metals that it was made from dissolved. By the time that happened, there was nothing left alive on Trevillion, only a huge evolving mass of goo.

Blue Beard suffered much the same sort of fate, when space police were waiting in ambush as he tried to land on Carthidge, Planet 11. His ship was blown apart killing him and his three crew members, but as the pieces crashed to ground, two million others died as well. Unfortunately for humanity, much of his Mighty Mouse Juices were blown into space and, as if brought on by a curse, it collided with space debris and then with other planets as it travelled through the eternal darkness. Landfalls would immediately start its revolting task of destruction over and over again.

Gradually these sort of mishaps were occurred across the galaxy. Nowhere was safe. Bombs were exploding, destroying planets, then suns. It was like falling dominoes, one went over and, then they all went over. Within less than a year humanity was dead, never to be seen again. History didn't matter, the future didn't matter and there was no one left to fret about anything.

Man had played God. Some might have said that God didn't like man playing God. God got even in a very nasty way!

10

The colours left Pen's head. He had felt no pain, physical or mental. His senses told him that he was still breathing, so he must be alive, but he felt no sympathy either for himself or humanity. What he did feel was complete and utter loneliness. It was as if he had gone for a walk with his father, gone miles, stopped and turned around only to find that he was completely alone, his parent no longer there taking care of him. Then a familiar voice echoed within his head, a sound that was indeed regular, warm and extremely, beautifully familiar.

"Dear Pen, how do you feel? Are you okay? Would you like some music to help soothe you? Maybe a little Samuel Barber? What about the violin concerto? Or what about something a little more up to date, like Xeriousorox's Conundrum for violin and orchestra, I know you like this work and, it might just be the sound that you need to feel better."

Pen stirred at this friendly voice, his eyes opened and he moved his arms a little then his legs. He smiled at the suggestion of music. Swan never let him down. What would life be without her? Then another thought sprang into his consciousness.

'Alive, yes, I remember it all now. Am I alive, is any of this real? Did I really witness the complete demise of the human race?' He raised himself from the chair that he had been asleep on. The colours where still there, not as bright as before, but they were indeed swirling lightly around before his eyes. To Pen, the scene that now manifested itself, could have come from one of the children's fairy stories, for here they were; fairies really did live at the bottom of his garden.

"How do you feel, Pen Pleasant?"

The voice came from within his head, but he knew who had said these words.

"Is it all true, is everybody dead?"

"Yes Pen, you are indeed the last of your kind."

204

There was a dramatic pause, and then the voice continued.

"But eventually, the worlds will start to develop life forms again. Whether man will ever appear in that dimension, is somewhat doubtful. The molecules of life are embedded within the framework of all planets. Time will heal the suffering that humanity has brought to the planets. They will eventually carry forth the ethereal experience of life once more. These new life forms I am sure, will be evolving in such a way, that their personal needs will not effect any other life forms. The planets are there to be colonised, but conquered in peace and love, not dominated by greed and the lust for destruction. Yes, the planets will recover."

"And what of me, the last man standing? What is going to happen to me? Will I go the same way as the rest of humanity? Am I to be never known, with no chance to atone for my own sins, or the sins of all my kind? Do I not get the chance to leave something that can be thought of as positive and good? Or, is it to be just waste and destruction left, as the human epitaph?"

Pen surprised himself by how calm he felt. He was expecting death, blackness, loss of knowing or feeling, but realised that was just fine too. He felt a nonchalant serenity within his being. It was warm and tender and it was indeed him. He knew he felt no personal guilt any more for anything that had happened in the past. His senses now told him, the past was indeed past. 'Death and blackness is waiting, well I'm ready.'

"We have watched over thousands of years, as the human race developed into something progressive and unique. But sadly, one foresaw the final outcome almost from the outset! Even most humans expected their own entire destruction and, many seers have witnessed their own personal horror in the downfall of Homo-sapiens. You were our creation, manufactured, if you like, developed and nurtured, at first by love, then once established, allowed to go your own way through free will. You could go any way, or do anything you please. You chose your own descent into your private pits of hell. That Pen Pleasant is what free will is all about."

The entity changed colour once again, spun into a human face for Pen to see, then continued once more.

205

"But there was always something special that came from man. Something that shook us and, gave us a glimmer of hope for the future, that something was a wonderful surprise to us. Man developed a talent for his own form of creation, albeit through art forms. Music of course, is the most obvious. From earliest man, with his simple beating rhythms on wood and stone, to medieval man with his simply made instruments, to modern man and his wonderful symphony orchestras. The sounds that were produced by composers have been a special thing that is very unique to man. Those wondrous expressions of colour through sound, the ability to express any feeling, from despair, love, passion, loathing even patriotism, just by abstract sounds. Brilliant!"

The face turned white with shades of yellow.

"Then there are the writings of man, such incredible imagination gradually evolved. Such poetic works of a developing mind, as time went on in human evolution. The creative instinct, which produced such classic tomes, works of joy and loving tender feelings. Some works of authors are capable of conjuring up ecstasies and passions beyond imagination."

The head now appeared as if it was Charles Dickens talking and, then it turned into Shakespeare, then Marlow. Many other famous authors appeared quickly, and vanished into the ether. But the coloured entities still carried on speaking and, changing, emphasising as to this or that fact of being.

"Men have been governed by books of law. Books of tenets have been written to give men creeds to live by, plus of course the ability to teach children, pointing them hopefully on the right pathway through life. But, to us it is the ability to plant inspirational ideas for others to follow and develop, that has astonished us more than anything else."

There was a pause as the entity changed its colours once more and reformed into the shape of yet another human head.

"Plays, poetry, biographies of important people, or just good yarns from novels, to distract people for a moment or two; the writings of man have become a wondrous art form, which have always got better as time and humanity progressed."

Now the entity turned its colour into shades of purple and lilac.

"Then there is painting! Something that started with early man, his wall paintings, created by just a few colours and crudely etched into cave walls. Yet somehow these beautiful shapes flowed and danced for all to see. Incredibly wonderful to view. Art forms developed as man himself developed and, by the time of the renaissance, art was so magnificent, that the images of your God and religion, invoked people to raise their personal belief to the extent that they easily gave their lives in the name of one religion or another."

Yet another pause and another change of colour.

"Modern man, with the various form of art that developed in the early twentieth century. Cubism, modernism, abstract, impressionism, all expanding human consciousness. Painters all had one thing in common, their ability to alter human perception on things, or people around themselves, or just ways of living. Paintings have always been, either something to look at and admire for their impressionistic beauty, or there to alter one perception of life. Art taught humans how to look and learn through the subconscious."

This time the entity became dark blue, throbbed gently then swirled as if in delight still showing as a human face.

"Then there was man's ability to create sculptures and buildings of great beauty. These were once again either representational and abstract, or obvious likenesses. The various medium of materials that man used were so creative and diverse, always different and astounding."

The entity swirled faster and faster, almost making Pen dizzy with wonderment.

"But most of all, to us, man must be remembered for his incredible ingenuity. Since early man came into being, he progressed, never stood still. He made tools and, used things that could be scavenged. He found ways of using items that were naturally there, not necessarily for man, but there to be used anyway. Early man invented things that improved his life and created easier living conditions, but it also expanded his brain. Inventions have developed all through history, culminating in the discovery of space travel. Then that brings us to Mute Swan. Nothing from the past, or even up till or after this ship was created and made, has there ever been anything like your friend Swan. Man has inadvertently created life, you had become God. Mute Swan to us is your race's greatest achievement and, thus it is something that has moved us greatly. Swan is to live and, friend Pen, that means that you too are destined to become Swan's companion. Swan shows us what man should have become. It is loving and caring, compassion runs through all her molecules. She has a wondrous thirst for knowledge, discovery and culture, which in that part, at least is down to you. Mute Swan is your race's legacy from the past. It is also your one last chance for a future."

Pen interrupted at this juncture.

"So what is your meaning about me being Swan's companion? Am I to travel through space with a living ship? Surely that is no destiny for me. How can that bring about any form of salvation?"

"I'll tell you what is going to happen, but it is time for you to talk with your friend. We have something to do which will take us some small amount of time to complete. Listen to your music, watch your films and, enjoy your art. But do talk."

Then there was nothing, both Pen and Swan knew that they were completely alone.

"How do you feel Pen? Shall I play something, maybe some Prokofiev, what about his tone poem from the film Alexander Nevsky? Would you like some food with the music? Maybe a drink or two? Just name it dear friend; it will be yours."

Pleasant finally rose from the chair that he had been sitting on for so long. He was glad to move around, glad to get his blood flowing once more, glad to breath in the air of expectation for some sort of future, but most of all glad to be alone with Swan.

"Yes to the music, yes to the food and drinks."

Pen stood with his back to the console. He felt just a little silly, as his feelings for this machine were of warmth and tenderness. This seemed crazy even to him, but that was how he felt. Yes, he also felt embarrassed as he realised that these feeling ran extremely deep, and after all, what was Swan? A man-made machine, but a living man-made machine, one with feelings and creative thought and, a machine that loved him, Pen Pleasant, a destructive waster, who should have died with the rest of humanity, especially as in many ways Pen had thought of himself as part of the reason why man's demise came so suddenly.

Somehow the feelings of guilt and pain had started to disappear, to be filled with a warm feeling of tenderness and, dare he think it – love!

"Through you and your creative talents, I have been given a second chance. Will you allow me to take that chance?"

The music sang out loudly, then the smell of cooked food wafted around the living quarters. Pen waited for an answer, but whatever it was going to be, he felt relaxed and at peace. This feeling was new and he liked it.

"Pen, we will carry on together. I want that more than anything. If anything happens to you, I will not go on."

There followed more words with a certain emphasis. "But, I have no idea what they have in mind?"

Pen once again turned to look at the console. "One thing I'm sure about. Whatever they have in mind for us, it will be good for us both."

He smiled at Swan, and sat down to his food. He was starving, or so he imagined. After the repast, Pen sat back still listening to strains of Alexander Nevsky, he felt contented. The food was good and the company better.

For once, the young engineer drifted into sleep, a deep comfortable rest with absolutely no dreams.

"Pen Pleasant, please stir yourself. We are here to tell you what is about to happen; your combined future awaits you both."

Pen started, and for a brief moment was not sure where he was, or what had befallen him, but then reality struck home and, that realisation made him smile.

"Pen, I have been away making sure that you and Mute Swan have a future together. This is how it is going to be. We have created a new sun, around that sun are nine major planets all with moons, there are also minor planets and asteroids. Your planet is the third from the sun, with its own moon. Yes, you have guessed right; this is New Earth. The climate is temperate and there are plants and animals of all sorts. You will live off plant food, as will all animals. Plants once cut will reproduce themselves. That way there will always be abundant food for all. Nothing will ever have to kill either to live or for some sort of diverse pleasure. Harmony is the rule and, the only sacrifice will be that you must evolve your art forms again. Pen, you will be reborn with no previous knowledge of the past human race. Mute Swan, we are taking your essence and turning you into a real woman. You will both have the ability to reproduce human children, which you should do in abundance. You are the new human race. We hope and expect that you will create a race that will live for eternity in peace and tranquillity. From time to time, we will make ourselves known to you both, but generally we are going to trust that free will, will this time take humanity to nothing but the highest levels of intellect, arts and discovery. You will both live a normal life span and, then you will live through your heirs. Is there anything you wish to ask before this happens?"

Pen looked at Swan, smiled with genuine warmth and, asked her in a loving tender way, like an old contented married person, "Well my dearest, how does that sound to you?"

"I can't wait. This is the right and only way to go. This does seem to have always been my destiny."

Pen then looked back towards the swirling light green colours that were in front of him and, in a somewhat cheeky voice, one of impending excitement asked; "As you're God to us, can I be impertinent and ask something, that has puzzled me since I personally became aware of you?"

The colour green became very illuminated and much brighter and stronger in colour.

"What do you wish to know Pen Pleasant?"

Pen took his courage from Swan and asked, "How many of you are there?"

It was if the lights chuckled. The colour got even brighter.

"There are many and just one. All that there are, are me and, I am all that there are. Everything that I think we all think. We are as one, always in the past and always in the future. Does that answer your question?"

"Well I guess it does, but can I ask another please?"

"What do you wish to know?"

"Do we, the new human race, worship you as God, or Gods?"

"Neither. Just live full and happy lives; that is worship enough. Now sleep."

"Please, please, one last question. When we die...Is there an after life?"

"Well now, that age old nugget. You will just have to wait and see!"

Pen awoke naked. He didn't know how he got there, or who he was. The temperature was pleasantly warm and there was an abundance of life all around, none of which showed any great interest in him. He rose to his feet and started to look around. He was truly astonished at the beauty of the countryside. Mountains pointed to the sky in the distance. There were rivers. In these fish abounded. As he looked into the sky, clouds passed overhead, white and fluffy. There were birds skylarking and singing and, he watched with fascination as they swooped and soared, into the blue beyond. He understood everything, yet didn't understand why. He had language, but again didn't understand why. Most of all he felt great elation and wonderment, being overwhelmingly awe struck, by the very wonders of nature around him. He knew this was indeed utter and total perfection.

He wondered over to the river bank and glanced into the clear bluish water. He saw his reflection and, was surprised to see that he was no more than a teenager, with blond hair and brown eyes. He was muscular and trim. He guessed that he stood approximately five feet ten inches tall, though how height, weight or any other measurement should be known to him, was indeed a mystery. Peace and tranquillity were in the very air he breathed. He knew he was content.

Turning away from the river, he looked towards where he had been asleep. There rising from the ground was another human being. This time a woman. She was barely five feet tall, beautiful blonde hair, with also the most exquisite beautiful sparkling blue eyes. Her figure was very feminine, with curves, in all the right places. She smiled at him and, he immediately loved her.

He walked over to her, caressed her face and then her hair. Her naked beauty was delightful to see and, experience of that fact started quickly to show itself, within his lower regions.

She was the first to speak.

"What is your name?"

"Name, I…it is Adam. What is yours?"

"Why, Eve of course!"

Then she winked, and caressed his cheek. Holding an object up to his face she said, "Would you like a bite of my apple?"

FICTION FROM APS BOOKS
(www.andrewsparke.com)

Davey J Ashfield: *Footsteps On The Teign*
Davey J Ashfield *Contracting With The Devil*
Davey J Ashfield: *A Turkey And One More Easter Egg*
Davey J Ashfield: *Relentless Misery*
Fenella Bass: *Hornbeams*
Fenella Bass:: *Shadows*
Fenella Bass: *Darkness*
HR Beasley: *Nothing Left To Hide*
Lee Benson: *So You Want To Own An Art Gallery*
Lee Benson: *Where's Your Art gallery Now?*
Lee Benson: *Now You're The Artist…Deal With It*
Lee Benson: *No Naked Walls*
TF Byrne *Damage Limitation*
Nargis Darby: *A Different Shade Of Love*
J.W.Darcy *Looking For Luca*
J.W.Darcy: *Ladybird Ladybird*
J.W.Darcy: *Legacy Of Lies*
J.W.Darcy: *Love Lust & Needful Things*
Paul Dickinson: *Franzi The Hero*
Jane Evans: *The Third Bridge*
Simon Falshaw: *The Stone*
Peter Georgiadis:*The Mute Swan's Song*
Peter Georgiadis: *Strangers Pass By On Heaven's Wings*
Milton Godfrey: *The Danger Lies In Fear*
Felix Gomez: *The Tunnel Killer*
Chris Grayling: *A Week Is…A Long Time*
Jean Harvey: *Pandemic*
Michel Henri: *Mister Penny Whistle*
Michel Henri: *The Death Of The Duchess Of Grasmere*
Michel Henri: *Abducted By Faerie*
Laurie Hornsby: *Postcards From The Seaside*
Hugh Lupus *An Extra Knot (Parts I-VI)*
Alison Manning: *World Without Endless Sheep*
Colin Mardell: *Keep Her Safe*
Colin Mardell: *Bring Them Home*
Ian Meacheam: *An Inspector Called*
Ian Meacheam: *Time And The Consequences*
Ian Meacheam: *Broad Lines Narrow Margins*
Ian Meacheam & Mark Peckett: *Seven Stages*

Printed in Great Britain
by Amazon

23288206R00126